The Devil Wears Timbs II
Baptized in Unholy Waters

The Devil Wears Timbs II

The Devil Wears Timbs II
Baptized in Unholy Waters
A Novel by *Tranay Adams*

The Devil Wears Timbs II

Email:trnayadams@gmail.com

Facebook: Tranay Adams

Cover design and layout by: Sunny Giovanni

Book interior design by: Shawn Walker

Edited by: Epic Kreationz

The Devil Wears Timbs II

Acknowledgments

I would like to first start off by giving all thanks and praises to my supporters.

Jane Pennella, Sharon Bell, Lashawn Green, Kizzy Stephens, Ravone Butterfield, Bry Heckard, Andrea Williams, Kim Leblanc, Deshawn French, Ann Cheeks, Priscilla Murray, Mary Davidson, Jennilee, Sabrina Darby, Marilyn Brown, Yara Kaleemah, Jeannette Ransom-Frazier, Naomi B. Johnson, Jessica Ward, Dachary James, Wendy Hall, Marcie Williamson, Tonsie Randall, Kastin Blak, Tumika Cain, Slowmotion Gary, Johnne Johnson and Melissa Porter aka Akia Boo. I have shared so many laughs with you two. I swear we're like old college buddies are something. I adore you both. Y'all my goons, str8 up. The Trini-nay's Lmmfao. If I forgot anyone, I'll get you on the next one.

Shouts out to Streetz aka Dolla Bill, Latrice Love, James Junior, Mike Northcutt, Artrell Allen aka Doe Boy and both my lil' Nephews (Amari and Aarie), Raynesha Pittman, Terry L. Wroten, Cool-Aide and The No Brakes Movement, salutations. Sylvia Spearman, Lola Bands, Jasmine Devonish, Ace Gucciano, my ninja, you know you ain't cook none of that shit you be posting. LOL Salute, I fucks with chu hard-body. Everyone at SIRR Radio, Treasure Blue for giving us new authors that good game, and my OG homie, Author Godfather Wesley.

The Devil Wears Timbs II Baptized in Unholy Waters
Let's get it!

Chapter One

Eureka lay in bed asleep, her nose twitching as the aroma of steak, scrambled eggs, and toast invaded her nostrils and caused her stomach to grumble with hunger. Her eyes fluttered open and she sat up in bed, wiping the scum from the corners of her eyes.

She looked to the window and saw the sun shining through the glass, illuminating the bedroom. The day was warm and beautiful. She could hear the birds chirping, a lawnmower running, and kids playing.

Eureka grabbed her Glock from under her pillow and shook Anton awake. He turned over, looked at her and rubbed his eyes.

"Rise and shine, my boy," she said groggily.

Anton sat up. "Something smells good."

"Yeah, somebody's over the stove," she told him. "Let's go see what's on the menu."

"Bet."

"Good morning," Eureka and Anton said after each other as they entered the kitchen.

Constance gave them a nod and took a bite of eggs.

"Good morning," Fear replied, holding a mug of steaming black coffee and the morning newspaper. "Your plates are inside of the microwave. Pull up a chair." He nodded to the two empty seats at the table.

Eureka grabbed her and Anton's plates and sat down at the kitchen table. She removed the foil and admired the breakfast before her. She couldn't wait to dig in.

Constance picked up her glass of orange juice. She took a drink and a devilish smile formed on her lips as she watched Eureka gather eggs on her fork. Eureka frowned as she was about to take her first bite. She looked at them, then back up to Fear who'd risen from his chair, taking another sip of his coffee.

"Who made breakfast?" She asked Fear.

"Constance," he answered. "It's good too, she can burn." He set the mug down, "I'm gon' take a shower."

"Alright," Constance said to him then turned to Eureka with a carton of Donald Duck orange juice. "Would you like some?"

Eureka narrowed her eyes at her, thinking, *something ain't right, this bitch couldn't wait to beat my ass and now she's acting all hospitable and shit? Where they do that at?*

"Nah, I'm straight." She finally answered.

"How about you, Ant?" She motioned with the carton. He was just about to take a bite of his food too. But just like his sister, he felt something in the pit of his stomach that told him he'd better not, especially with how nice Constance was acting.

"Nah, I'm alright." He sat his fork down on the plate and pulled his empty glass into him.

"Well, more for me then," Constance refilled her glass.

Eureka and Anton exchanged glances. She watched Constance eat her food as if she didn't have a care in the world. The bitch took a bite of eggs, looked at her and cracked a slight smile before she continued with her meal. Something was definitely up. She didn't know exactly what it was, but she for damn sure wasn't about to eat that breakfast. Fuck that!

"Eat your food before it gets cold," Constance told Eureka.

"We ain't eating this shit." Eureka picked up her and her brother's plates.

"What's the problem?" Her brow furrowed.

"We're allergic to eggs." Eureka lied.

"You aren't allergic. You were just about to eat 'em," Constance told her.

"Fuck off." Eureka spat back.

"Wait a minute, are you finna throw that food away?" She scowled. "Bitch, have you lost your goddamn mind?"

"Don't worry about it, Ant, we'll go out to get something to eat." Eureka told him. Turning to head to the trash can, her eyes came across Constance who didn't look too happy about what she'd planned to do with the food.

"See, this is exactly the type of shit I warned Fear about," Constance said to no one in particular, "Picking up people from off the streets like they're dogs and shit."

"Fuck you!" Eureka said over her shoulder.

"Bitch, fuck you!" Constance spat back sharply.

"Whatever, I don't do the back and forth."

"Me either, I'm all about action like a Schwarzenegger flick, boo boo. And we can shoot the ending to your movie right now." Constance bit into a crisp strip of bacon.

While Eureka was raking the food out into the trash can something caught her eye. She moved the loose trash aside and uncovered two empty boxes of rat poison. That confirmed what she'd suspected all along.

Several lines formed across her forehead and her mouth dropped open in shock. She picked up one of the empty poison boxes and read over its contents. She looked over her shoulder at Constance and she was wearing that same devilish grin on her face. Eureka's own face contorted into something ugly. She was so angry she found herself trembling. Fire danced in her eyes and she clenched her teeth so tightly her jaws pulsated.

In a flash, she whipped around and charged toward Constance, who shot to her feet and kicked her chair over.

"Come on, bitch!" Constance motioned Eureka over with both hands. She couldn't wait to tax that ass. "Come to momma!"

Eureka roared as she leapt forward. Constance used her momentum against her. Using her hands, she shifted Eureka's direction in midair and slammed her down on the table. Eureka hit the table, knocking over glasses and mugs. The impact caused stabbing pains to needle her back. She was paralyzed with pain, but swiftly moved once she saw Constance snatching a steak knife to send crashing down above her head.

Wooooooooof!

There was a shift in the air as something flew toward Constance. Her head snapped up and Anton was flying at her with a Liu Kang kick.

Thud!

The assault sent the steak knife up in the air and Constance flying backwards. She slammed against the kitchen cabinet and hit the floor hard on her ass. She groaned.

Shaking the daze off she looked up to see Anton helping his sister off of the table."Oh, you wanna kick people, you lil' runt?" Her eyes glinted with murder and her lips peeled back in a sneer. Getting up off of the floor, she said, "Alright, both of you bitches getting it now."

"Grrrrrr!" Eureka growled, charging toward her.

"Yeah," she smiled fiendishly, holding her fists before her.

Constance fired off on Eureka's face with rock hard jabs, making her head jump back. She struck and moved, laying into her ferociously, faking her out and landing solid blows. Eureka ate that shit like she had a face made of iron.

"Uh huh," Constance said, feeling herself as she stared beyond her fists. Her knuckle game was official. She was trained by one of the best. Her only options were to win or die. "Talk that shit now."

Crack! Wop! Whrack!

Eureka's face met with a crushing left, right, and then a round house kick across her jaw. She fell off to the side on her hands and knees, grill leaking blood. She spat blood on the floor and wiped her lips with the back of her hand. She looked up at Constance with hateful eyes and red clenched teeth. A length of bloody saliva hung from her chin, making her look like a mad dog.

"Bitch, get off my sister!"

She turned around just in time to meet a powerful right. The blow was so hard that her dreads jumped and a ripple went through her cheeks. Specs of blood flew and splattered through the air as she went sailing backwards. She hit the kitchen counter and fell down on her hands and knees. She looked down at her blood pelting the floor and then back up at Anton.

Her eyes registered rage as she clenched her jaws. She spit on the floor and pulled a loose steak knife into her palm. She gripped the knife so tightly her knuckles turned white.

"I'm gonna carve that face of yours up like a fucking Jack-O-Lantern." She stood to her feet, doing fancy tricks with the knife in her palm.

"Step aside, baby boy," Eureka shoved her brother out of the way. "This is between me and her."

Eureka snatched a knife as well, then she tossed it over her back and caught it. She brought it around and flipped it over in her palm. Lowering her head slightly, she peered up at her rival menacingly as she licked her lips. "Let's dance!"

Anton moved out of the way like his sister ordered.

She kicked the table over, spilling all of the dishes upon it. The table clanged when it hit the surface and all of the dishes shattered into broken pieces. There was now a clear path that lead from her to the femme fatal.

"Come on then, ho!" Constance spat.

"First draw of blood was yours, but your life is mine!" Eureka swore.

"We'll see."

"Ahhhhh!" Constance charged in her direction.

"Ahhhhh!" Eureka charged right after her.

They moved to claim their pound of flesh and blood, but right before they could lock ass, Constance was snatched up. She screamed and kicked her legs as Fear held her up off of the floor.

"Let me go Alvin, I'm gonna cut her fucking head off!"

"Stop it, goddamn it!" He ordered his protégé. "Calm the fuck down!"

"Noooo! Let. Me. Go!"

"Anton, grab Reka." Fear struggled with Constance. One arm was around her chest, keeping her back while the other held his .9mm at his side.

Eureka was enroute to carve her foe up something nasty when Anton snatched her up by the waist, kicking and screaming. She and Constance performed as they both couldn't wait to claim a piece of one another.

"Ant, I swear to God you better let me go!"

"Nuh uh, sis, you gotta chill out."

"Fuck a chill! I'm on one, baby boy!"

"Constance, drop the knife now. Remember your vow." Fear brought up her pledge of unquestioning loyalty to him and to follow his every command.

Nostrils flaring and chest heaving up and down, she took a deep breath to calm herself. She closed her eyes and then opened them, letting the knife drop to the floor with a clasp. "Let me down.

He lowered her to the floor and stood between her and Eureka.

"Sis, you've gotta calm down, you disrespecting homie's house and he letting us crash here," Anton said in a hushed tone to his sibling.

Remembering that made Eureka quiet down a little bit, but she was still on fire. She took a deep breath and released a little pent up tension.

"Okay, alright," she said. "I'm cool now."

"Drop it like it's hot, lil' momma," Fear referred to the knife Eureka was still holding and she dropped it at her feet. "Now what the fuck is going on in here?" His head snapped between the two women heatedly, veins ran up his neck, his temples throbbed. He loved peace and quiet at his house. He had enough noise in his line of work, he'd be damned if he dealt with the drama inside of his own home.

"She put rat poison in my food," Eureka answered.

"I didn't put shit in your food," Constance claimed. "You're losing it, bitch. You're delusional." She twirled her finger around her temple, insinuating that Eureka was crazy.

"I know what I saw," Eureka said. "The empty boxes are in the trash can."

Fear massaged the bridge of his nose and shook his head. "Lil' momma," he addressed Eureka. "I laid rat poison out in the garage a couple of days ago. I caught that filthy mothafucka and threw 'em out. I threw the boxes away this morning."

Eureka suddenly felt like a Jackass, she didn't know what to say after that revelation.

"You need to check her." Constance folded her arms across her chest and tapped her foot. She hated Eureka with a passion and the look on her face made that public knowledge.

Fear's head snapped in her direction and he gave her a look that could kill faster than lethal injection. "Shut up."

She sighed and looked off to the side, rolling her eyes and talking shit under her breath as she tapped her foot.

He stepped to Eureka so close that she could smell the breakfast on his breath. He wore an expression on his face that was as serious as cancer.

"Lil' momma, I cannot and will not have all of this drama going down in my spot," he began. "If any more trouble arises between you and Constance, I'm gonna have to ask y'all to leave. Do we understand each other?" He looked from her to her brother. She nodded and he said *yeah*. "Good. I want you and Anton to clean up this mess. Me and Constance have an engagement."

While Eureka and Anton got busy cleaning up the kitchen, Fear and Constance took it up stairs.

Chapter Two

Constance walked in the bedroom behind Fear, en route to the dresser. She rifled through the top dresser drawer until she found her pack of smokes. After firing up the square, she tossed the lighter upon the dresser. She smoked on the Joe as she watched Fear go through the clothes hanging up inside of the closet.

"I can't believe that lil' skank tried me." Constance shook her head as she blew smoke out of her nostrils and mouth. She was genuinely pissed off at Eureka because she'd tried to drop those thangs on that ass *and* she didn't eat the breakfast she'd actually contaminated.

She'd put just the right amount of rat poison in their food and sat the containers back out in the garage. By the time Fear had gotten up that morning and checked the garage, he found that big ass rat he'd been trying to catch for a month. He was ecstatic when he found the beady eyed vermin belly up in the corner.

He had dropped the filthy little fucker into an old sneaker box and dumped it into the black trash can outside, but discarded the empty poison containers in the trash can inside of the kitchen. If he hadn't done that, Eureka and Anton would have been lying stretched out dead some time later.

"I should run back down stairs and ring that heifer's neck. She thinks she's slick with that shit she pulled. Humph, seducing my man so her and that lil' bastard in there can have some place to stay."

"Is that what this is all about? Some dick?" Fear tilted his head to the side and made a face that Constance read as *Bitch, are you serious?*

"Yeah, I'm in my feelings, but so what!" Constance snaked her neck.

"See, this the type of shit I was afraid was gon' happen. I should have never given yo ass no dick," Fear stated. "I knew you weren't going to be able to handle it."

"So, I guess this is just all my fault, huh?" She asked accusingly as she tapped her square and dumped ashes into an ashtray. "What did you think was going to happen, Alvin?" She hit him with his government name. "You're laying the pipe to me, cuddling up with me every other night and whispering that good shit into my ear. How am I not gonna feel some type of way? I've tried to fight this shit, thinking it would somehow pass, but it hasn't. I'ma G about mine, so I'ma keep it a stack with you. I love you."

"I got love for you too, but—" the words died in his throat as she raised a hand and retorted.

"Nah, you aren't hearing me." She mashed the cigarette out in the ashtray and hopped up from the bed, approaching him. Her delicate, soft hands cupped his face and she stared into his eyes. "I'm *in love* with you."

The revelation struck him like a sniper's bullet. He was taken completely off guard. His mouth opened, but he didn't know what to say. For that matter he was sure he couldn't form the words if he tried. His mind drew a blank. The moment those words left her lips the world stopped spinning. Everything was silent, still, calm, undisturbed. Fear burrowed into those hazel brown eyes of hers. They bled with emotion.

"Well, say something. Has the way you feel about me changed in the slightest bit?" She asked, hoping and praying he didn't feel the same as he always had. She searched his eyes as if they were a word search puzzle, looking for just a tinge of what she felt for him.

Fear grasped Constance's wrists and took her hands from his face. He shook his head and said, "No."

Through her eyes she saw his mouth moving in slow motion and *no* rolling off of his tongue dramatically. It was as if his lips had fired an AK-47 bullet and it had pierced her heart. She could literally feel the blood rimminginside of the hole in her heart and trickling down.

He read the hurt on her face like the drawings on the walls of an ancient Egyptian temple. She looked like she had been shot with a live round at that precise moment. Right before his eyes, she seemed to revert back to the scared young woman he had met many years ago. That rough exterior and that rugged demeanor were now gone. She was like a flower, precious, delicate, fragile.

And he was scared to touch her for fear she may die.

For a moment, Fear had forgotten she was a cold blooded killer standing before him. Constance had broken several laws of the Ten Commandments multiple times, especially the sixth one. But looking at her in that hour, Fear almost believed she wouldn't harm a fly. However, he knew better than anyone what she was capable of. He couldn't believe she had the stomach to do some of the things he had seen her do, but then again, he'd done the same things she had without losing a wink of sleep.

"What happened to *fuck feelings*?" Fear grabbed her arm, outstretched it and turned it over. Tattooed down the inside of her arm was *Fuck Feelings*. "I guess this always rang true until it came to me, huh?"He probed her eyes in search of the ruthless assassin he'd trained himself, hoping to find that raging, blood thirsty beast that lived for the thrill of the kill. He wanted to see that now more than ever. He hated to think his greatest creation had flaws because he prided himself on what he'd contrived. "I told you how it was going to be between us and you agreed to it. So, don't make me out to be the bad guy here, alright?"

Fuck, Constance, say it ain't so, ma. I told you before that a killer with a heart doesn't have longevity in this game. Show no love, love will get chu killed, he thought of the quote Majestic said in the Get Rich or Die Tryin'.

Constance snatched her arm back, "True, but that was before and this is now. You mean to tell me after all of this time you don't feel anything? I took a gun charge for you. We almost had a child together. Shit, nigga, it's my blood that courses through your fucking veins. I was the one who gave you blood when you got shot up by the Mexicans." She jabbed him hard in the chest with a crooked finger. "That's a tie that binds us together for the rest of our lives. I am a part of you. You mean to tell me that after all of the shit that we've been through together you don't feel a lil' something more for me?"

"Didn't we have this talk before?" His brow furrowed and he tapped his temple with his finger. "Get it through your fucking head. I will never have those kinds of feelings for you."

He knew he'd gone at her too sharply. The devastated look that masked her face made it known, so he'd have to go at her with a different approach. Fear ran a hand down his face and exhaled, thinking for a minute before he spoke.

"Constance, you're my partner-in-crime, my road dawg, and my mothafucking ace." He touched his fist to his left peck where his heart resided. "I'd kill for you, I'd die for you. Whatever it is I have, you can take as yours. I'll give it to you no questions asked but—"

"Your heart," Constance blurted, cutting him short. "That's all I want from you. This," she touched the left side of his chest where his heart rested.

He shook his head and responded, "Constance, *we* could never be, not in this life or the next." He watched as her bottom lip slightly quivered. Tears rimmed her eyes and threatened to drip. True to her hardcore nature, she refused to allow them to make their debut. She tightened her face and drew them back, swallowing that moment of vulnerability she'd just displayed.

"You're right, Fear, we could never be." Constance conceded. "We're much better as partners. That love shit complicates things. We don't need that fucking up what we've got going. L.O.E, we're all we got, right?" She flashed the *Loyalty Over Everything* ink on her hand that they both shared.

"Come here." He opened his arms for an embrace.

"Nah, I'm gucci. I don't need no love right now." She plucked her Joe from the ashtray and sparked it up.

"Maybe *I* do." He cracked a smile as he approached.

"Ol' tender heart ass nigga," Constance grinned and hugged him, careful not to burn him with the ember of her cigarette.

"Let me hit that," Fear spoke.

"This?" She held up the square, "Or this?" She patted that fat twat in her boy shorts.

He chuckled and shook his head. He took the Joe that Constance had pinched between her fingers and took a couple of drags from it. He then passed it back to her and grabbed a wife beater and boxer-briefs from out of the drawer.

"You about to jump in the shower?" she asked. He turned around to her and nodded. "Let me pee real quick 'fore you go in there," she said.

"Alright." He twisted up his wife beater and smacked her on her ass with it as she passed him, heading toward the bathroom.

Constance closed and locked the door behind herself before approaching the porcelain sink. She sat the square down on the soap dish and stared at her reflection in the mirror. She watched as her face slowly began to transform into a mask of grief. Her eyes grew moist as the tears obscured her vision and spilled down her cheeks. She held onto the porcelain sink and got down to her knees. A whimper escaped her lips.

Knowing she was about to break down, she flushed the toilet to drown the noises she would make. Her head bobbed as she cried aloud. The tears fell in abundance, hitting the floor one after another, appearing to be attacking the white tiled surface. Constance cried so hard she felt her nose drip, so she wiped it with her shirt and sniffled.

Once the toilet had finished making its noise from the flush, she turned the dials of the faucet on. As the water flowed, she sobbed until her heart was content. Afterwards, she splashed water on her face and straightened herself up. She gave herself the once over in the medicine cabinet mirror to make sure she was decent before opening the door.

"She's all yours." Constance smirked at Fear as she abandoned the bathroom.

When she left, Fear went in behind her. He was none the wiser that he was breaking the most fragile possession of a woman. Her heart. He may not have known to what degree he had broken it, but he would know soon enough.

17

Chapter Three

Fear stood under the showerhead, allowing the hot water to beat down on his head and body. Lathering up his form with a bar of soap, his hands ran over the keloids, old stab wounds, bullet wounds, and burn marks. He'd never forget the day he'd gotten the old bullet scars.

Fear lay back on the couch as Good Times played on the flat-screen TV. His hand had a loose hold on a Heineken. His eyes were narrowed and every couple of minutes his head would drop as he dozed off. For the umpteenth time, he'd nearly spilled his beer into his lap and every time he almost did, he'd wake up just in time to catch it.

No more than twenty minutes prior, he had devoured a hearty meal of T-bone steak, shrimp, cheese potatoes, and a Caesar salad. No sooner than he drank half of his beer, The Itis had taken him. He'd had hopes of catching up on his favorite show growing up, but the Sandman had paid him a visit.

Hearing his cell phone ring, woke Fear from his sleep. He swallowed the last of his Heineken and sat the bottle down on the coffee table. He picked the cell phone up and saw the call was 'Blocked'. He started not to answer it, but figured it was old girl he bumped into at the Del Amo Mall. Fear pressed 'answer' and placed the cell phone to his ear.

"What's up with it?" He spoke. The caller said something, but he couldn't hear him over the blare of the show. "Hold on, family. Let me turn this TV off, I can't hear you." Fear told the caller. He turned it off. "Now, what were you saying?"

"I said, 'you're a dead man, mayate!" The caller hung up.*

Fear saw a masked gunman standing behind him through the tinted black glass of the television, raising a ratchet to the back of his head. With lightning fast reflexes, he snatched the bottle and broke the end of it off at the edge of the coffee table. Just as the masked man pointed the gun, Fear sliced him across the wrist.

"Arghhhhh!" he gritted his teeth. Feeling a burning sensation in his wrist, he dropped his weapon.

"You break into my house, mothafucka!" Fear barked with arched eyebrows and a crinkled nose. His lips were twisted and veins were bulging in his neck. He snatched the man over the couch and turned him around. He pulled his chin back and exposed his throat. He stabbed the broken half of the green glass bottle into his neck with a grunt, and dragged it around to the other end, spilling a crimson fountain.

"Argggg! Gurgle. Gurgle. Gurgle." Blood filled the intruder's mouth and quickly overflowed his grill, splattering on the cushions of the beige couch.

Bathoom! Bathoom!

The door rattled and Fear's head snapped up, seeing the door lurch back and forth. The only thing keeping it from swinging inward was the chain, but then—Boom! Two more masked men spilled in, ratchets in hand.

Fear snatched the dead man's blood speckled ratchet from off of the couch and hoisted him up to use as a human shield.

Choot! Choot! Choot! Choot! Choot! Choot!

Bullets whizzed through the air, narrowly missing him, pelting the dead body of the masked man that Fear used as a human shield and tattering the back of the couch.

The masked men let off in unison, trying to air their target the fuck out. Fear hunched behind the slab of mutilated flesh, keeping his head down and waiting for a chance to respond as the projectiles flew all around him. Seeing his chance to react, he responded with bursts of rapid gunfire.

Choot! Choot! Choot!

Waves of heat snatched off the left side of one of the masked gunners face's, tore off his bottom jaw, and left a gaping hole through the center of his forehead. He dropped to the floor dead, his soul spiraling toward that inferno below ground. Fear swept his ratchet around to the last shooter and let loose.

Choot! Choot! Choot!

"Ahhhhhhhh!"

When the first bullet hit him in the neck he grimaced like he was about to bite something and slapped a hand over the spurting hole. The second one struck his chest and the last marred his shoulder. Fear closed one eye and took aim before sending that third one at him. There was a whistle and then splat, the shooter's blood and chunks of his brain went flying out the back of his skull. When that shit hit the hardwood floor, it looked like someone's vomit. The lifeless man hit the surface right after the killer's human shield did once Fear released him.

Fear advanced upon the two masked men he'd dispatched cautiously. He kneeled down to them and pulled off their ski-masks, tossing them aside. Lines creased his forehead as he realized he recognized them. They were Gustavo's men. The Mexican kingpin who was pissed that Fear didn't execute his rival's entire family. Fear had terminated all of the adults, but allowed the children to live. He couldn't bring himself to take the life of innocent children,so now he had to pay for his reneging, with his life.

Choot!

Fear grimaced as he took one in the back. He whipped around and there was a fourth masked assailant that had entered his apartment. Fear noticed the opened window at the end of the hallway, ruffling the sheer curtains with a cool breeze passing through. Fear realized he'd gotten inside of the apartment through the fire escape.

Fear went to lift his ratchet, but the assailant had the drop on him. He sent a hot-one through Fear's thigh, causing him to drop his gun when he went to clutch his leg. The assailant took his sweet time approaching, taking shot after shot at him.

Choot!

Choot!

Two shots slammed Fear up against the wall, but one more left him bleeding on the floor on his side. Seeing the gunman moving in to finish him, he reached for his dropped weapon. His palm had just grazed its handle when the intruder mashed his boot against his hand, pinning it to the handle. He looked up at the gunman who had just pointed his silenced .380 between his eyes. A wicked smile formed on his lips.

He pulled off his mask and his malicious eyes penetrated Fear's. "Adios, primo," he said.

The gunman's malicious expression melted into one of confusion and excruciation. His eyes bulged and when his lips peeled apart, a red river spilled over them. Dropping his silenced .380 to the floor, he slowly turned around as he grabbed at his back.

Looking up, Fear saw a butcher's knife buried down to its handle in the man's back. When he peered beyond him, he saw Constance lunge forth, gripping a meat cleaver with both hands. She released a snarl right before she buried the cleaver in his face, nearly splitting it in half. Blood poured out of the split in his face and splashed on his black thermal. He dropped to his knees and fell on the side of his face, dead.

"Oh, my God, baby! What did they do to you?" Constance said, seeing Fear lying on the floor bleeding like a stuck pig. She grabbed the cordless telephone and dialed 911. She then tossed the telephone aside and rushed to his aide. She laid his head into her lap and caressed his head. He tried to talk, but she hushed him. "Shhhh, don't say anything, save your strength." She placed a tender kiss on his forehead and continued to stroke his head. "Everything is going to be all right, baby. You just hang in there."

"Hide the guns—hide the—hide the drugs," Fear's eyes blinked and he coughed up blood, struggling to escape the cold hands of Death. His crimson hand grasped Constance's hand, squeezing tightly. "Stash—stash—stash the money." He stared up into her eyes in what could very well be his last hour.

"Alright, alright," Constance nodded, wiping her tears with a curled finger. She ran back and forth across the apartment gathering what he'd told her to and stashing it in the secret compartments inside of the unit.

****

Fear survived his wounds and recovered at UCLA hospital. During his stay, Constance brought him what she believed was good news. She was pregnant. Constance was all smiles. She was overly excited about the life growing inside of her. Though Fear wasn't feeling fatherhood, he put up one hell of a front. He wasn't nearly as happy as Constance was about the baby. Constance thought he was though but she was as wrong as two left sneakers.

Fear made no illusions of who he was and what he did for a living. There was no way he could raise a child given his lifestyle. Even if he turned his back on the game he still had to worry about his past coming back to haunt him. His enemies could use the love of his child against him and have him in a fucked up situation. He didn't want to have to deal with that. He felt life would be much better without having to worry about taking care of a child. In his heart he knew he was right, but it would be impossible to convince Constance to go through with an abortion. She had her heart set on welcoming a little boy or girl into the world. And he was positive she would turn a deaf ear to whatever he had to say contrary to it.

One day tragedy struck while Constance was moving about in the kitchen fixing a bag of popcorn. The microwave dinged, and when she went to remove her snack an excruciating pain jolted through her stomach and southern region. She doubled over, blinking and wincing in pain, holding her stomach. The next thing she knew she was waking up on the floor in a small puddle of blood that was coming from between her legs.

She pulled herself up on her feet, grabbing her car keys and jacket. She didn't bother to change her bloody clothes before she left the house, she wanted to get to the hospital as soon as possible to see if her baby was alright. Constance banged Fear's line on her way there. She and Fear reached Kaiser at the exact same time.

He walked her inside and they rushed her to the back. Constance and Fear discovered she'd had a miscarriage. She was devastated. She hollered to the Heavens asking God why he would bless her with such a precious gift and then rip it right out of her life.

"Oh, God, why? Why me Lord?" The tears flowed down her cheeks and she brought her hands to her face. She was lying in a hospital bed, in a sky blue hospital gown with an IV hooked up to her arm. The doctor stood beside her rubbing her back and doing the best he could to comfort her. "What have I done?" she looked up at the ceiling. "What have I done to deserve this,Father? Haven't I been through enough? Haven't I been dealt enough pain in my life?" Her hands trembled uncontrollably and she looked at them as if they weren't apart of her body. She breathed sporadically with her body twitching ever so often. She was hurt, broken, devastated, and overwhelmed.

"Get off of me, don't chu fucking touch me!" She swung on the doctor and missed, but her next one connected, sending him sailing back.

He bumped into the neighboring bed, holding his jaw. She yanked the IV out of her hand and attacked him, throwing punches. He subdued her, wrapping his arms around her in a bear hug. She snuggled her face into his chest and sobbed her heart out. The nurse entered with a sedative, he motioned her in. He placed a finger to his lips telling her to be quiet. She crept in and gave Constance a shot. She went wild for a spurt, but eventually fell woozy and met with sleep. The doctor placed her in the bed and covered her up, turning off the light.

Hours later, Constance stirred awake. Her eyes were swollen from so much crying that it looked like she'd gotten into a fight. She looked beside her and found Fear lying asleep. A slight smirk formed on her lips seeing he'd stayed there the whole night with her.

"He stayed, he stayed the entire time." She spoke softly to no one in particular. She caressed the side of his head and kissed him on the temple.

Constance slid out of bed and made her way into the bathroom. Flipping on the light switch, she stepped before the sink and stared at her reflection in the mirror. She studied the altered version of herself. She couldn't help thinking about what her appearance and life had in common, they were both ugly. The thought fucked with her head. She found her shoulders shuddering and the tears rimming her eyes. She gripped both sides of the sink and bowed her head, her tears hit the sink and floor as she sobbed. The volume of her sobbing grew louder and louder.

"Shhhhhh." She heard him at her back, and when she looked up he was wrapping his strong muscular arms around her. Fear kissed her on the back of her head and nuzzled his nose in the nape of her neck. He placed two gentle kisses on her neck and looked at her reflection in the mirror.

"It's okay, it's alright." He whispered in her ear. "Everything is going to be just fine." He assured her.

She turned to him and her arms snaked around his body. She nestled the side of her face against his chiseled chest. "Hold me tight, Fear."

He did like she'd asked.

"Tighter, please."

Fear tightened his hold on her, pinning her against his warm body. He continued to whisper in her ear, slightly rocking her and rubbing her back. She didn't know what it was about his touch and his voice, but they made the perfect couple to soothe her pain in that moment.

"Tell me you love me," she said.

"Constance, I—"

"You don't have to mean it, I just need to hear you say it."

Fear closed his eyes as he took a deep breath, "I love you, Constance."

"Again."

"I love you, Constance."

Constance sobbed long and hard into Fear's white T-shirt, staining it with her tears and snot. Fear continued to comfort her with his gentle voice while rubbing her back. This was the first time he had ever shown that kind of affection to her. He didn't want to confuse her with what their relationship actually was, but seeing how she was breaking down, he had to step in and let her know he was there for her.

Constance decided to have a funeral for the baby she'd lost. Although she and Fear didn't know the sex, they both wanted it to be a boy, so they agreed to name him Nasir. They didn't have a body to bury so instead they put a memory in the ground. A beautiful burgundy wood stained coffin just big enough to fit a newborn was committed to the earth at Compton Cemetery. Surprisingly, Constance didn't shed a solitary tear that day. She lovingly kissed the casket and placed a long stemmed rose upon it. She then left the cemetery on Fear's arm.

Fear killed the water and stepped out of the bathtub, snatching his towel off of the rack. He dried off and wrapped the towel around his waist. While brushing his teeth he couldn't help but think, *Damn, me and Constance have been through some shit together. I can't front, I got mad love for ma. It's just not that love love that niggaz have for a broad. Still, I can kind of see how she could catch feelings for a nigga. I know she wants more than what we got, but I'm just not feeling her like that. Besides, I'm not tryna wife up nan chick right now. I'm on my get money tip and all that love shit gon' do is make shit com-*

plicated. It's M.O.B on mine, Money Over Bitches. She can either soldier up and deal with it or take her walking papers, fuck it.

Fear spat tooth paste out in the sink, gargled Listerine, and washed his mouth out with water. Once he finished shaving, he slapped on some aftershave and made his exit. When Fear stepped back into the bedroom, he saw Constance had his clothes, his sneakers, his Kevlar bulletproof vest, and his .9mm with two magazines laid out for him on his king-sized bed. A smile formed on Fear's lips as he looked upon the layout. *Ain't nothing like a ride or die, nothing like it at all,* he thought to himself.

Chapter Four

Not long ago, Malvo had sent Crunch out into the streets looking for Ronny. The stalwart young soldier was given orders to find his childhood friend and execute him if he discovered he had his money and dope. If not, he was to bring him back to face an interrogation or a firing squad if he determined he was intentionally trying to bend him over and fuck him.

In the meantime, he had a meeting with his counterfeit money plug. He planned on using the knock off dollars he purchased from him to purchase a couple of birds of dope to get his traps back cracking again.

See, the plan was for Malvo to take the money just outside of the city where he knew of these dudes who were letting kilos of heroin go for a reasonable price. Malvo knew the dudes through a homeboy of his that used to cop from them, but he left the game to start up a legitimate business. His homeboy had linked him with this new connect, now shit was going to be sweeter than new pussy.

Ernie sat inside of the McDonalds on the corner of Imperial and Crenshaw, hunched over the tray of his number 7. He wiped his mouth with a napkin and took a sip of his orange HI-C drink. Looking up, he saw the man he was supposed to meet that day entering the establishment. When the man stopped before him, he motioned a hand toward the chair across from him, signaling for him to sit down. Malvo pulled out a chair and sat, placing a Ralph's brown paper bag on the floor between his Timberlands. He leaned over the table and grabbed a couple of Ernie's fries without asking, garnering a nasty look from the man.

"Sure, help yourself," Ernie said sarcastically.

"Don't mind if I do." Malvo replied, not giving a fuck how he felt about it. After he'd eaten the fries, he grabbed his drink and removed the lid, taking a long drink. He belched and sat the drink down, wiping his mouth with the back of his hand.

"What's up? You got that for me or what?"

Ernie nodded his head and looked around to make sure there wasn't anybody watching him. Everyone seemed to be engrossed in eating and talking so he went about his business. Using his foot, Ernie pushed a Marshall's shopping bag across the floor to him under the table. Malvo pulled the bag in to him with one foot and pushed his bag over to Ernie with the other. Looking down, Malvo opened up the bag and peered inside.

"This 300k, right?" Malvo asked.

"That's right." Ernie nodded. "300k."

"Alright then, I'm out." He rose from his chair, grabbing a few more of his fries. Then he stuffed them in his mouth on his way out.

Ernieshook his head saying, "I fucking hate that guy."

As soon as Malvo departed from McDonald's, his cell rang with a call from Crunch. He had some information he wanted to drop in his lap, so they agreed to meet up at Target on 120th and Crenshaw, which was only a few blocks away. Fifteen minutes later, Crunch pulled into the lot and parked all of the way at the back beside Malvo's whip. Crunch killed the engine and murdered the stereo. The front passenger door opened and Malvo jumped in, closing the door shut.

"Tell me you got something on your boy."

"Nah," Crunch shook his head sadly. "I combed the streets and ain't nobody so much as heard a peep from that nigga."

"You holler at his people?"

"I went by his mom's and his girl's crib, said they still haven't seen or heard from 'em." Crunch spoke honestly. "Mom's stressing like hell, though. She said she filed a police report and is staying prayed up, suggested we do the same."

"Humph." He shook his head shamefully as he played with the stubble of his goatee "I never could understand how mothafuckaz could believe in anything they couldn't hear nor see."

"Blind faith," Crunch analyzed.

"We gon' have to see one of 'em. Either moms or old girl," Malvo said. "One of their asses knows something."

"You sure about that, fam? Maybe Ron just blew town without saying a word."

"Nuh uh," Malvo shook his head.

"Between moms and his bitch, there's something there. Someone's holding out and we're going to find out who it is."

"I hear what chu saying, Boss Dog, but they're like family."

"Family." He frowned and abruptly stopped playing with the stubble of his chin hair. "Let me tell you something, them mothafuckaz ceased being family the day they people ran off with my dope. Fuck them, the whole lot of 'em. Feel me, my nigga? He played with the Devil now his loved ones gotta feel his wrath."

Crunch raised his eyebrows and exhaled. He didn't really want to get at Ronny's people, but if that's the way Malvo wanted it, then fuck it, he was going to roll with him.

He didn't have a choice after all, he had pledged an allegiance to the man when he was just a snot nose.

Crunch could remember the day Malvo put him and Ronny on as if it was yesterday. They were only thirteen and fourteen years old then and had been living on the streets after having ran away from their group home. From sun up until sun down they'd stand on the block hustling They treated the corner like a job, clocking in at 6 o'clock in the morning and taking it back in at 7, only to wake up at the crack of dawn to do it all over again.

Unbeknownst to them, Malvo had been watching them in his car from afar for the past two weeks. He saw how ambitious they were and thought they would be an asset to his budding organization. Having seen enough, he whistled and waved the boys over. Seeing that they were hesitant to come, he flashed them a wad of money to entice them.

It worked.

He got the boys to take a ride with him to get a bite to eat. During that time he picked their minds to see where they were at with it. Not long after, the trio found themselves sitting at a table inside of Bertha's Soul Food restaurant on Century and Western Avenue.

"I'ma let you lil' niggaz eat with me, but chu gotta set the table and do the dishes." Malvo told them, pulling a thick ass wad from his pocket. He peeled off four one hundred dollar bills, placing a pair in front of Crunch and Ronny, respectively. "All I ask for in return is your devotion, loyalty and honesty, nothing more and nothing less. Y'all picking up what I'm sitting down?" He looked from Crunch to Ronny and they nodded in unison. Crunch went to pick up the money, sparking Malvo to grab a steak knife and stab it into the table top near his hand, startling him.

"Slow your roll. Now when I say loyalty, I mean your undying loyalty. That shit that'll never wither and die. If I was to tell you to put your man here to sleep," he pointed to Ronny, "then I'd expect it to be done, no questions asked."

"But that's my nigga, though," Crunch made it known. He and Ronny had come up on free lunch together, so he couldn't see himself peeling his cap back.

"You think I give a fuck? If I say he goes, then he's gone, for whatever reason. The same goes for you, do you follow me?" He stared Ronny directly into his eyes. Crunch and Ronny nodded their heads. "Good, 'cause all I need is soldiers, that's it. You either fall in line or get rocked to sleep." He looked from Crunch to Ronny. "Make your choices gentlemen, either eternal damnation living the rest of your lives as a couple of broke ass niggaz,, or salvation working for me and getting more money than you know what to do with."

"Salvation," Crunch nodded.

"Salvation," Ronny spoke after him.

"Alright now, I'm set y'all out with three hundred packets of Kryptonite," Malvo told them. "You're gonna get it on the same avenue you've been on, but this time I'ma post a trigga-man and a lookout out there with chu. Cool?" He looked back and forth between them, awaiting their answer.

"Cool," Crunch and Ronny spoke in unison.

"Smooth."

Crunch and Ronny then took the glasses off of the twin hundred dollar bills and tucked them. They went on to devour their meals like a couple of starving puppies. Malvo sparked up a square and lay back with his arm stretched over the top of the neighboring chair. He puffed on the square and blew out clouds. The smile on his face made him look like the horned overlord of the hottest place imaginable.

Malvo was a master manipulator. He knew just what to say and what to do to get people to move to the beat of his drum. If you weren't his wife or his daughter, he couldn't give a flying fuck about you. Everyone was expendable to him, even Crunch and Ronny, and he was practically their father. The two thugs were everything he wanted in soldiers. They were dedicated, determined,and willing to kill. That didn't matter, though, because once they'd outgrown their usefulness or served their purpose they would be discarded like a shitty diaper. Everyone in his operation was nothing more than pawns on the chest board of the deadly game he played. And he would move them around and place them where ever he saw fit.

"Alright," Crunch began, "you wanna take it there?Cool. But we aren't getting at moms and his girl. You gon' have to choose up or your ass is going at this shit solo."

Malvo shook his head and said, "Old Marshmallow heart ass,which one?"

"I don't know nigga, you decide."

"Fuck it. We'll flip a coin." Malvo leaned to the side and fished around inside of his pocket until he found a silver dollar. He held it in his palm so Crunch could see it. "Heads for moms, tails for wifey." He flipped the silver dollar, caught it and smacked it down on the brown side of his hand. Staring down at his hand, he slowly removed it to reveal what side the coin was on. A sinister smile formed on his lips and he looked at Crunch who raised an eyebrow.

"It's settled, then." Malvo tossed the coin against Crunch's chest and hopped out of the car.

****

The Desert Eagle bucked in the Russian's hand, releasing a hot bullet just as the rickety chair collapsed beneath his feet. The sizzling rock simmered through the rope, burning and severing it. Ronny fell just before the rope could snag him back up. He hit the basement floor hard on his side, coughing hard and loud. The Russian approached Ronny with the Desert Eagle at his side. His shadow completely swallowed his form.

The Russian placed his foot on Ronny's throat and pressed down on it. The pressure against Ronny's esophagus caused his eyes to bulge and him to gag. He looked like his eyes were about to explode out of their sockets.

"I want to know everything there is to know about Malvo," the Russian gritted with insanity peeking in his eyes. "His hangouts, the streets he puts his product on, where his kid goes to school, where his wife works, everything. Do you understand?"

"Yes! Yes!" Ronny gagged, his eyes pooling with tears from the pressure on his esophagus.

"Good." The Russian's gritting morphed into a jovial expression and he took his shoe off of Ronny's esophagus. Ronny turned on his side with his forehead against the floor, coughing violently as he struggled to suck the precious air into his lungs.

The Russian turned around to his men, looking back and forth between the two as he spoke. "Nicolay, Mikhail, I want you to clean this man up. Call up the good doctor, Eme, and see to it that he receives the best medical care. I want this man in tip top shape. He's going to take us to every trap Malvo runs, every strip joint he frequents, and the homes of every piece of ass he's ever entertained. I'm going to turn this man's most beautiful dream into his ugliest nightmare."

"Yes, Vladimir," the men said in unison, moving to pick up Ronny.

Vladimir handed the Desert Eagle back to the man he'd gotten it from and headed back up the staircase. Coming out of the house, he approached a Lincoln Town Carlimothat had a chauffeur standing beside it. The chauffeur opened the backdoor and he climbed aboard. Once the Lincoln pulled off, he sat back in his seat and poured a glass of Louie XIII. He sat the glass down and pulled a Cuban cigar from his suit. He clipped the end of the cigar and placed it between his lips.

"Fugazi," Vladimir shook his head and took another sip from his glass, "Fucking fugazi."

The money Malvo sent Ronny to buy the heroine with was counterfeit. Normally, Vladimir didn't bother checking the authenticity of the money when he did business because all of his customers were on the up and up with him. But recently he had discovered he had close to $650, 000 dollars that was counterfeit. He didn't know who had slipped him the money, so he decided to play it forward. The next time someone came to cop he would check the money they spent with him.

All of his customers had passed the test, leaving Malvo left to deal with. Although the proof was right there staring him in the face, Vladimir wanted to be positive his heroin peddler's money was indeed fake before he handed down his death warrant. So he ran a Drimark Counterfeit Detector pen over three stacks of the money. When the markings turned black this confirmed it for him, the money wasn't legit. If the money was the real deal, the markings would have been yellow, amber, or clear.

"You have crossed the wrong man, my friend," he said of Malvo as he stared out of the window, watching the scenery change through the black tinted glass. "Once I catch up to you, you'll be begging me for a bullet after the torture I put you through." Vladimir partook of his cigar and liquor thinking of the different ways he could torture Malvo once he caught up with him.

An hour later...

A black pillowcase was pulled over Ronny's head and he was thrown into the back of a van. Vladimir's henchmen took him to an old warehouse and stored him in an office. Inside there was two buckets. One for him to shit in and the other for him to piss in. A thin blue mattress was lying against the wall along with a pillow and a tattered blanket. Ronny was given a half jug of water, two slices of bread, and some shit that resembled oat meal.

About thirty minutes later, Doctor Eme showed up and gave him a thorough examination. He discovered that Ronny suffered from fracture ribs, a fractured eye socket, and a concussion. The doctor wrapped his ribs, gave him a couple of painkillers, and prescribed that he gets at least a month's worth of bed rest to fully recover.

Later that day, Ronny lay on the mattress staring up at the ceiling thinking, *No matter what happens I'm not giving them Malvo. I'd die 'fore I roll over on my dawg. I just gotta bide some time so I can get a hold of him and let 'em know what's up. They may take me to the grave, but I know my nigga got my back. He'll take care of my lady and my family, that's what I'm sure of. Real niggaz do real things.* Those were Ronny's last thoughts before he closed his eyes and sleep invaded him.

Only time would tell if he was right about Malvo.

Chapter Five

"I'm telling you, sis, we should have pounded that bitch out." Anton held the dustpan while Eureka swept the broken pieces of dishes into it."Matter of fact, it ain't nothing stopping us from charging up them stairs and giving her a crucial beat down."

"As much as I'd like to take you up on that offer, I'm gonna have to pass." She stated regretfully.

"Why?" he asked disappointedly.

"Baby brother, you heard what Fear said, any more drama and we're out on our asses." She told him. "We get kicked outta here then where are we gonna go?" He didn't respond. "Exactly."

"All we need is money."

"Yeah, well, where are we gonna get it?"

"I already told you where it's at." Anton reminded Eureka about his plan to jack Trap Boys for their grips. The little nigga loved the rush he got from robbing cats. Stealing cars gave him a hard-on, but jacking niggaz for their shit got him off like a Taiwan hooker.

"I'm still milling that over, but I don't want you taking part in it." She spoke earnestly.

Anton exhaled as he tilted his head back and rolled his eyes. "Here we go again," he said, sounding like DMX.

"That's right. *Here we go again,*" Eureka repeated. "Now, dump that and take out the trash."

Anton dumped the trash from the dustpan into the trashcan and grabbed the black garbage bag out of it. He tied it up and carried it outside.

Eureka dipped the mop inside of the bucket and smacked it down on the floor. She was moving about mopping the floor until she heard someone coming down the steps. She looked over her shoulder and saw Constance approaching, tucking a pair of designer shades into the collar of her shirt. Eureka went back to her business, paying Constance no never mind.

Here comes this busted Timberland rocking bitch, Eureka thought as she shook her head. *I am so not in the mood for her shit, so I hope she keeps it moving.*

Boomp!

The mop bucket hit the linoleum and the hot sudsy water spilled all over the floor. Eureka's forehead creased and her lips twisted. She looked to her left and Constance was tapping a pack of Newport 100s in her palm. Once a cigarette rose up from the pack, she pulled it free with her lips and pulled out a Bic lighter. She went on to spark up the square as if she didn't just kick over the bucket of water.

A cloud of smoke rushed from Constance's mouth as she formed her lips into the shape of an O. She tucked the lighter into the small pocket of her baggy, black denim jeans and the cigs into the pocket of her shirt. She then looked Eureka up and down like,*Bitch what? I wish you would say something.*

Eureka remained tight lipped as she narrowed her eyes at Constance,her mouth was quaking she was so hot. She wanted to whip Constance until she caught on fire, but she didn't want to kick up anymore shit in Fear's house for fear of getting tossed out on her ass.

"What's up? You got something on your mind?" Constance asked, trying to provoke a fight. "If so, speak on it, youngin'.Don't hold that shit in,it's bad for your health." She narrowed her eyes at Eureka as she took a slow, casual pull from her square, daring her to stunt so she could give her a reason to act the fuck up. She unleashed a roar of smoke directly into Eureka's face, blatantly disrespecting her.

"I'm good," Eureka answered, narrowing her eyes into slits as the smoke was blown into her face. She ignored the nicotine fog and continued mopping the floor, paying Constance no mind.

Constance stepped up to Eureka with her nose nearly touching hers. "Say what, now?"

"I said, *I'm good.*" Eureka repeated, she gritted her teeth and the skin on her forehead bunched together as she tried her damndest to keep the beast inside of her chained and shackled.

A smile formed on Constance's lips and just like that it disappeared, replaced by a maddening expression. "That's what I thought." She turned around and headed for the front door, kicking the bucket one last time as she walked passed it. The bucket deflected off of the kitchen cabinets and hit the floor.

Eureka spat obscenities under her breath as she picked it up.She poured Pine Sol, Clorox beach, Fabuloso, and a little Dawn dishwashing liquid into it. She then refilled it with scolding hot water again and started back mopping.

Constance crossed paths with Anton as she headed for the front door. Locking eyes with him, she gave him that,*What the fuck are you looking at nigga?* look. Anton waved her off as she disappeared through the front door. Entering the kitchen, he noticed the agitated expression on Eureka's face.

"What's up, sis?" He asked, concerned. Eureka shook her head like,*Ain't shit.* Anton looked back at the door Constance went through, then back at Eureka. "It's

Constance ain't it?" Eureka nodded. He exhaled and ran his hand down his face. "What happened?"

"That bitch is this close, bro, this close." With her finger and thumb, Eureka showed Anton how close Constance was to getting a chest fullof something blazing hot.

She had already dropped two bodies so a third would be as easy as reciting her ABC's. She knew she was going to end up having to take Constance out. She hadn't known her long and she had proven to be a headache. Eureka refused to live her life walking around on pins and needles, wondering when that bitch was going to try her. She wasn't about to sleep with one eye open on her account, she'd much rather put something in her head and get that shit over with.

"If you want that ho gone, that's one magic trick I can perform.He licked his lips and smiled sinisterly, rubbing his hands together.

The statement and the expression on his face caused Eureka to stand erect like a hard dick. She narrowed her eyes at Anton as the thought ripped through her brain. She had an idea, but she had never been for sure. She figured now was as good of a time as any to ask.

Eureka stopped mopping the floor and rested her hands on top of each other on the end of the mop's handle. "Baby boy, I got something I'm gonna ask you and I want chu to keep it one hunnit with me."

"Always do, sis, Watts up?" Anton wore a serious expression.

"Kilo…" Eureka paused and allowed the name to marinate in his mental before she went on. "You did that?"

"Did what?" He faked ignorance.

"Do you really want me to bust your balls about it?"

Anton exhaled and looked away. He turned back around, looking Eureka in her eyes and nodded.

"Fuck it. Yeah, that was me."

"What happened?"

"You really wanna know?"

"I asked didn't I?"

"Alright." Anton exhaled and recounted the story.

It was 2 o'clock in the morning when Kilo came hustling down the steps of his house, wiping his shiny forehead with the back of his hand. He had been in the middle of cooking crack when he'd gotten a call from his girl's sister saying she was in labor about to have his baby boy. This was his first kid so needless to say he was excited.

After he finished turning the soft white powder into hard white rocks, he straightened up the spot. Once he grabbed his strap and his jacket, he headed for the front door. Coming out of the yard, he gave a cautionary scan of the block, making sure karma hadn't come back to bite him in the ass. He'd done a lot of dirt in his lifetime and was well aware that when you did dirt you got dirt.

Kilo hopped behind the wheel of his rental. He stuck his key inside of the ignition and was about to turn it until a flicker of movement at the corner of his eye stalled him. He reached for the gun on his hip and was about tolet something go until someone came into view. It was Crack Head Fred.

"What chu know good, Big Time?" The lanky man greeted, he was in a big sun hat and his bony hand was wrapped around a lacquered oak wood staff he'd crafted himself.

"What the hell is yo problem, sneakin' up on a nigga like that at this hour of night?" Kilo fumed with arched

eyebrows and a scrunched nose. "You almost got cho mothafuckin' head knocked off!"

"My bad, folk, I don't mean no disrespect." He held up his hand and his staff submissively. "I was just tryna get me a lil' something, something 'fore I went in." He thumbed his nose and sniffed, flashing a couple of wrinkled dollar bills he hoped would lighten the mood with Kilo.

Kilo's massive hand shot out ofthe window and snatched the wrinkled bills out of Fred's hand.

"Look out for yo peoples one time, Big Time. I'm shorter than a midget on his knees," he said as he watched Kilo count the money he'd snatched from him.

Kilo seemed to become angrier once he'd counted the money he had to spend with him. "Three punk ass dollas nigga?I should peel ya cap for disrespectin' my hustle!" Kilo fumed. "Do I look like a nickel and dime nigga to you? You fuck with me you know to come with at least twenty or don't come at all."

"I know, man,but help me out. I'm tryna get right for the night," Fred pleaded.

"Gon' get outta here, fam, and charge this lil' paper to the game." He held up the wrinkled dollar bills then deposited them into his pocket.

"Ah, come on, Kilo, I'm hurting out here.Don't do me like this," he held his hands together, begging. If there was anything Kilo hated in the world, it was a weak ass man.He was an Alpha Male and only respected such.

Kilo reached into his pocket and tossed Fred something copper and shiny. Fred caught it and his brow furrowed, wondering what it was. He held the object up to the street light and it gleamed like a flawless diamond. It was a copper bullet.

"We're gone find out if you can catch the next one if you don't breeze." Kilo shot him a deadly expression that could kill a nigga faster than an LAPD officer with an itchy trigger finger. Fred knew as well as anybody how Kilo gave it up in the streets. His penalties for violations were swift and unmerciful.

"Alright, man, I'ma just take the L," he spoke submissively.

"That's what I know you gon' do." Kilo rubbed his defeat in his face and fired up the rental. The car roared to life and thunder erupted.

Bop!

A Look of confusion seized Kilo's face as a red dot quickly expanded at the center of his white T-shirt. He lazily looked through the passenger side window and met the black hole of a blue steel, .38, snub-nose revolver, wafting with smoke. Kilo went to snatch his banger off of his waistline, but Fred grabbed his hand before he could pull it. He turned around, trying to fight Fred off, and thunder erupted four more times. A quartet to the dome left Kilo's thoughts in his lap. It looked like crumbled raspberry cobbler sitting on his crotch.

"Fuck man, you got blood in my eyes." Fred complained, wipingaway the residue with the inside of his tattered, Lakers basketball jersey.

Anton dressed in a black hoodie and jeans, ran around to the driver side of the car. He opened the door and rifled through Kilo's pockets, taking whatever cash he had on him. He then got a firm hold on Kilo's Cuban link chain and yanked it clean from his neck. Police sirens wailed in the distance as he stuffed the hefty chain inside of his pockets. He tapped Fred's arm and together they made a hasty getaway, fleeing up the street like a couple of track stars.

Anton and Fred ducked off inside of an alley about four blocks from where he'd given Kilo his issue. Anton pulled his hood from over his dome and leaned his head back against the brick building, panting, out of breath. Fred was hunched over with his hands on his knees. He too was out of breath.

"Man," Fred wheezed, "I haven't run like that since I was on the high schoolVarsity football team back in '77."

Anton pulled the money he'd taken from Kilo out of his pocket. He shuffled through the crisp bills, counting out Fred's take from the robbery.

"How'd you get that?" Anton pointed to his arm with the .38 revolver.

Fred looked at the bloody gashes and said, "Mothafucka scratched me back there, got me pretty good, too." Seeing Anton's sneakers as he stepped before him, Fred's head snapped up to see him pointing the blue steel .38 dead at his ass. Fred's eyes bulged and his mouth dropped open, revealing all of the teeth he had missing. He took a cautious step back, looking like he saw Jesus walk on water. "What I do, man?"

"It ain't about what chu did, it's about what chu could do, G." Anton said with a solemn face, settling his finger on the trigger. Fred's head snapped from left to right as he looked for a place to escape. Anton saw he was about to make a run for it. "Don't run, my nigga, I got love for you. I don't want to take you from the back, just take this shit like a man and get it on out the way."

"Hel—" The rest of the word was knocked right back down Fred's throat as a bullet slammed into the front

of his skull, snapping his head back and knocking the big sun hat off of his crown.

Fred dropped down to his knees, where he stayed for a second, before falling over to the side. Anton approached his lifeless body. Looking down on him, he crossed his heart in the sign of the crucifix. He then chucked the empty .38 down the dark alley and threw his hood back over his head. Anton made his way to the end of the alley where he peered out to make sure the coast was clear. Once he saw that the boys weren't anywhere in sight, he emerged from the alley and strode off casually.

The world appeared to have stopped and all seemed to have grown quiet as Eureka stared into the eyes of her little brother. She was stunned by his revelation. She knew more than likely he had murdered Kilo, but to find out he had murdered someone else had taken her by surprise. His soul had been stained and his thoughts had been tainted just as hers had.They both had been purged of their innocence and there wasn't any way either of them could get it back.

"What?"

Eureka shook her head, "Nothing."

"Nah, Watts up?"

Eureka exhaled and replied, "Why'd you kill Crack Head Fred? He was alright by us. Sometimes he would help me carry groceries home and wouldn't ask for shit. Hell, before he got all strung out, he and Daddy used to play Tonk at Ms. Charlene's house every Saturday night before she died."

"I know, but I had to do what I had to do." Anton spoke from the heart. "Kilo scratched 'em, so Fred's DNA was definitely underneath his fingernails. The Ones would have come looking for Fred eventually and who's to say he wouldn't have given me up? I couldn't let that man hold my life in his hands. The way I saw it, it was either my ass or his."

Eureka looked off to the side, nodding her head as she thought about where Anton was coming from.

"Right. You did what you had to do." Eureka conceded. Gazing into her little brother's eyes, it hit her like a Pimp Slap. Those eyes no longer belonged to a fifteen year old boy, they belonged to a fifteen year old killer.

The truth was a hard pill to swallow and it turned her stomach. She realized she had gone wrong somewhere in her raising of him. She held herself accountable for what he had become. She felt if she would have done a better job, his hands wouldn't have become dirty. Eureka's eyes stung as they began to water, tears threatened to spill down her cheeks but she quickly wiped them away with the back of her hand.

The skin on Anton's forehead furrowed as he approached his sister, laying a hand on her shoulder.

"What's wrong, Reka?"

"I'm sorry."

"Sorry?" He looked at her eerily.

"I'm sorry, Anton. I'm so, so sorry, baby brother." Her voice cracked under her emotions as she staggered back, breathing like an asthmatic in desperate need of an inhaler.

Her eyes stung like they'd been pierced with hot sewing needles and the tears she swiped away before came flying down her cheeks, dripping onto the floor. Her chest was moving up and down sporadically, causing her shoulders to rise and fall, rapidly. She was hyperventilating.

She felt like she'd been shot through the chest. She grabbed the edge of the kitchen sink, holding on for dear life. She looked up at Anton like she was having a heart attack, clutching on the cotton of her wife beater where her heart beat. Eureka looked around, eyes wide and gasping for air.

"It's my—it's my fault that you—you turned out this way," Eureka's heart acted as a ventriloquist, using her to relay exactly how she felt. "I should have—I should have protected you!"

She broke down slobbering and crying. She had allowed her baby brother to be tainted by the wickedness of the world. His innocence had been lost and there wasn't anyway he could get it back. Eureka felt like it was all her fault. Her father made her promise to take care of her baby brother before he was ripped from the bosom of life. She'd failed miserably and she just knew that old Bootsy was turning over in his grave at that moment.

Anton tore off a couple of paper towels and balled them up. He held Eureka by her chin as he wiped her face dry. She blew and wiped her nose with the paper towels, dropping them in the trash can as he led her into the living room. Eureka sat on the sofa, closing her eyes and taking deep breaths, trying to gain control of her breathing. While she was doing that, Anton left and returned with a glass of water.

"Here, drink this," he told her, rubbing her back as she drank from the glass thirstily. "Take it easy, sis. You'll be alright."

"Okay. Alright," she responded, closing her eyes and trying to slow her breathing to a normal pace.

Once Eureka got her bearings, Anton kneeled before her,tookher hands into his own and looked into her eyes.

"How I turned out isn't your fault, you hear me? That burden doesn't lie upon your shoulders," he spoke sincerely. "We got a raw deal, sis. We were fucked the moment mommy pushed us outta her womb, the very day we took our first breath of air. The world wrote us off early. You did the best you could to keep our family together. Shit, you were just a kid yourself when you took the responsibilities on,but somehow you persevered, pulling off miracle after miracle. You're smart, clever, pretty, loyal, and you got my back."

With each compliment he gave her, the grim expression her face slowly withered and died. After its death, her face gave birth to a smile and a blush. She partially hid her face against her arm, feeling giddy. It was nice to know that someone thought so highly of her and believed she was so special. She needed to hear such kind words, especially with all of the heartache and turmoil she'd been through.

Anton hadn't a clue that his praise was strengthening and uplifting his sister. She was going to store away that moment in time and use it to get through whatever obstacles life threw her way. She'd silently recite them to herself and remember just how unique she really was. Anton's words were like the temperature of the sun and they were slowly melting away the icy balls of guilt that had formed in her chest.

"Truthfully, I couldn't ask for a better ride or die, Queen." He held her hands together and kissed them, treating her like the royalty he saw her to be. "Now, as far as Kilo is concerned, I got that dick sucker up outta here 'cause he laid hands on the most precious person in my life—you." That caused the tears to return, but they weren't of guilt. Nah, they were ones of happiness. Happiness that there was someone out there that held her in such high regard. Eureka quickly wiped the tears away with a curled finger. "I know if it was me that dude had beaten like that,you would have rode for me.That's why I rode for you. You aren't just my big sister, you're my nigga, and I'd die—I'd die for you."

For the first time since he was nine years old, Eureka heard her baby brother's voice crackle and saw his eyes mist with tears. He loved Eureka just as much as she loved him and no matter what life saw fit to hurl their way, they knew that they'd be right there to face it. Together.

Eureka shot up from the sofa and hugged her baby brother like she'd never hugged him before. They stood there, wrapped in one another's warm embraces, feeling closer than they ever had before.

Anton wiped the tear that trickled from his eye and chuckled lightly.

"Man, you got a nigga in here crying and shit like a lil' ol' bitch," he said. "What would the homies think if they were to see me now?"

"Shut up, punk ass, you're ruining the moment." She squeezed him even tighter, kissing his cheek and the side of his head. "I love you, Ant."

"I love you too, sis." He replied. "This shit bet not get back to The Bricks, though. Baby brother gotta rep to uphold."

"It won't, you dick." She laughed and broke their tender moment, shoving him away.

"What y'all doing down here?" Fear asked, descending the last step as he slipped a graphic T-shirt over his head.

"Ain't nothing, big homie. Just a lil' brotherly, sisterly bonding going on." Anton threw his arm over Eureka's shoulders and pecked her on the cheek.

"Is that right?" Fear asked. "Well, look, me and homegirl out there 'bout to bust a move. Y'all ain't got no problems holding it down here, do you?"

"Nah, we're good. Gon' and do yo thang, my nig-ga," Anton told him.

"Yeah, we'll be alright here."

"Cool."

Fear dapped up Anton and Eureka before making a beeline for the front door.

Chapter Six

Darkness fell on the city of Watts, calling forth the wayward souls that owned the night. The underworld was in full effect as drugs sells were made, pussy was bought, niggaz were robbed, and police were on the prowl to put some poor bastards in shackles. Fear pulled up three houses down from Bugsy's trap and killed the engine of his '76 Buick Regal.

Bugsy was a young knucklehead that made the mistake of putting his hands on Bemmy's daughter. With that slap to the face, the OG took his leash off of his most vicious dog and sent him on his trail. Fear had a pretty simple job to do: kidnap the Jordan Downs thug and torture his ass to death for what he'd done to his employer's offspring.

Fear slipped on a pair of black sunglasses, tied a red bandana around the lower half of his face and pulled the drawstrings of his hoodie, enclosing the hood around his head. He took a moment to give himself the once over in the rearview mirror before sticking his hands into a pair of black leather gloves. Once he'd strapped the gloves on and made sure they were secured on his hands, he pulled out two guns: one a silenced .9mm automatic, and the other a tranquilizer gun.

He chambered a live round into the head of the .9mm and laid it down on the passenger seat. He then picked up the tranquilizer gun and jammed a fresh tranquilizer dart into it. He strapped a belt, lined with tranquilizer darts, around his thigh, grabbed his weapons, and hopped out of the car. Lifting the trunk, he grabbed a red gas-can and slammed it shut.

Fear speed walked his way up the sidewalk, occasionally looking over his shoulder as he went along. When he made it to Bugsy's trap, he circled it and doused it with gasoline. Once the gasoline was spent, he tossed the gascan aside and pulled out a book of matches. He struck a match and tossed it into the dry weeds surrounding the house. The weeds went up quick, wrapping a ring of fire around the house.

"Five. Four. Three. Two. One." Fear counted aloud on his fingers.

A moment passed and then the backdoor rattled from powerful impacts. *Ba-thoom! Ba-thoom! Ba-thoom! Boom!* The backdoor flew open, sending a chunk of the door frame flying. A horde of dope fiends came spilling out of the house, falling over one another and trampling over those that hit the ground.

Fear brandished his weapons for the task at hand. Cautiously, he approached the backdoor and stepped inside, allowing his weapons to lead the way. Coming through the door, entering the kitchen, emerging into the hallway, a beanie rocking thug crossed Fear's line of vision. He whistled. The young man whipped around and took two in the sternum, dropping to the floor. Fear stepped over him and heard what sounded like two sets of footsteps hurrying down the staircase. His head shot up and two hoodlums in white T-shirts had just come into view. He turned their white T's crimson and moved along, seeking out his real target, Bugsy.

Hearing shuffling inside of a nearby bathroom, he ran to its door and kicked it open. He was about to pop off until he saw a dope fiend hiding inside of the bathtub, cradling her young son. She stared up at him with sad, pleading eyes that begged for him not to give her a new hairstyle.

"Nigga, get the fuck out the way!" Fear's head snapped to the bathroom's door, hearing the voice out in the hallway. He darted out into the corridor just in time to see Bugsy shoving another young man aside so he could open the front door. Fear lifted his .9mm and steadied it so he could push the youth's wig to the front. He was about to pull the trigger when something loud exploded.

Bloom!

The shotgun roared and Fear stumbled forward, nearly falling as he gritted his teeth. Thwarting off the pain in his back, he whipped around to find a fat hoodlum he'd missed cradling a long ass chrome shotgun.

Bloom!

Another blast sent Fear sliding across the floor through the drug paraphernalia and loose trash. Looking up, he saw his hefty assailant running up on him to finish him off. Fear gripped his .9mm as tight as he could and brought that thang up, spitting flames. The searing bullets tatted up the assailant's thighs and belly. He fell to his knees and dropped the shotgun. He then fell on his face with his ass hiked up in the air, like he was waiting for a nigga to come fuck him doggy style.

Fear heard the rapid squeaking of sneakers on the hardwood floor as someone else was hastily approaching. He knew it had to be the youngster that was with Bugsy at the front door. His theory was confirmed once he saw a pair of black All-Star, Chuck Taylor, Converse with purple laces in them enter his line of vision.

He rolled over on the floor like he was on fire as the youth shot at him, trying to give him a closed casket. Still in motion, rolling around on the floor, he extended the hand that held the silenced .9mm. He allowed it to puke bullets after bullets, tagging the young man's chest. He lifted the .9mm a little higher and sent one more at his forehead. The impact of the bullet snapped his head back and a chunk of his brain was caught in his doo-rag before he could hit the floor. The youngster slammed into the floor, making a thud and shitting in his Dickies for the final time.

Fear slowly staggered to his feet, rubbing his chest and wincing in pain. The Kevlar vest he wore underneath stopped the shotgun's pellets from snatching his life and he couldn't be more grateful. But the truth of the matter was those pellets were a son of a bitch. They hurt like hell even through the vest. He could only hope his ribs weren't broken. Nonetheless, he had to move along before his target got away.

Fear inched toward the open hallway and quickly glanced down the corridor. Bugsy had just ran outside. Fear tucked his .9mm. Gripping the tranquilizer gun tightly, he ran after Bugsy to serve him some street justice.

Slowly pulling the front door open,Fear poked his head out. Before he could make another move, Bugsy sprayed that Tec-9. The quick burst of hot lead stabbed the door like a dozen butcher's knives, one after another. Fear managed to snatch his head back before he got his hat split. He waited a few moments before kicking the front door open and stepping out,both hands firmly wrapped around the handle of the tranquilizer gun as he hurried down the steps.

Looking up the block, he spotted Bugsy running for his life.You would have thought he had a horde of zombies on his heels. Fear scurried out of the yard of the trap and took aim at Bugsy as he struck up the sidewalk. As soon as he pulled the trigger he heard Bugsy yelp. The tranquilizer dart lodged into his thigh, slowing him down, but not stopping him. Fearloaded another dart and hugged the trigger. Thatone stuck to Bugsy's back like a magnet. His buff neck ass slowed to a trot before he eventually collapsed on the sidewalk.

Fear jogged over to Bugsy and took a quick scan of the block to see if anybody had been watching himbefore kneeling down and checking his pulse. The tranquilizer had knocked Bugsy out cold. He tucked the gun on his waistline and popped the trunk. He strained as he pulled Bugsy's thick ass back toward his car then hoisted him up and deposited him inside of the trunk. Slamming it shut, he hopped back inside of the Regal and pulled off.

A few blocks down, after figuring he was in the clear, Fear mashed the gas pedal to the floor and the hooptie blew through a stoplight just as it turned red. As soon as he crossed the intersection, he heard something he didn't want to hear, the very familiar chirp of Five O's siren. He looked up into the rearview mirror, and sure enough, there was a police cruiser at his rear.

Fear spewed obscenities and shook his head. *That's all a nigga need is for these mothafuckaz to show up.* He thought about sending the pig on a high speed chase, or pulling over and letting his banger melt his face, buthis cooler head prevailed and he chose the option behind door number three.

After storing the black sunglasses, bandana, leather gloves and the weapons into a stash box he pulled over. Seeing the buzz cut rocking police officer approaching through the side-mirror, he mentally prepared himself for the confrontation.

The police officer stepped to the driver side door, shining his flashlight inside of the interior of his car. The light the flashlight illuminated was so bright it caused Fear's eyes to narrow. He was so irritated he could feel himself submerging into the heart of his anger. Brushing off the officer's blatant disrespect, he mustered up a smile and addressed him.

"Hi, how are you doing tonight, officer?" Fear said with a jovial expression.

"You know you ran through a red light back there?" The officer clicked off the flashlight and stashed it on his waist.

"You got me there, boss," he said. "I was tryna make it home to take a shit."

"Take a shit, huh?" The police officer said, disbelievingly. "Where are you coming from?"

"My girl's house," Fear told him. "I couldn't take a shit over there. We've only been together a couple of months. You know how that is. I'm not quite comfortable yet."

There was a silence between the police officer and Fear that seemed to have lasted forever.

If there is a God, he better give this pig the notion to keep it moving 'cause if not, that ass is sure 'nough gon' be another notch under my belt.

The police officer had a feeling Fear had come from the area where gunfire and a fire was reported. Initially, he was going to let him go with a warning for speeding, but something told him that he'd better look into things. The cop stepped back from the door with his hand on his holstered gun.

"Driver, step out of the car for me, please," the police officer ordered.

Fear frowned, "What's the problem officer?"

"Step out of the car now!"

It's your funeral, mothafucka, Fear thought with a hardface as he unbuckled the safety belt. He moved to hop out of the car. If shit went south then he was going to snap the pig's neck and leave him with his dick in the dirt.

****

Constance lay back in the driver seat, maneuvering her black rag top BMW through the streets. She listened to Nipsey Hussle's *Rose Clique* as she took casual pulls of a burning joint. Her eyes were moist and bloodshot, but no one would be able to make them out through her oversized designer shades. She sat up in her seat and mashed out the joint in the ashtray. She made a right at the corner, sped through two stop-signs, and nearly hit a wino crossing the street before she made a sharp left onto a residential block.

Turning the volume down on her stereo, she coasted down the street, checking her whereabouts. When she saw a few hoodlums posted up outside of a yard, smoking, drinking, and talking shit, a wicked smile formed on her face. She removed her .45 automatic from the console and clicked the safety off. She killed her BMW's headlights and held down a button that descended the driver side window. The hoodlums grew silent and watched the BMW attentively, some of them even pulled out their burners.

"Who dat, cuz?" One of the hoodlums asked.

"I don't know, but I'ma 'bout to light that bitch the fuck up," another hoodlum said.

"Straight like that."

Constance mashed the brake pedal and brought her .45 around. She pointed it out of the window and squeezed its trigger with rapid succession.

Poc! Poc! Poc! Poc! Poc!

The eruption of gunfire sent the hoodlums scrambling and scattering. Niggas broke from off of the pack, trying to get the fuck out of the way and avoid catching some hot-ones. Constance sat her smoking .45 in her lap and pulled off laughing manically. A couple of the hoodlums ran out into the street and pointed their burners. They cracked off shots and sent hot rocks at the back of the fleeing BMW.

She slumped low in the driver seat looking from the windshield to the side-view mirror. She watched as the hoodlums ran out into the street, popping off in her direction. Two bullets struck the bumper of her car while a third struck the side-view mirror, hollowing and shattering its glass. She snapped her head to the right to avoid any shards of glass slicing her face.

"Cock suckas," she fumed. "I should roll back on their asses."

She hung a right at the end of the block and sped off.

****

"Driver, step out of the car for me, please," the police officer ordered.

Fear frowned, "What's the problem officer?"

"Step out of the car now!"

It's your funeral, mothafucka, Fear thought with a hardface as he unbuckled the safety belt. He moved to hop out of the car. If shit went south, then he was going to snap the pig's neck and leave him with his dick in the dirt.

Something told him this wasn't going to end well as he moved to break the cop's neck. But at that moment, he was frozen by the sudden burst of gunfire that plagued the night's air.

Poc! Poc! Poc! Poc! Poc!

The sound of gunfire made the police officer look alive. His neck snapped from left to right, wondering where the shots had come from. When several more shots followed, he knew the firefight was just a couple of blocks over from where he was. The radio transceiver attached to his shoulder crackled as the voice of the dispatcher came through. Fear didn't understand what kind of codes the dispatcher was spewing, but whatever they were, they must have been important because it got the officer hyped up and in a hurry.

"Get out of here, you're free to go!" The police officer told him.

Fear watched the law haul ass back to his cruiser, shouting something into the radio. A devious smile came across his face. He then hopped back inside of his Regal, fired it up and drove off.

A horn honking snagged his attention. When he looked, a white, BMW 640i was driving alongside of him. He cracked a smile as he let down the passenger side window.

"You're getting rusty, ma. I almost had to sit that pig on his ass."

The wind blew through Constance's thin dreads, ruffling them and causing them to move like animated fingers. She pulled the designer shades off of her face and projected a devilish smile in his direction as she gave him the middle finger.

"You play your cards right and you just may get chu some tonight," he said of the *fuck you* finger Constance had given him.

"Whatever, nigga," Constance retorted. "Where are we headed?"

"The Spot."

The Spot was actually the broiler room of an old building Fear and Constance took niggaz to bleed them for information or to teach them a lesson. Once a cat was taken to the The Spot, he was guaranteed two things. One, that he'd tell them whatever they wanted to know, and two,that he wasn't leaving there alive.

Down in the boiler room there was a big chair made of black leather and iron. You would think the Devil himself had handcrafted such an evil contraption. The chair was comprised of an abundance of straps, metal bracelets, and shackles to keep its victims held in place for torture. It was equipped with a variety of bladed weapons, drills, electric saws, swords, daggers, and spikes. The seat was even rigged to electrocute its victims every three minutes.

The Death Chair was operated by a remote control that was as big as the controllers that were used to operate one of those expensive toy helicopters. It had taken Constance four months to get that contraption up and running, but once she did, she felt that it was her greatest creation.

"The Spot?"

Fear nodded with a wicked smile. "No one will hear 'em scream down there."

"The Spot it is." Constance slipped the designer shades back on and drove off with Fear tailing behind her. Together, they hopped on the freeway taking the 105 East, heading toward Paramount.

Chapter Seven

Fear was approaching the Garfield exit when he heard his front passenger tire burst. He pulled onto the shoulder of the freeway and Constance pulled up behind him. He hopped out of the Regal, made his way around the car, and kneeled down to examine the tire. It was busted flat.

"Shit!" He rose to his feet and kicked it.

"You gotta donut?" Constance asked.

"You already know where it is." He nodded to the trunk.

"Damn," Constance cursed, hating to hear that. She massaged her chin. "Highway patrol rolls through here, like every couple minutes. We can't risk getting bagged tryna pull that nigga out to get to that spare."

"Shit, you don't have a donut in your trunk?"

"Nah, I let my cousin, Kantrell, get it when her shit busted, bitch never gave it back."

"Man." Fear shook his head and thought on it. He turned to her, "Alright, well, look, my house ain't too far from here. I can roll this mothafucka in the garage and change it."

"Aren't you forgetting that you've got *guests*?" She asked, referring to Eureka and Anton who were back at the house.

"Nah, I haven't forgotten," Fear told her. "We're just finna roll up in there, change the tire, and roll out so we can torture Mr.Woman Beater here." He patted the trunk where Bugsy was lying unconscious.

"Alright, bet."

They hopped back into their respective whips and rolled to his house.

Six minutes later...

Fear and Constance drove into his driveway. He pressed the button on the controller that was clipped on the sun visor's flap and the garage door lifted up. They rolled inside, he pressed the button again and it closed. He hopped out of his ride and made his way around to the trunk. Constance slid out of her ride, closed the door shut, and went to stand beside him. She screwed the silencer onto the barrel of her .45 automatic and rested it at her side.

Fear pressed his ear to the trunk and listened closely. When he didn't hear anything, he unlocked it with his key. As soon as he lifted it up, he was struck across the head with a tire-iron. Constance pointed her .45 at Bugsy and he threw the tire-iron at her head. *Thunk!* The metal object struck the side of her forehead and she slung the .45 upwards, sending a bullet through the ceiling and causing debris to fall.

She staggered backwards, holding her forehead and falling up against the garage door. Seeing his opening for an escape, Bugsy hopped out of the trunk and hauled ass to the door that lead into the house. He snatched the door open and ran inside of the kitchen, straight to the wooden knife block.

Snikt!

He snatched a butcher's knife from the block and whipped around. His head was on a swivel as he looked for some place to run. Fear and Constance ran into the house behind him. The side of Fear's head was bleeding and a knot the size of a golf ball was forming on Constance's forehead. Silenced guns in hand, they moved forward, looking to leave Bugsy wetter than a pool party when Eureka entered the kitchen and flipped on the light-switch.

Her abrupt appearance startled everyone in attendance as theirs startled her. Her head snapped back and forth between Bugsy and Fear and Constance. The line across her forehead deepened as she tried to figure out what was going on. She made to run, but Bugsy grabbed her by the back of her shirt and pulled her into him. He grabbed a handful of her curly hair and yanked her head back. Her eyes bulged and her body stiffened as he brought the knife to her throat. His eyebrows arched and his eyes shifted between Fear and Constance as a malevolent smile formed on his lips.

"Y'all back the fuck up, or on Geo I'ma slit this lil' bitch throat!" He tightened his hold on Eureka and gripped the butcher's knife tighter, pressing it against her neck and causing a red dot to form and trickle.

"What the—" Anton emerged, taking in the sight. "Bugsy, what the hell are you doing to my sister?" He moved in Bugsy's direction, but seeing him buck like he was going to slice Eureka's throat made him freeze in his tracks.

"Back up lil' cuz, 'fore I do big sis greasy," he warned sternly. He'd known both brother and sister for years, but with his life at stake anybody could get it. He didn't give any fucks whatsoever.

"Wait a minute, y'all know this nigga?" Fear asked Anton.
"Yeah, we're from the same neighborhood," Eureka winced, feeling the tip of the butcher's knife in her skin. Any sudden movement and Anton would be getting a R.I.P tattoo. "But fuck this nigga!" Anton spat.

"Fuck you, too!" Bugsy spat as beads of sweat ran down his forehead. He was in a bad situation and was desperate to get himself out. "Y'all back up! Back the fuck up, cuz! I ain't playing!" He shouted, trying to instill terror in the hearts of the persons assembled, but his threats meant little to anyone present besides Anton and maybe Fear.

"I told you *you* shouldn't have brought these fucking kids in this house," Constance said with clenched jaws, hating Eureka and Anton more and more with each minute that passed. If she had it her way, she'd allow Bugsy to dust Eureka off and lay his ass right after.

"Now isn't the time for your pissing and moaning," Fear said with clenched jaws as well, his eyes never wavering from Bugsy. "You think you can get 'em from here?" He whispered.

"Yeah, but I don't think I want to." She whispered back, eyes stuck on Bugsy.

"What?"

"Fuck her. What's she supposed to mean to me?"

"Constance."

"Constance nothing, she's tryna take my position with you."

"Can't nobody take your position, we're a team." He assured her. "L.O.E, remember? Loyalty Over Everything." He held up his hand, showing her the L.O.E ink between his thumb and trigger-finger.

Constance glanced at the tattoo they both wore on their hands. Remembering the vow they'd made to one another, she nodded her head.

Choot! Choot!

She fired two well-placed bullets. The first one struck Bugsy's elbow and the second his rotator cuff, rendering his arm useless. He howled in pain like a broke dick dog and dropped the butcher's knife, staggering backwards. The blood from his wrist and arm fell fast and vastly, splotching the white tiled floor.

He turned and tried to run, but his shot at freedom was short lived once a hot rock pierced the back of his knee and exited his kneecap. Bugsy greeted the floor hard, bumping the side of his head. Eureka took a step back, rubbing her neck and looking to her hand. There was a small smear of blood, but she'd live. Anton rushed over and hugged his sister dearly.

"You good?" He asked as he held her at arm's length.

She nodded *yes*.

"Let me see your neck." Fear lifted Eureka's chin and examined her neck. "It's okay. It's not nothing we can't take care of here." He looked to Constance. "Finish 'em."

"No," she replied as she stood over Bugsy, watching him writhe in agony.

"What chu just say?" Fear questioned with a raised eyebrow.

This was a big deal because Constance had never disobeyed him before. She pledged her life to him the night he rescued her from the brothel. She was to do what he said, when he said it, without complaint. That was the vow she made, to have unquestionable loyalty.

"I kill him and they," she pointed to the brother and sister, "become witnesses. We don't leave witnesses. You want 'em gone then they participate." She looked him dead in the eyes with a seriousness that could never be misconstrued as anything else. He knew she'd stand her ground firmly and wouldn't budge. He'd taught her that. *Stand for something or you'll fall for anything* he'd told her time and time again.

Fear nodded and said, "Okay."

He tucked his .9mm in the small of his back and stepped to Eureka and Anton. The look in his eyes was unrelenting.If they didn't submit then they had to go, too. After he explained to them what was going to happen, they looked to Bugsy then back to Fear, nodding.

Together they approached Bugsy, looking upon him like a dissected frog on the table of a laboratory.

Fear picked the remote control up from the coffee table, turned on the flat-screen TV and escalated the volume to its max. He then took the .45 from Constance, pointed it at Bugsy and pulled the trigger. A black, bleeding hole appeared in his shoulder and stomach as he lay there screaming like he'd gotten his dick caught in a bear trap. Fear passed the .45 to Eureka and she popped off without hesitation, making fire explode in Bugsy's dick and chest.

Bugsy lay on his back with his chest heaving up and down as he gasped for air. All he could do was watch as Anton stepped to him with his five foot seven shadow eclipsing him. His eyes poisoned by malice and his lips morphing into a sneer. Anton said something that Bugsy couldn't hear due to the high volume, but made out through the movements of his lips.

"This is for putting your paws on my sister, pussy!"

Choot! Choot! Choot! Choot!

The .45 kicked like a wild bull as it splattered Bugsy's noodle and gave him his Death Certificate.

Fear held out a cloth and Anton laid the .45 down in it. He wrapped the murder weapon up and turned the volume down on the flat-screen. He turned around holding up the .45 he'd wrapped up in the cloth for everyone else to see it. He then addressed them.

"This is the tie that binds us," he told Eureka and Anton. "This is our guarantee that no one here will rat the other out. 'Cause if one burns," he held up a finger and then swept it around the three of them, "then we all burn."

The Jackson kids nodded their understanding while Constance examined her finger nails. She was already familiar with this process because Fear had taken her through it. Fear stashed the .45 in a safe and returned to the kitchen. He and Constance wrapped Bugsy's body up tight in black garbage bags and dumped it into the trunk of the BMW. Eureka and Anton were left with the task of gathering the shell casings and cleaning up the blood from the floor.

Once Fear and Constance left to bury Bugsy's body, they locked up the house and took a shower. Afterwards, they climbed in bed for a night's rest. Anton slept like a baby, but Eureka had trouble falling asleep. Hearing Fear and Constance inside of the kitchen, she hopped out of the bed and went to see what was up.

She entered the kitchen to find them lounging about, passing an L between them. They were covered in smudges of dirt and looked exhausted. But when she entered the fold they looked alive, especially Constance. Eureka could almost feel the heat from her gaze causing her body to simmer.

"Lil' momma, you're still up?" Fear cracked a smile as if he didn't just catch a body with her a couple of hours ago.

"Yeah, I couldn't sleep." She took a seat at the island.

"Where's baby boy?" he inquired.

"He's K.O'd."

"After what just happened I don't know if you still wanna kick your feet up here, but you're welcome to."

"What?" Constance blurted, not feeling Eureka and Anton staying there. Fear's head snapped in her direction and he shot her a look that made her shut her mouth and take a pull from the L.

She was on fire, but remembered what he'd said about overstepping her boundaries. The last thing she wanted was to fall out of his good graces and ruin any chances of them being together.That wasn't going to happen any goddamn way, but you couldn't tell her that shit. She was determined to have him to herself.

"Listen, I'm not tryna come between you and your girl," Eureka began. "Just gimmie a couple of weeks and I'll be outta your hair."

"Constance isn't my girlfriend, I thought I made that clear," he corrected her. "She's L.O.E, so she's family."

Eureka nodded her understanding and looked to Constance. Constance shot daggers at her as she blew smoke from her nose and mouth. Eureka could tell she was trying to intimidate her, but she wasn't the type of bitch to fold. She *had* a pussy, but she wasn't *a pussy*.

"Yeah, we'll kick our feet up for the time being," she said to Fear, but kept her intense gaze on Constance. "But if you really wanna look out, put me down with the crew."

"Humph," Constance said, passing the dutchie to Fear as she cracked open a bottle of Hennessy and poured up a glass.

Fear's forehead crinkled and his neck recoiled when he heard Eureka's request.

"Put you down with the crew? What chu know about the crew?"

"I know y'all about money and murda, and I want in."

"*We* want in." Anton made his presence known as he approached.

Eureka wanted to speak up and tell Anton to fallback, but said fuck it. She'd already done dirt with him and knew he was going to take part in whatever she did from now on. It sadden her, but she'd done as best as she could when trying to raise him. Now she was going to let the chips fall where ever they pleased and hope for the best outcome.

Fear looked up at Anton, but focused his attention back on Eureka. He blew hard and ran a hand down his face saying, "What chu know about popping the lid on a nigga, besides what you've done here tonight?"

"My soul has been stained and my hands are already dirty." Eureka informed him. "You know those niggaz I told you we robbed back at the motel?"

"Uh huh," he replied as he poured up a glass of Hennessy.

"Well, I gave 'em strong doses of Zzzquil, left 'em sleeping forever." She morphed her hand into the shape of a gun.Fear raised an eyebrow to this, but Constance wasn't impressed."Do I regret it? Hell naw! You know why? 'Cause I done it for me and my brother's survival. Peep this," she outstretched her arm and showed him the ink inside of it, *Only The Strong*, it read.

She'd gotten the tattoo when she was just sixteen years old, the day after her father's funeral. She understood life was going to be as hard as it had ever been. From that day forth the world was going to give her hell, but she was going to give it right back. "I did this to remind myself that the strongest of the strong survive inside of this concrete jungle. Contrary to the Bible's popular belief, it is not the meek that will inherit the earth, but the strong. The strong are a club of very few, but I will be among their ranks. I'm living by Malcolm's motto: By Any Means Necessary."

Fear took a sip from his glassas he thought about Eureka's request. If he were to bring her and her brother into his outfit then he'd have three guns watching his back instead of one. They could play the shadows as Constance had in case he needed them in a tight squeeze.

Licking his lips, he turned to her and said, "Alright, I'ma put y'all down but—"

"Wait a minute!" Constance blurted, looking at him as if he had a booger peeking out of his nostril. "I know you aren't seriously thinking about putting them down with our thing?"

"Yes, I am." He gave her a stern look. "I am the boss of this fraternity," he jabbed his finger into the counter top. "and my will shall not be questioned." He gritted his teeth. "Not even by a senior member." The look in his eyes gave her a warning to stay in her place or face the consequences of her insubordination.

For a time she mad dogged Eureka, narrowing her eyes into slits. She hated her so much her upper lip twitched uncontrollably. Finally, she lowered her head and took a deep breath, relaxing. She took another pull and launched a missile of smoke.

"Okay, alright," she nodded. "They've gotta get initiated like I did, blood in blood out."

She kept her eyes on Eureka, blowing a cloud of smoke in her direction on some disrespectful shit. She sincerely thought the threat of having to put in some work would make her second guess her decision. What she didn't know was The Jackson kids were just as built as any nigga in the life.

Fear nodded his head in agreement. Looking to Eureka and Anton, he said, "That's right. Everyone earns their spot in this crew. It's a rite of passage."

"What do we have to do?" Eureka asked.

"Make a nigga lie down forever." He answered.

"I thought we proved ourselves tonight," she reminded him.

"That was to gain our trust," he told her. "But this here will be your introduction into L.O.E."

"Alright, fair enough," she nodded. "Who's on the hit list?"

"As soon as I get the word on the next job, you'll know. But I want y'all to understand something," he said. "This is a blood pact and it cannot be broken." He looked the siblings straight in their eyes. From the expression on his face they could tell that he was dead ass. "Once you've walked through this door you're about to open, you'll be one of us, and the only way outta this thing of ours is death. Have I made myself clear?"

"Crystal." Eureka nodded.

"I got chu, big homie." Anton said off of Fear's look.

Constance lay back against the sink, sipping her glass of Hennessy as she stared off at nothing, in deep thought. She didn't know what task Fear had in mind for Eureka and Anton to execute, but she was going to be there to make sure they didn't succeed and that they wound up dead once everything was said and done. A devilish smile stretched across her face as she brained stormed ideas of how to rid herself of Eureka and Anton.

Chapter Eight

"Pleasure doing business with you," Blair shook Malvo's hand. He was a five-foot-nine cat rocking a hoodie and Nike boots.

"The pleasure is all mine." Malvo cracked a sinister smile.

"If you need to cop some mo' just—"

"Oh for sure," Malvo interjected. "I got cho math, so I'll be in touch. You got that fire so I know that we'll most definitely be doing business soon, real soon." He rubbed his hands together like Birdman from Cash Money records.

"Alright then, my nigga, we're outro." He touched fists with Malvo and tapped his homeboy in the oversized camouflage Cardinals jersey. They hopped into a black on black Escalade truck on them pretty chrome thangs. The beast roared to life and smoke exhausted from the shiny pipes. Meek Mill's *Young and Getting It* thumped hard from the speakers and then the SUV pulled off. Malvo smiled like he knew something they didn't know. He waved goodbye as he stared at the bright, red taillights of the truck. Then he converted his wave into a middle finger and saluted them.

"Them two niggaz are gonna be as hot as fish grease once they find out they got their heads bumped," Crunch shook his head.

"Fell for the Okey Doke," Malvo said. "Gets them every time. You'd think these niggaz would be hip to this shit. I ain't complaining though. They stay dumb and I stay with a grip." His meaty palm patted his jeans pocket as he turned and grinned at Crunch.

Blair and Aaron were the cats just outside of the city that were holding a couple of birds of raw that Malvo was talking about. He had successfully made the exchange without so much as a slingshot being fired. The deal went as planned and now the janky fucker was six kilos of heroine richer. He and Crunch had removed the bumper of the rental and stashed them thangs there for safe keeping. By the time Blair and Aaron realized that they were bent over and fucked up the ass, it would already be too late. Malvo and Crunch would have already been gone.

"Yo, man, take this shit to the spot and have the youngins' do what they do and package it up," Malvo told Crunch. "Make sure them mothafuckaz spell Kryptonite on the packets right this time, too. Smalls had them fools labeling them as Dynamite the last time."

"I got chu, Boss Dawg. Don't wet it," Crunch said from behind the wheel of the rental. "Where are you headed now?"

At that moment, Malvo's cell phone rang and vibrated inside of the pocket. When he pulled it out and looked at the screen, a grin morphed his face when he saw the name. He held up one finger for Crunch to give him a second as he answered the call. He was on there about a minute before he told the caller he'd be pulling up on them in about half an hour.

"Who was that?" Crunch threw his head back a little bit.

"That was pussy talking to me right there, something you may not ever know nothing about." He replied, sounding like Mike Epps off of All About the Benjamins.

"I heard that, fam." He smiled and stuck his fist out of the window. Malvo touched fists with him and said, "Yo, be sure you call to let me know that you made it back safe."

"Alright, I gotchu," Crunch fired up the car and pulled off while the big man trekked back to his truck.

****

"We're about to cross over into the dark side, baby boy." Eureka told Anton as she sat on the edge of the bed, wrapping her head up in a scarf.

"We've been living on the dark side, big sis, or have you forgotten?" He responded, kicking off his sneakers.

"I hear you, but this is different." She looked him in the eyes. "Blood doesn't wash off, no matter how much you scrub."

"You're telling me? Have you already pushed what I've done to the back of your mind?" He asked as he plopped down beside her in bed.

"No. I haven't forgotten what I've done either," she told him. "All I'm trying to tell you is that we're on a different playing field now. Our whole outlook on life is about to change in the next couple of days and I need to know that you're a hunnit percent sure about being down with this."

Eureka and Anton stared into each other's eyes for what seemed like a decade. The little nigga had a cold look in his eyes as if he'd seen the horrors of a harsh life twice over. He didn't say a word. It was like he was trying to read her just as she was trying to read him. Finally, he cleared his throat and licked his lips saying, "I'm with this shit and I'ma represent it 'til the day I die," he said straight up.

Eureka was quiet for a second before saying, "Alright. As long as you're sure we're going through with it."

"Cool."

Smack!

His head snapped to the side when her open palm went upside of it. They both got to their feet, slap boxing. *Smack! Smack! Smack!*

"Come on, punk!" Eureka said.

"Hahaha, I'ma fuck yo ass up!" Anton said, playfully studying his sister's form.

Smack! Smack!

He tagged her good twice. She swung on him again, he ducked her and lifted her up. He tried to throw her on the bed but she held tight to him, putting him in a headlock. They fell to the floor and he tried to wiggle his head out of her grip. "Let me go, Reka."

"Nope." She laughed. "Not 'til you say uncle."

"You got me fucked up. I'll never throw in the towel."

"Whoaaa!" Her eyes grew big and her mouth opened in an O as he lifted her up and slammed her down on the bed.

He brought his head up, breathing hard and smiling, "You can't hold me." He flexed his arms as if he was a body builder.

"Whatever, nigga, I was kicking that ass," she said out of breath as she waved him off. "Help me up, I gotta pee." She extended her hand and he pulled her out of the bed and to her feet.

She flinched at him like she was going to hit him and got into a fighting stance, fists up and ready.

"What, you wanna go again?"

"Nah, we're good, baby boy." She extended one hand and when he went to shake it, she smacked him upside of the head. She laughed and giggled as he chased her out the door. She pulled the door closed behind her and held the knob, listening for noise on the other side. Once she didn't hear anything she headed toward the bathroom.

She had just reached for the bathroom doorknob when it came swinging open. Warmth escaped and fog rolled out into the hallway. A short, muscular silhouette moved forth until it was visible. Out stepped Fear, body beaded with water. A white towel was wrapped around his waist. Eureka licked her lips as she took him in from head to toe, her hand pressed to her chest. His calves, legs, and arms were all rippled with muscles. He was as solid as a rock, looking like he was carved out of a hunk of chocolate.

Shit, baby, it's like that? Goddamn, she thought, feeling slight moisture build between her legs. Her eyes took a tour of every inch of his body until they settled on his grinning face.

"My fault, you weren't waiting long were you?" he asked. "Constance has the one in my room sewn up, so I ducked off in here real quick."

She didn't say anything because she was still under the hypnosis of his sculpted physique. Smiling, he snapped his fingers before her eyes and waved a hand.

"Hello, earth to Reka."

"Oh, my bad," she snapped back to the here and now.

"You gotta use the bathroom?"

"Yeah, I gotta pee." She moved to head into the bathroom, but he called her. She turned around.

"Yo, I was finna roll up, you tryna chief something?" He hit an imaginary blunt.

"Hell yeah, let's smoke that shit."

"Cool." He went to turn around, but looked back to her. "Damn, you know what? I gotta get some more chocolate Cigarillos."

"Ain't it a store around here that's open all night?"

"There's a 7-Eleven not too far from here." Fear responded.

"Aye, I'ma roll with chu, I wanna get me a few things. Is that alright?"

"Yeah, let me throw on something." He told her. "I'll meet chu down stairs."

"Alright, cool."

****

Malvo made his way inside the 7-Eleven, brushing past patrons as they came and went. He headed straight to the refrigerator doors where all of the cold beverages were stored. He massaged the stubble of his goatee as he tried to make his decision. Making up his mind, he grabbed a Red Bull and headed up to toward the front, snatching up a Ho Ho along the way.

"Hey, how're you doing?" The Indian store clerk asked him once he stepped to the counter.

"I'm alright." Malvo said, studying the bottles of liquor behind the clerk on the shelf. He looked like he was attempting to read the letter chart at the DMV. "Let me get a pint of Hennessy, a pack of grape swishers, some Maggies, and about six of those Lucky Day scratch offs."

While the clerk got busy obtaining the items he desired, Malvo looked over his shoulder to see a white Dodge Charger pull into the parking lot. At that moment, his cell phone rung diverting his attention. He answered it in a jovial tone, seeing it was the trim he had lined up for the night.

"What's good, baby? Yeah, I'm at the store right now. You want something?" He asked, peeling off a couple of dead men and passing them to the clerk as he bagged up his items. Through the glass window of the convenience store the Dodge's front passenger door swung open and someone stepped out. They were en route to the store when they suddenly stopped and looked up, seeing something that made them retreat back to the car.

****

Fear pulled the Dodge into the parking lot of the 7-Eleven and bodied the engine.

"What chu want?" Eureka asked.

"Chocolate Cigarillos, A fruit punch Arizona, and a bag of Doritos. And get whatever you want. Here," Fear went to reach inside of his pocket, but she grabbed his arm, stopping him. His head snapped in her direction.

"I got it," she smiled. "Least I can do with you letting us crash at your place and all."

"You sho'?"

"Uh huh," she nodded. "Cigarillos, Arizona, and Doritos?"

"You got it."

Eureka threw the door open and hopped out. A smile graced her face as she headed for the entrance of 7-Eleven. She'd just stepped upon the curb when she saw something that slapped her across the face. She lowered her head, scowling and clenching her teeth, causing her jaws to throb. She balled her hands into fists so tightly that they turned white at the knuckles. Moisture poisoned her eyes as they took on a heinous glint. She headed back to the car unraveling the scarf from her head and dipping her head into the open window of the front passenger seat.

"Gimmie yo strap, Fear," she said seriously.

"What?" He frowned.

"Gimmie your burner."

"For what?"

"You see that nigga in there?" She pointed to the window where Malvo was passing the Indian clerk the money for his items.

Fear nodded, "I see 'em."

"He's the one that's after me and my brother," she told him. "I have to take 'em out and I have to take 'em out now."

Fear looked ahead, frowning with a tight jaw causing his temples to jump. He thought about how to go about handling the situation. He looked to Eureka and said, "I got it, fall back."

He hit the hazards, the AC, and knocked on the dashboard. The stash spot shot out, revealing his loaded, black,.9mm automatic. He went to grab it when she leaned over into the car and snatched it.

"He's mine," she growled from behind the scarf that was now wrapped around her mouth.

"Handle yours. I'll be waiting," he told her, firing up the Charger. The name plates were fakes, so they were all good in the hood if a surveillance camera were to capture them.

She nodded and turned around just as Malvo was stepping out. He was cradling his cell to his ear and scraping a quarter across a scratch-off. He was so engrossed in his activities he hadn't a clue of the black shroud of death blanketing over him.

Eureka's heart was beating so hard that the sounds of the night's traffic had become lost to her. All she could adhere to was the explosive sound of the thick muscle located behind the left side of her chest-plate. She moved forth, almost in slow motion, eyes glued on her victim and hand hugging the .9mm. She was consumed with all of the bullshit he'd taken her through. She could hear his voice in her head during their numerous encounters.

"The next time you put your hands on me, I'm gonna put a bullet through your eye, ya hear me?"

"If you don't return with every dollar of my money accounted for, I'm going to execute your mother and your brother, one by one. I don't wanna hear any stories about you getting jacked, extorted by crooked cops, or none of that shit. If you can't come back with my trap, then you may as well stay where you are and make the funeral arrangements from there."

"Bitch, you brought a knife to a gun fight?"

"Move the fuck outta my way 'fore I open up your face with some hot shit."

"You've got some set of balls on you, girl. I hope they'll do you some good where you're going."

Malvo's voice sounded like a recorded cassette tape playing inside of her head. She grew angrier and angrier the more she listened to it. Her face had tightened with a scowl so much that it felt like the veins in her temples were going to erupt. Her victim had just stepped off of the curb when she pointed the .9mm dead at his face.

"Malvo? Malvo? Hello?" the caller called out. There wasn't any use though. The big man was so shocked to see Eureka standing before him with that banger in her hand that he could have pissed on himself. He dropped the cell phone, then the scratch off and his plastic bag of items at his feet. His eyes were as big as saucers and his mouth was wide open, twitching.

"Eur—Eur—" he stammered, not believing she was there, right before his very eyes.

"Eureka muthafucka!" she barked. "Let these eyes be the last ones you see before you meet with your Lord."

She gave the trigger pressure but he swooped in, not Malvo, Fear. Swiftly, he lowered her hand and pulled her scarf down. He kissed her hard and passionately. She confusingly fought off the kiss until she succumbed to his will. He then pulled his lips from hers but at this point she was in a daze by the overwhelming kiss. He nodded his head to the left and she looked, a police cruiser was just pulling into a space two cars down.

"See?" he asked.

"Yeah, good looking out." She looked at his lips and then his eyes as if she was waiting for him to finish the kiss. He smiled, knowing exactly what she wanted, but now wasn't the time.

They both looked over their shoulder to find that Malvo was gone. The only thing that was left behind was his bag of items and the scratch-off.

"Damn," she said in a hushed tone.

"Come on. Let's get outta here." He threw open the door and deposited her inside. He slammed it closed and ran over to the opposite side, tucking his banger. He hopped in and pulled out of the parking lot.

****

"Holy shit!" Malvo wiped sweat from his forehead with the back of his hand. He peeked around the corner of the building he was standing up against and saw the Charger rolling out of the parking lot. *That was close, real close, fo' inch bitch almost got me up outta here,* he thought as he tilted his head back and gasped for air. He looked to his cell phone and could see that the trim he had lined up was still holding on.

"Malvo, are you okay? Malvo?"

"I'm good."

"Oh, okay, well, are you still coming over tonight?"

"Bitch, I almost lost my life, hell nah!" He disconnected the call and stuffed the cell into his jacket's pocket. He trekked over to his truck, recovered his gun from underneath the seat and tucked it on his waist. Looking both ways, he jogged across the street to a telephone booth. He snatched up the receiver and dropped two quarters into the slot before punching in a number. He pressed the telephone to his ear and listened as the line rang. All the while he was doing this, he peered over his shoulders, making sure Eureka wouldn't come rolling back on him.

Yeahhhh, I see now. I should have been addressed this situation. I was supposed to have been on it. My fault though, I'ma take care of it now.

"Hello? Ernie?" He spoke into the receiver. "You know that cat you were telling me about that cleans? I need you to put me in contact with 'em. Yeah. I gotta big mess that needs to be gotten up ASAP."

****

"I had 'em right there, right where I wanted 'em." Eureka sneered, slamming her fist into her palm. "I was so close I could smell the stink on his breath."

"You should have taken 'em out." Anton frowned, wishing his sister would have blown Malvo's face off.

"If she would have, she'd be getting booked for murder down at 77st division precinct." Fear spoke sternly.

"Yeah, you're right." Eureka came down from her adrenaline, realizing he was telling her the truth. "It's just that I wanted that dick-sucker so bad. You know how much shit me and Ant had went through because of him?"

"All 'cause his punk ass wanted to G us for that forty racks." Anton shook his head.

"Don't worry.Fat boy is going to get his in the end. I'll see to it." Fear assured them. "Even if y'all don't make the cut, I'm going to help you get that ass."

"G' looking." Ant slapped hands with Fear.

"Thanks." Eureka said.

"Don't mention it." Fear replied. "We're family, and family rides for each other."

"Straight up." Anton nodded.

Fear looked up at the digital clock and saw how late it was.

"Alright, y'all, I'm finna turn it in," he stated. "Goodnight."

"G'night, big homie."

Fear left the bedroom, pulling the door closed behind him. Seconds later, Eureka came out behind him, garnering his attention once she'd called his name. He turned around with his eyebrows raised.

"Sooooooo, that kiss though." She smiled.

"Oh, my bad," he said with a straight face. "I had to do something to throw The Ones off."

"Is that the only reason why you kissed me?"She looked disappointed.

He stared at her with a face chiseled out of stone, not uttering a word. She took from it what she did and looked to feel let down. She turned around to head back to the bedroom when he called her back.

Fear grinned, "No, that wasn't the only reason why I kissed you,but it did give me the perfect excuse."

The world's biggest smile stretched acrossEureka's face. She didn't walk back to her bedroom, she floated.

Chapter Nine
The next night

When Fear had gotten the call from Bemmy for the meeting location, he could detect something off in his tone of voice. This made him uneasy and he decided to take some precautions before agreeing to the meeting place because for all he knew he could have been walking into a setup. Although the OG had always been on the up and up, he could never be so sure of another man's intentions, especially in the game he was in.

Fear crossed the threshold of Zell's restaurant, toting a cooler and twisting a toothpick at the corner of his mouth. The uptight host came from around his podium to address him about his attire, but he shot him a deadly look that made him change his mind. Taking a quick scan of his surroundings, he located a section of the establishment enclosed in glass. You could see right through it.

The man he'd come to see was there amongst other men sitting at a table, eating and talking to each other. This made the creases on his forehead deepen. He had only expected to see Bemmy that night, not the rest of the fellas. Thinking nothing of it, he trekked through the restaurant, looking at all of the people sitting at the tables enjoying their meals and conversations. Along the way he scooped up a flute of champagne the waiter had just poured at a table for a couple. The waiter and the couple's necks snapped in his direction as he moved past their table, taking sips from the flute. The couple wanted to protest but there was something about his demeanor that gave them second thoughts.

Fear winked his eye at a brown skinned chick at a nearby table. She was in a white shoulder-less dress and wore her hair like Cleopatra. She winked at him and gave him a sexy smile. Turning his head back around and sipping his bubbly, his eyes came across a young black couple sitting off to the side. The man gave him a slight nod and he returned the gesture.

Fear threw back the last of the sparkle and sat it on a table he was walking past. He wiped his mouth with the back of his hand and approached the sectioned off area Bemmy was in.

Kirby, Bemmy's body guard, was posted up in front of the door with his hands clasped at his waist. He was staring ahead and wearing a perturbed expression.

Kirby looked alive when he saw Fear approaching. When the killer greeted him, he didn't acknowledge him.

"I gotta pat you down, bruh." Kirby said with a solemn face.

"Let me save you the trouble, family." Fear pulled his .9mm from his back and passed it to Kirby. Kirby took the .9mm and stashed it inside of his suit. "What's going on here, Kirby? You're searching me now? I ain't never had to go through a pat down with Boss Dawg. Me and old head have been doing business for years."

"I'm just doing what I'm told, homie," was all Kirby said.

"Bemmy told you to search me?" Fear frowned.

"That's who I take my orders from," Kirby replied. "Do me a favor and turn around, so I can pat you down."

"Alright." Fear turned his back to Kirby, spreading his arms and legs apart. Had it been anybody else he would have barged right past him and made his way inside of the enclosed glass dining area. But Fear had love for Kirby, he had always been a cool ass, down to earth type of dude. For the most part he was a humbled cat that was just trying to keep a roof over his family's head and hot food on the table. Fear respected that, so he chose to oblige him when he told him to assume the position for the pat down.

Fear thought about the old man's reason for having him searched. If he didn't want him armed then he could very well be walking into a setup. But then again, he wouldn't murk him inside of a restaurant. Even if he did own the place, there were still plenty of potential witnesses around.

Thought after thought shot through his mental like a hollow-tip as he tried to think of a reason why his employer would want to give him a eulogy. The best he could come up with was him putting the love on someone near and dear to him that he didn't know about. Fear had been called upon to kill a number of folks. He didn't ask any questions. As long as a nigga had that paper, one more soul would be cast out into the afterlife.

"Alright, clean." Kirby announced, standing back upright, having given the hit-man a half-ass pat down. He had love for him too and didn't want to pat him down like he was some common thug. "Let me check that cooler."

Fear passed Kirby the cooler and he opened it. He raised an eyebrow once he saw what was inside of it, looking from what was stored to Fear. He closed the cooler and gave it back to him.

"We're good?" Fear asked, ready to holler at old head so he could get his issue.

"Yeah, we're straight." Kirby nodded. "My fault about all of this, but I gotta do like I'm told if I want to keep this gig. I need this mothafucka, my family gotta eat."

"Don't wet it, big bruh, I know what it is." Fear patted him on the shoulder and opened the door to the glass enclosed area. He'd entered just in time to hear the end of a joke.

"So I say, '*Well, if she doesn't like the ring I got her, she can use the dildo to go fuck herself*'." Mike Huggins burst out laughing and the rest of the men fell in line.

Fear looked around at all of the men laughing heartily. With their eyes squinted and their mouths open. They appeared to be moving in slow motion through his eyes. Fear's head swept around at all of the men present at the dining table. He knew each one by name and reputation.

Mike Higgins was somewhat of a legend. That man's story was almost the same as his, only backwards. He'd started his affair with the streets when he was just sixteen, making his bones slicing niggaz throats in the name of a dollar. From there he got involved in the drug game, first managing traps and then almost overnight sitting at the head of his own empire. Mike had a nice chunk of Compton on smash, he was the man to see if you wanted quality coke.

The light skinned cat sitting beside him, who looked like a throwback Ice-T when he played Scotty in New Jack City, was Arkane. This ponytail rocking miscreant had a strangle hold on a little more than half of the real estate in Watts. Although he often clowned around, people were fools if they'd let his sense of humor fool them.He wasn't above getting his hands dirty.

"You are one funny ass guy, Mike." The only Mexican sitting at the table claimed, wiping the tear that dripped from his eye from his laughing so hard. Honcho was a vato straight out of Lynwood. He had an army of gangsters and a couple of donut eaters on his payroll. He had his hands in some of everything illegal you could name, but he made most of his profit off of cocaine.

"Him regular standup comedian," Mr. Jun laughed as he held his stomach and smacked the table top. Mr. Jun was a short, big head, Chinaman with craters in his cheeks. He ruled all of China Town through murder and intimidation. The coke he had on deck kept his pockets lined and the latest European whip in the driveway of his three million dollar home.

The gentleman sitting at the head of the table was none other than Niles Bemmy, one of the most ruthless men to have ever worn a tailored suit and a pair of Mauri Gators. He'd literally started from the bottom and moved his way up to the top. He went from lookout to the Top Dawg of his own criminal enterprise. When he finally closed his eyes, his name would be mentioned right along with some of the most notorious cats that had ever touched a Los Angeles block.

The five men collectively made up what was known as The West Coast Connection. As a whole they bought their weight from one of the most abominable drug lords in the United States, Black Jesus Arturo. Each man sitting at the table was more dangerous than the next. They had enough money and power to have a nigga's entire family tree wiped out.

But ask Fear did he give a fuck and he'd tell you: *Fuck all of them niggaz and the pussies they came out of! They all can get it! Straight up!*

Bemmy came down from his merriment and wiped his mouth with a cloth. He sat the napkin on the table and started up a Blu electronic cigarette. He took a pull and blew a smoke ring up into the air. Bringing his head back down, he found Fear at the far end of the table.

"We have a guest." The old school gangsta spoke and silence spread throughout the room like the plague. The rest of the men sitting at the table looked to the assassin, some of them coughed and cleared their throats to ascertain a more serious demeanor. Fear wasn't a stranger to those men. In fact, they were well acquainted. They'd all taken out a contract with him at some time or another. "I see you brought me a gift.For what? It's not my birthday."

He smiled and the men sitting at the table chuckled. Bemmy was easily the most powerful man there, so when he raised a hand, everyone became deathly quiet. He picked up a remote control, pointed it, and pressed a button. At that moment, the curtains were activated and they swept around the enclosed glass, blocking the outside patrons' view of their business.

He tossed the remote down on the table and motioned for Fear to give him the cooler. Fear handed it to the man closest to his end of the table and he passed it down, then the other man passed it, then the other until the cooler finally made it to the H.N.I.C. Electronic cigarette wedged between his fingers, he picked up the cooler and shook it, listening closely. He was trying to make sure there wasn't a bomb stored inside. He and Fear were cool, but he didn't make any illusion about how he made his living.

Cautiously, he opened the lid and peered down inside. A smile emerged on his lips as he picked up what was inside with both hands. When he brought his hands up, they were gripping the wrists of Bugsy's cold, severed hands. He held them up for all of his business associates to see.

"That nigga put his hands on your daughter, so I brought you his hands," Fear said. "If he would have seen something he shouldn't have, I would have brought you his eyes. And if he had snitched, I would have brought you his tongue. That's how I give it up."

"Did this cock sucker die screaming?"

"Like a fourth grade sissy."

This made the OG grin and say, "Good." He placed Bugsy's hands inside of the cooler and closed it shut. Reaching beside him, he picked up a briefcase and passed it to Arkane who passed it down. His briefcase was in circulation until it was in the killer's hands. Fear didn't bother to pop the locks to make sure all of the money was there. The OG had always given him his due and sometimes a little extra.

"Gentlemen," Fear addressed the room, his eyes sweeping across every face. "It's been a pleasure." He gave a nod and turned his back to leave when Bemmy called him back. He froze with his back to the table. Slowly, he turned back around to see exactly what it was that he wanted. "What's popping?"

"It is with great regret that I must inform you that The Connection is no longer in need of your services."

"Excuse me? Come again." He narrowed his eyes and angled his head.

Bemmy exhaled. He knew that the hit-man had heard him the first time, but decided to oblige him anyway.

"Your time with us is up," he told him. "I threw in a couple more thousand as severance. No hard feelings, huh?"

"You're letting me go? For what?" Fear growled, clenching his jaws. Veins bulged on both sides of his neck.

"You had business with a favorable man by the name of Gustavo El Rey about a year ago."

The name struck Fear in his chest like a fist. He'd never forget Gustavo El Rey. His henchmen had broken into his apartment, looking to bring his head to their boss.

Fear managed to dispatch most of them, but one had gotten the drop on him. He put more holes in him than a cheese grater and if it wasn't for Constance saving his skin there wasn't any doubt in his mind he'd be sleeping with the worms and maggots. However, he caught up with the Mexican kingpin and made him regret the day he'd sent his men for him.

Gustavo lay back in the barber's chair with a face foamed with shaving cream, snoring. He slowly began to stir awoke, hearing the straight razor being sharpened against the strap. His eyes fluttered open and he sat up, snorting, wiping the drool from the corner of his lips. When his vision came into focus, he almost shit himself seeing Fear standing before him holding the sharp blade. His face was balled up and he was smiling devilishly. Gustavo went to scream, but before the sound could leave his lips the razor swiped across his thick, flat nose.

Snikt!

His severed nose went flying across the shop and sliding across the floor, leaving a smear of blood. Fear spun the barber's chair around, leaving the Mexican kingpin face to face with his horrifying reflection. His eyes bulged and his mouth widened. He couldn't believe that it was him he was staring back at. He looked like a Mr. Potato Head without the attachable nose.

"Ahhhhhhhh!" He bellowed as he stared at the mutilated image in the mirror. His wails of terror were quickly cut short when the straight razor slipped under his chin and yanked around. The soft flesh of his throat split and a black river of blood flowed. "Gaggggaaaa!" He stuck out his tongue and went cockeyed as he grabbed for his neck. His blood drenched his white dress shirt and stained his light gray suit.

"That'll be twelve dollars," Fear said, staring at his handiwork through the mirror.

He watched the chunky Mexican bleed out until he went still. Afterwards, he washed off the razor and his hands. He gave himself the once over in the mirror, checking his nostrils for long hairs and his teeth for food. Once he was done, he closed the razor, stuck it into his back pocket, and headed for the door. He took one last look over his shoulder before pushing through the door, causing the bell above to ring as he made his exit.

Absentmindedly, Fear rubbed the healed bullet wound in his arm that he'd gotten the night of the botched hit. That wound was one of many and he'd never forget the eight others. They didn't hurt anymore, but when the winter came they felt just as raw as the night he'd gotten them.

"Yeah, what about Gustavo?"

"You fucked up when you murdered him, son."Bemmy shook his head regretfully. "Gustavo was the nephew of a late friend of Black Jesus. Black Jesus didn't take it too kindly when he discovered it was you that sent Gustavo to his eternal resting ground. He knew of all of our ties with you. He gave us an ultimatum, exile you from our affairs or be cut loose from his product."

"So what! Fuck 'em," Fear retorted, agitated. He didn't see what the big deal was. If this Black Jesus character wasn't trying to supply them with their drugs anymore then they could find another plug. To him it was that simple.

"Not only does this cat have the best product on the market, he has political connections we very much need if we plan on staying at the top of the food chain in this business."

Fear's eyebrows arched and he looked aside, twisting his lips.

"Ain't this about a one legged, big eyed, buck tooth bitch?" He fumed and gritted his teeth, still rubbing the arm with the old bullet wound. His head snapped in Bemmy's direction and he found him looking dead at him, casually smoking his Blu cigarette. "You mothafuckaz are gon' cut me off? Me? After all of the work I done put in for your ungrateful asses? Fuck all of y'all…" His crooked finger did a tour across the ensemble sitting at the table, "…with a bumped up, gonorrhea dripping, AIDS infected dick!"

"You little fucking brat!" The OG grumbled. "Do you have the slightest inkling of what we had to do to stop this man from having your head mounted on his wall, huh?"

"I never thought I'd see the day where you'd start sounding like a bitch, Niles." He looked him up and down, with disgust.

Fear's reaction brought scowls to every single man sitting at the table. Although they all moved to react, Arkane suddenly sprang to his feet gave them pause. His forehead was wracked with creases and his jaws pulsated from him clenching his teeth so hard. You could tell he was hot from how tense his body was and from the trembling of his trigger-finger. He was a millisecond from snatching that heater off of his waistline and leaving Fear flat-lined.

"Who the fuck do you think you're talking to?" Arkane slammed his fist down on the table, rattling the dishes and causing his glass of wine to tip over and spill. The glass hit the white table cloth and soiled it red. Bemmy grasped Arkane's arm, trying to calm him down, but he snatched away.

"If the shoe fits, buy a bag to match!" Fear shot back.

"Fuck you!" Arkane retorted.

"Fuck you!"

"Fuck you, mothafucka!"

"Suck my dick." Fear grabbed at his crotch.

"To hell with all of this talking!"

Arkane and the rest of the men went to draw their guns on Fear. As they went to point their weapons, he reached inside of his Dickies and pulled something free with a click. When his hand came back up, a shiny silver ring fell and a length of string came loose. He raised his hand up for all to see what he held clutched inside of his palm. The men's faces went slack when they saw that it was a pineapple grenade.

"You don't have the stones, pandejo." Honcho challenged.

"Oh, I got stones, and they're the size of bowling balls!" Fear swore, staring him dead in his eyes as he smiled wickedly. "They don't call me Fearless for nothing. I ain't scared to die, how about chu, nigga? What about the rest of y'all?" His neck twisted as his eyes took in all of the men standing around the table. Not a soul spoke and their silence was all he needed to know that they weren't ready to take it there. "That's what I thought. Now put your guns down before I send this bitch up in smoke." The men were reluctant to lower their weapons. Seeing this, pissed Fear off. At that moment, he was about to say fuck it and set it off up in there. "Y'all bitches think it's a game, family? Keep playing with me and see if I won't let this mothafucka rock!"

When the men didn't budge, Fear shrugged his shoulders. He was just about to let the grenade do what it do when Bemmy gripped Arkane's shoulder and threw up a hand.

"Wait!" He shouted, then looked around at all of his business associates. "Everyone do as he says and put your guns down." The men were still hesitant. "Now, goddamn it!" With that said, the men tossed their weapons down on the table-top, causing the dishes to rattle.

Fear's eyes shifted around at all of the men at the table. All of their eyes glinted with murder. He could literally feel the heat exhausting from their bodies. Their body language told him they might try something, so he kept the grenade visible in case they tested his gangster. He had no reserves about dying. He was sure when the streets heard about the way he went out in the restaurant; his street legacy would only inflate, leaving his name on every tongue of every nigga who sought to take it to the streets for salvation.

Fear stepped back toward the door, keeping the grenade in sight. With his eyes stuck on the men that rounded out the table, he reached back and knocked on the door. Moments later, Kirby opened it. His eyebrows were raised and his mouth gapped open when he looked at Fear. He couldn't believe what he was seeing.

"Kirby, don't try anything, leave him be," Bemmy urged.

Shieetttt, I wasn't gon' try nothing anyway, Kirby thought.

It wasn't because Fear had the grenade that he wasn't gon' try him, it was moreso that he had a great deal of respect for the hit-man. His attitude was so ill earlier because he knew his boss was giving him the boot.

Once Fear made it out into the corridor, he stuck the pin back inside of the grenade.

"You know this shit ain't over right, big man?" Fear asked the OG and his associates as he emerged fromthe enclosed glass area.

"Oh, you can bet it's not, mothafucka," Bemmy countered, chuckling sinisterly as he re-buttoned his tailored suit.

Fear stashed his grenade inside of his Dickie pocket and speed walked through the dining area. Eureka, Anton and Constance fell in line behind him. Together, they made a quiet escape that went unnoticed by the other patrons.

****

The lady with the Cleopatra hair style sat at the table pretending to look over the menu. What she was really doing was watching the door as she was waiting for someone to arrive. She sat up straight when she saw her charge finally enter the restaurant. She watched as he was given a hard time by the host at the door. Her eyes shifted over to a young African American couple seated across the way from her. Seeing the young man about to engage, she shook her head no, signaling for him to stay where he was and allow things to unfold.

When her eyes shifted back to her charge, he was making his way past the host. She watched as he snatched up a flute of champagne from a couple's table and kept it moving. She was pleasantly surprised when he turned to her and winked. She returned the gesture and smiled sexily at him. Once he was out of her line of vision, she focused her attention back on the menu.

"Are you ready yet, Miss?" The waiter approached. He was a white stud in a white button-down and black vests. In his hands were a small notepad to jot down orders and an ink-pen.

Constance rolled her eyes and exhaled when she saw him step to her table. He'd been on her ass about ordering something since she'd gotten there and he was getting on her last nerve. If it wasn't for her being on the mission, she would have told him where to stick it and kept it moving.But she knew that Fear was counting on her to pull his ass out of the fire if things went left in the meeting, so she decided to play it cool. Constance mustered up a halfhearted smile and cast her eyes on the young waiter.

"I'd like a bottle of your finest red wine please."

She watched him jot it down on his notepad.

"Will that be all for tonight, Miss?"

"Yes. Thank you."

The young waiter gave Constance a slight nod and flipped the small notepad closed, heading off to get what she'd acquired.

Constance's brow furrowed when she heard something through the earpiece. Clutching the menu, she stared at nothing as she listened in on the conversation.

"If the shoe fits buy a bag to match!" Fear shot back.

"Fuck you!"

"Fuck you!"

"Fuck you, mothafucka!"

"Suck my dick."

"To hell with all of this talking!"

Constance's eyes shifted up and she saw the young African American couple shoot to their feet. She shook her head no rapidly and spoke into the small microphone attached to her white Vera Wang dress.

****

Eureka and Anton sat at their table with bowls of Gnocchi soup before them, they hadn't touched it since they'd ordered it an hour ago. The soup had grown as cold as the whores that patrolled the blade of Hoover and

103

Figueroa. Eureka and Anton were engrossed in the mission at hand so they weren't worried about eating.

"What're you doing?" Anton asked.

"Trying to make sure this shit is working right," Eureka answered. She looked to him. "Is yours working okay?"

"Yeah." Anton nodded, adjusting the earpiece in his ear. "My shit A1."

"You hear that?" Eureka looked at Anton with a wrinkled forehead.

"Hear what?" Anton asked, taking a sip of ice cold water.

"Fuck you!"

"Fuck you, mothafucka!"

"Suck my dick."

"Fuck all of this talking!"

Eureka and Anton exchanged furrowed expressions, communicating what was on one another's mind. Eureka pulled her banger from her purse and Anton pulled his from his suit. They shot to their feet at the same time, ready to make some niggaz lay down forever. They were about to take action when they heard Constance over their small microphones.

"No, no, y'all sit your asses down!" Constance grumbled over the microphone. "We do not move until he gives us the word."

"Are you crazy? He could be food in there right now," Eureka spoke into the small microphone attached to her off the shoulder dress.

"Stand. The. Fuck. Down." Constance said through gritted teeth. "I've been down with Fear a lot longer than you have. I know him. He has the situation under control.

You move now and a shit storm is gonna rain on your heads."

Eureka locked eyes with Anton.

"Fuck that bitch," Anton said, ready to defy Constance. "You give the word and we're crashing the party."

Eureka exhaled and continued to listen to Constance as she kept her eyes on Anton.

"...Fear's got this, have some faith."

"Alright," Eureka spoke into the small microphone. She nodded to Anton and they sat back down in their chairs.

They weren't seated long before the door of the enclosed glass area came swinging open. Fear backpedaled, holding up a pineapple grenade in one hand and gripping a briefcase with the other. As he slowly walked backwards, Bemmy and his business associates began to emerge from the room. Eureka and Anton heard Fear say, *You know this shit ain't over right, big man*? to the old head and his associates before sticking the pin back inside of the grenade and walking off toward the exit.

Eureka, Anton, and Constance fell in step behind him, taking their leave.

Chapter Ten

Fear, Constance, Eureka, and Anton sat around the living room table passing a blunt and sipping glasses of Hennessy. "What happened back there?" Constance asked.

"They cut us off, Constance, they fucking cut us off! Shit!" Fear shot to his feet and threw his glass at the wall. It exploded. The sudden action startled everyone. Breathing hard, with his chest leaping up and down, he sat back down in his chair. Constance set another glass before him and rubbed his shoulder as she poured the brown liquor. Fear exhaled and ran a hand down his face.

The West Coast Connection cutting Loyalty Over Everything off presented a big problem for them being that they saw majority of their money from them. The syndicate forever needed a couple of niggaz rocked to sleep. Fear made his living etching tombstones for them. With them out of the equation he'd take a huge hit financially. With The Connection severing business ties with him that meant that everyone that they supplied would be turning their backs on him as well. This was the last thing he needed to happen, especially with his finances already dwindling.

From now on he was going to have to watch how he handled his money. There would be no more of his frivolous spending. He'd have to cut out all of his splurging on those ancient artifacts and furnishings that he loved so much. That would be hard for him to do. Fear was used to a certain kind of lifestyle and he knew that it would be in jeopardy without the kind of loot he was used to flowing in. He would have to make his dollars wherever he could get them. If the killer thought that the world was cold before then, it was about to get colder.

"Who?"

"The West Coast Connection," he told her. "We won't be getting money with them anymore. When I went to pick that up, Bemmy laid the news on me, said it had something to do with some nigga named Gustavo winding up on the wrong end of a straight razor."

He looked into her eyes and silence past between them. They didn't have to say anything, they both knew what he'd done to Gustavo.

"Fuck, they think you did that?"

"Yep," he nodded.

"Where's the proof?"

"The OG's don't give a shit about proof. They go on their suspicions," he told her. "You know that."

"True," she nodded, looking away and thinking, then turning back around. "What're we gonna do?"

"You know what time it is, girl. We're about to get on some ski-mask shit," Fear said. "You still down for a nigga?"

"You know don't nobody got cho back like me."

"And us," Eureka spoke up for her and Anton.

"That's right," Anton added. "I'ma always ride for my nigga."

Fear looked to them and smiled. It felt good knowing that he had two more guns on his side.

"That's love," he responded.

"Nah, that's real life," Anton corrected.

"True dat," Fear replied.

"Well, listen, I'ma take it upstairs," Constance said. "I'm tired as hell."

She stood up, stretching and yawning before turning to leave.

"Yeah, I'm up too." Anton rose to his feet and threw back the swallow of liquor in his glass. "Good night." He pecked his sister on the cheek and staggered up the staircase behind Constance.

Eureka smiled and shook her head. "You need some help?"

"No. I'm fine." He threw up two fingers as he ascended the steps.

She looked back to Fear and saw the worried expression he wore.

"From what you've told us about this West Coast Connection, I think it's safe to say that they're pretty powerful cats." Eureka spoke her thoughts. "Am I right?"

"They're some of the most powerful men assembled on this side of the West Coast,"he admitted. "They've got more than enough influence to wipe me out. I'ma tiny spec in their universe, but ask me do I give a mothafuck." He looked into her eyes, allowing the silence to pass. "No. Seriously, ask me."

"Do you give a mothafuck?"

"Hell no. And do you wanna know why?"

"Why?"

"'Cause all of them old niggaz bleed," he told her. "And if they can bleed, then they asses can die just like me." Eureka nodded her head, seeing where he was coming from. "Call me crazy, but as long as I got heart and guns any nigga and his baby momma can get it, you feel me?"

"I feel you," she answered. "And I'm on it the same way."

"I know," he said. "That's why I fucks with chu the long way." He pounded his fist to his chest.

"Listen, now that these gangster niggaz are salty, they're gonna be at us."

"I know," he conceded. "That's why we've gotta hit first. We're few, but with the four of us on 'em, they won't know what hit 'em.Straight up."

"Whenever you're ready, you know baby girl's got cha back."

"Glad to hear it." He took a sip of his drink and said, "After losing this plug, money is gonna be tight. So we're going to have to seek out other endeavors." Eureka stopped the cup at her lips as she was about to take a sip. "Like?"

"Kicking in doors," he said like there was nothing to it. "Robbing traps, Brink trucks, kidnapping niggaz for ransom.Whatever we gotta do to get to the money. Now I can't rightfully put chu down with the team until you've made your bones, but if and when you do, we're on it. We're headed straight up to the mountains for training. I'm going to have to cram six months of everything you need to know into a month before we start busting moves out here, so I hope you're ready." He looked to her to see her reaction to what he'd said. Her expression was as solid as a standup nigga that took his charge and refused to snitch.

"I was born ready, let's get it."

Fear nodded and took another sip from his cup. From the corner of his eye he could see Eureka staring at him.

"What're you looking at?" He asked without turning his head.

"Nothing," she cracked a smile, looking away and tilting her cup.

The silence between them stood for a while as they finished off their drinks. Fear picked up the bottle of Hennessy as he was about to pour some into his cup.

Noticing that he'd already killed it off; he lowered the bottle to his side.

"Well, guess the party is over," he slurred.

Eureka rose to her feet, mashing out what was left of the blunt. She turned to Fear who was just rising to his feet, empty Hennessy bottle in hand. She could see that he was shit faced by the look in his eyes and his wobbling legs. He rocked back and forth, barely able to keep his equilibrium. Eureka quickly caught him as he was about to greet the ground. She threw one of his arms over her shoulder and snaked her arm around his waist.

"Come on, big daddy, let's get cho drunk ass in the house," she laughed.

Eureka helped Fear up the steps and down the corridor. She made sure he could keep his balance before taking his arm from around her neck. Looking to his hand, she grasped the Hennessy bottle and said, "Gimmie this, I'll throw it away."

"Alright," he released the bottle.

"Goodnight."

She turned to leave and he grabbed her arm, pulling her into him. His strong chocolate hands cupped her face and his mouth met hers. His tongue pierced her lips and met with her tongue. Their mouths groped one another gently, passionately, sensually. Slowly, their kissing became slightly more aggressive. The sight was beautiful, amazing even. It looked like they were making love to one another with their mouths.

Eureka dropped the Hennessy bottle as they were getting it in and it hit the floor at their feet. Her hands held him at the hips and he pressed her up against the wall. Their faces turned at opposite angles and their tongues explored one another's. Their breathing through their nostrils became sporadic and loud as they were going at it hard.

Her small hands unbuckled his belt while his hands slipped underneath her shirt in an attempt to free her small breasts from bondage. Her bra fell at their feet at the same time his jeans met the floor. She slipped his boxer-briefs off of his waist and his black pole was standing at attention.

She pulled back from their kissing and looked down at his third arm, licking her lips. She was anxious to feel it inside the warm comfort of her walls, dying to feel all of it stuffed inside of her mouth. She hastily unzipped her skirt and pulled it down. She was so wet that her panties clung to her pussy, giving him a visual. It was like looking through a department store glass at one of the clothed mannequins.

He hiked her up against his abs and she wrapped her legs around his waist. Her arms slithered around his neck in a tight hold as their mouths devoured each other hungrily. While his mouth was occupied, his hands got busy. He pulled her drenched panties aside with one hand and took hold of his dick with the other. He rubbed the head of it up and down the slit of her pussy, teasing her. She threw her head back and licked her lips thirstily. She closed her eyes in anticipation of feeling him fill up that space that had been vacant for quite some time.

She was burning up, on fire, ablaze, and he was the only one that could extinguish the flames. He looked up at the expression she was making as he played with her second pair of lips. He smiled wickedly as he listened to her tantalizing moans, knowing that he held the key to her orgasm.

"You want it?"

"Yes."

"You need it?"

"Yess, yesss, yessss."

He slid that whole thang inside of her walls, causing her eyes to widen and her mouth to drop open. Her gooey hole was filled to capacity and there wasn't any room for him to maneuver, so he'd have to take his time to break her in. Pressing her up against the wall he felt her arms and legs tightened around him. From the way she was breathing he could tell she was preparing herself for him, but years of preparation couldn't have her ready for the thorough dick down she was about to receive.

He moved his hips in a slow circular motion at first to loosen her up. Once he felt her internal grasp welcome him, he dove into the depth of her pussy, punishing it with angry, long strokes. The muscles of his back and buttocks flexed and contracted as he worked her middle. The sweat that beaded upon his form ran down his V shaped back and got lost down the crack of his ass.

The temperature rose to such a level that she thought that she saw the walls sweating while she was getting dug out. She clawed at his back and sank her teeth into the soft flesh between his neck and shoulder. He was slinging dick like he had a license to do so, diving in and out of her slickened sex tunnel. He pumped hard, fast, furious, and with a vendetta. He and that pussy had a beef and he was there to settle the score.

Now was the best time, being that both Constance and Anton were passed out drunk in their bedrooms.

"Sssssss, ah, shit. I'm 'bout to cum, I'm 'bout to cum," she whined, feeling that long, fat piece of meat pushing her to the cliff of her pleasure. Her face, shoulders, and chest were shiny from perspiration.

"Shhhhhh, be quiet before they wake up and hear you," he said, beating that thang up like it was a nigga that got caught wearing the wrong colors in the wrong hood.

When she kept making noise, he placed his hand over her mouth and pounded her out. His face tightened and crinkled all over as he gritted his teeth. Even when he felt her legs loosen around him and shake as if they were electrocuted, he still didn't stop. She'd gotten off so it was only right that she let him get his too.

Holding her against the wall and slipping both of his arms under her arms, he locked them in place. He then sucked on her throat as he fucked her tight twat mercilessly. Her eyes rolled into the back of her head and her mouth stayed open as if it were on pause. He was fucking the sound out that ass.

"Uh."

"Uh."

"Uh."

They moaned in unison as he thrust three last times, releasing inside of her sacred hole. His body twitched, having gotten off to what he'd deemed some fire ass pussy. He still held her up against the wall, licking up her neck and sucking on the soft flesh of her throat. A slight grin accented her lips as he did that. Her eyes met his just as he came up from sucking on her throat. This time she cupped his face with her hands and kissed him, pecking his lips one last time before he let her down from the wall.

They gathered up their clothes and parted ways, but not before kissing one last time. She headed for the bathroom to clean up while he headed for his bedroom. They turned the doorknob at the same time as they were about to walk inside and looked over their shoulders. They exchanged smirks and walked through their respective doors.

The next morning…

Fear's eyes moved behind their lids from left to right before they fluttered open like the wings of a wasp. His forehead wrinkled with lines as he tried to gather his wits, sitting up in bed. He looked to the digital clock on the nightstand. Its red numbers read 10:47 A.M. He sifted through the cemetery of blunt roaches until he found a sizable one to smoke. He stuck it between his lips and fired it up. Expelling smoke from his nostrils and mouth, he thought back to the sex he had the night before with Eureka. He had bedded a number of women and he hadn't experienced like he had with her in quite some time. It was kindred to the intimacy that he shared with the love of his life, Italia.

Italia was a hood chick that was street smart and book smart. She had wound up pulling his heart's strings. He had fallen head over heels for her and even had considered leaving the life behind and starting a family with her. Everything was sunny skies and blooming daisies until he came to her house one morning and found her murdered. The tragedy left him howling like a wolf.

Losing the love of his life changed him drastically.

After that day, he buried himself into his work and never came back up for air. He vowed to never give his heart to another woman for as long as he lived. This was his way of honoring Italia's life. He promised himself to be cold toward women. To never allow himself to catch feelings or get emotionally involved, because if something was to happen to that special someone he knew that he would never be able to recover again. Things had been going exactly how he wanted them, that was until she came wandering into his life.

Eureka.

He didn't know what it was about her, but he was drawn to her like a moth to a flame. Her personality, her smile, her style, the way she carried herself all seemed to draw him in like a magnetic force. They hadn't known each other that long, but he enjoyed every minute of every hour that she was around. And he could feel it in his gut that the feeling was mutual. Now here he was thinking that maybe that there was something brewing between she and him. He couldn't be for sure, but she stayed on his mind constantly.

Even before the sex, which was explosive, he found his thoughts always drifting to her. He knew she was something unique. He wanted her, he needed her, he deserved her, but he was afraid that if he allowed himself to love again, it would end up bad. Just like with Italia. Feelings were contagious and he couldn't afford to catch them, at least not right then he couldn't. He was spiraling toward broke so his attention had to be focused on his grips.

Hearing a loud snort that sounded like it would have come from a pig, the skin on Fear's forehead bunched up and he looked over his shoulder toward where the noise came. Butt naked and lying half way underneath the sheets was Constance with her left buttock exposed. She was sprawled across the bed with half of her body hanging over the edge. Although Constance was a slender woman, she grunted and snorted like a four hundred fat man with asthma when she slept.

Since Constance was asleep, he thought it was as good a time as any to check and see how much money he had left. He slipped on some red Fruit of the Loom boxer-briefs, a pair of sweatpants, and crept to the closet door, opening it. He pulled the flap of carpet back, revealing the in-floor digital safe. He punched in the combination on the key-pad of the safe. The door of that thang popped open.

He stole a glance over his shoulder before he started pulling out the racks out of the safe. Once he saw that Constance wasn't watching him, he went about his business. When he was finished counting all of the money he was disappointed. He only had forty-eight thousand dollars. That was all of the money he had in the world. That was some all right paper, but he was used to a lot more. He was definitely tightening his belt now. There wasn't any question about it.

Fear closed the door of the safe and threw the flap of carpet over it. He stepped out of his bedroom to welcome the day. He was journeying down the hallway, taking tokes and blowing smoke when he noticed the bathroom door was open and two shadows shuffling about. Posting up right outside of the door, he attentively watched Eureka and Anton.

They stood before the medicine cabinet mirror looking over their reflections as they modeled themselves. Anton was formally dressed in a simple, navy blue suit, sky blue button-down, and tie. Earlier that morning Eureka had come across Fear's hair clippers and decided that she'd hook her little brother up with a close fade.

Anton looked brand new out of the box fresh with his haircut with the hook in it. Eureka was amazed at the difference a haircut and some new clothes could make. Anton looked nothing like the young hoodlum he actually was. Nah, that day he looked like the pastor's handsome teenage son.

Although Anton was fresh to death, Eureka's attire couldn't be denied either. She donned a pink, leopard print dress with a thick belt that resembled the one that Santa Clause wore with his big red suit, and matching leopard print heels. A fake pearl necklace and matching earrings hung from her lobes. Her short hair was done to be slicked on the sides and spiked at the top. Eureka and Anton looked like a couple of Christians draped in their Sunday's best about to be on their way to church.

Fear took a toke of the L and it sent him into a coughing frenzy that garnered Eureka and Anton's attention. "Good morning," he managed to say through his coughing with a fist to his mouth.

"Good morning," Eureka replied, smiling and winking at him. He smiled and winked back at her.

"Rise and shine, big homie.Let me hit that," Anton approached, holding his pinched fingers out toward the blunt roach. Fear's eye shifted up at Eureka, looking for her okay. When she shrugged, he passed Anton the roach.

"You let the lil' homie smoke?"

"I've let Ant do a lotta things that I shouldn't have," Eureka said, turning from side to side and looking herself over in the medicine cabinet mirror. "Besides, with all of the drama we've been through these past couple of weeks, he deserves a toke or two. Shit, I do too for that matter."

She took the L from Anton and took a couple puffs, tainting the air with the vile odor. She tried to pass it back to Fear, but he declined with a wave of his hand.

"Nah, you go ahead and finish that, ma. I'm Gucci," Fear told her, "Where y'all off to?"

Eureka allowed a small cloud to emerge from her mouth before zapping it back in and blowing it back out."To visit a relative."

"A relative?" Fear frowned. "Who?"

"No one you'd know."

Fear nodded and said, "Well, I was about to leave, I could take you to see 'em if you want."

"Nah, we don't want to impose."

"You ain't imposing, believe me," Fear assured."

Eureka thought on it for a minute, then said, "Alright. I guess it is better than catching the bus."

"Cool." Anton turned to Fear, slapping hands with him. "Good looking out, my nigga."

"That ain't about nothing, I'ma gon' and get dressed." Fear clapped the doorway before walking down the hallway. He was nearing his bedroom door when Eureka called after him. He turned around and she approached him.

"About what happened last night," she began, blushing and twiddling her fingers. "I don't want chu to think lil' of me 'cause I've never done anything like that before. It was just that I'm really feeling you and—"

Before she could finish, he engaged her, tilted her chin up with a curled finger and kissed her like her lips were glazed with the nectar of a peach. He pulled his head back and smiled, they both did. Eureka was glowing, floating on cloud nine.

"I know exactly how you feel and it's mutual," he told her. "I'm not saying let's jump right into anything, but let's take whatever this is slow and see what happens.Cool?"

She smiled hard and nodded, "Cool."

With that said, he left to get dressed.

Chapter Eleven
Meanwhile

Antoinette stood over the stove with flour stained hands, frying chicken. Her eyes were bloodshot and moist. Every so often, she'd stop to wipe the tears that ran down her cheeks. She had been having a rough time keeping it together since the disappearance of Ronny, her boyfriend and her son's father. He'd been gone for nearly a month and no one had seen or heard from him in just as long.

Her mind had began taunting her as she thought about a number of things that could have happened to Ronny. The one that stood out in her mental was of him wearing a bullet hole in his forehead, lying slumped only God knew where. As of now, she could only expect the worse and pray for the best, because given Ronny's line of work, him lying dead somewhere wasn't farfetched. In fact it was more than likely.

Ronny wasn't anybody's Saint and that was apparent to anyone with a set of eyes and ears. He'd done some wicked things in the past and in the present, but she loved him, all of him. And if the Lord saw fit to allow him to be alive and well, she'd do all she could to convince him to leave the life.

Feeling something pulling on her skirt, Antoinette looked down and found the love of her life, her son, her everything, five year old R.J or Ronny Junior. He was draped in a blue Spider Man T-shirt and holding a crayon in one hand as he was coloring in a coloring book on the kitchen table. RJ was standing on the tips of his sneakers and holding a balled up paper towel up at her. This brought a smile to Antoinette's face. No matter how down she was feeling, the little dude always seemed to brighten up her day.

"Here, mommy, stop crying.Okay?" It hurt him to see his mother's sadness.

"Okay," she nodded.

"Kneel down here," she did as he said and he dabbed her face dry with the balled up paper towel. Once he was done, he kissed her on the lips and said, "There. You feel better now?"

Antoinette smirked and nodded, saying, "Yes. But you know what would really make me feel better?"

"What?"

"A hug and another kiss from my little man."

He wrapped his little arms around her neck and squeezed tightly, kissing her on the cheek. Antoinette closed her eyes as she embraced her son, rubbing his back and kissing him on the side of the head.

"I love you so much," she told him.

"I love you, too," he replied. "Don't cry no more, okay? Daddy will be home soon."

"Alright," she kissed him on the cheek and stood erect to take out the chicken.

She held a plate with several folded paper towels on it, which she used to place the chicken on as she took it out of the hot skillet. She'd just placed the plate down on the kitchen table when the cordless telephone rang in the living room. Anxious, she pulled off her apron and used it to wipe her hands as she made a mad dash into the living room, RJ on her heels. Antoinette snatched up the cordless from the living room table and pressed talk, placing it to her ear.

"Ronny?" She spoke hopefully. As fast as her excitement rose, it fell just as quickly with disappointment when she heard the caller's voice.

"Nah, this ain't Ronny, this Malvo."

"Oh," she said, defeated. She looked to RJ who was standing beside her, beaming brightly and jumping up and down.

He was hoping that the call was the one that they'd both been looking forward to. His flame of hope was quickly extinguished when she looked to him and shook her head no. He stopped jumping around and hung his head. She pulled him into her and stooped low, kissing him on the top of the head as she rubbed his back.

"Well, don't sound so excited to hear from me."

"Believe you and me, the last thing I am is excited to hear from you."

Ouch!

Antoinette had never been too fond of Malvo and she didn't make it a secret. Whenever Ronny would bring him around she didn't give him anything more than a hi and/or bye and she made sure to keep her distance from him. She'd heard about his exploits in the streets and how he'd manipulated weaker women with drugs for sexual favors. It disgusted her and the only reason she tolerated him was because her nigga worshipped the ground that he walked on. You couldn't say anything about Malvo without Ronny threatening to bring World War III your way. Ronny praised the man like he was his father and in his eyes he couldn't do any wrong. Shit, he loved him so much that he made him and Crunch RJ's Godfathers when the boy was born.

"Oh so, it's like that?"

"Real life," she responded. "I know you know more than what you're letting on about Ronny's disappearance, and I swear 'fore God Malvo, if my man comes up dead and you have anything to do with it, I'm marching my ass straight down to the 77th division precinct and telling them everything I know about cho trifling ass."

"Bitch, knock it off with all of the dramatics, you ain't fooling nobody," Malvo spat angrily. "I know you know where that mothafucka is so you better start talking before something real happens to you." He spoke with a chill to his tone that could freeze a ninety three degree summer day.

Antoinette looked down to RJ who was looking up at her. He looked like he was worried so she flashed him a smile and told him to cover his ears. Her face tainted with hostility as she focused her attention on the conversation with Malvo.

"Fuck you, you ol' fat ass nigga. You don't scare me with your empty ass threats," she talked that shit in the cordless like she was bout that life and would bring it to a nigga's doorstep with twin nines. "Suck my dick!"

She said it how a turned up nigga would and he felt it like a punch to the jaw.

"Fuck you just say to me, bitch?"

"I'll say it again for your slow ass." She talked that shit, gripping the cordless tighter and clearing her throat. Bobbing her head, she said with attitude, "Suck. My. Di—"

Ba-thoom!

The front door rattled upon impact, startling Antoinette and causing her to drop the cordless telephone. Her heart nearly leapt out of her chest. She whipped around to the front door, her eyes as big as saucers and her mouth wide open. She gripped her son's hand as the door was struck again, again, and again. This time the door snapped open and a wood splinter shot across the living room. Crunch stalked forth, his malevolent eyes bloodshot and glassy as he gritted his teeth. His gloved hand gripped a ratchet as he advanced in Antoinette's direction. She shrilled and hauled ass toward the back bedroom, pulling her son along. RJ fell to the floor as his mother was moving too fast for his little legs to keep up. She yanked him back upon his feet and they fled to the back bedroom, with Crunch on their asses like a hemorrhoid.

As soon as they crossed the threshold, she slammed the door behind them, pinning Crunch's arm in the doorway as he reached in. Crunch grabbed a handful of Antoinette's dookie braids, pulling and yanking them as she continued to slam the door on his arm. Her face balled up, feeling the stinging in her scalp. RJ sobbed and hollered, wanting to help his mother, but not knowing what to do.

Antoinette opened her mouth, bearing her teeth like a wolf would his fangs. With a snarl, she bit into the Crunch's gloved hand, drawling a blood curdling scream from him. Antoinette bit and chewed on his hand until it slithered back out of the door. She slammed the door shut and locked it, rushing over to her sobbing son with red stained teeth.

The bedroom door rattled with back to back punches with vulgarities coming right after them. Each time the door met with Crunch's fist it caused a banging sound and made RJ scream, louder and louder.

"Fucking bitch!" Crunch's voice boomed from the opposite side of the door.

Antoinette picked up her son and carried him over to the other side of the bedroom. He sobbed into her shirt, clinging to her like Spider-Man would to a wall. She rocked him and said what she thought would calm him, but he kept at it. Antoinette picked the telephone up from off of the receiver. Hastily, she punched in a number and brought it to her ear, her forehead deepened with creases when she didn't hear anything.

"Hello? Hello? Shit." She cursed, realizing that the line was dead. She dropped the telephone to the floor.

The lights inside of the bedroom flickered on and off until they went out completely, blanketing them in darkness. Antoinette rocked RJ in her arms and caressed his back, trying to comfort him in his emotional state. She slowly stepped backwards until she was in a corner with her back against the wall. The bedroom door continued to rattle as it was assaulted with punch after punch as Crunch was trying to break through the door.

Antoinette slid down in the corner onto the floor, listening to her son's sobbing as tears slicked her cheeks. She didn't know what was going to happen, but Crunch had come there to claim her life she only hoped that he'd spare her son's.

Abruptly, the rattling of the door stopped and all that could be heard was RJ's sobbing, but eventually she got him to quiet down. For a time Antoinette sat on the floor in the corner waiting for what was to come next. After a while she got up off the floor and crept toward the door cautiously. By this time RJ was wiping his face with his small hand and trying to see what was going on.

Antoinette swiftly stepped around the door as if it would burst into flames at any given moment. She took a cautionary step toward the door and placed her hand gently against it. She looked to RJ and put a finger to her lips, silently telling him to hush. When he nodded his head, she pressed her ear against the door and listened closely. She didn't hear any movement on the other end, but she was sure that there was someone there. She didn't know what their next move would be or hers for that matter.

Antoinette held her ear pressed against the door, her eyes settled in their corners as she listened for movement on the other side. A long while had passed before *thok* and half of a meat cleaver splintered the door, misting the air with debris. The sudden assault against the door startled Antoinette and sent her sailing backwards. She tripped over her loose Manolo boot and fell down on her back, grimacing.

She came back up, holding RJ against her chest, his head snapped in every direction as he wondered what was going on. Antoinette looked up at the door, watching the meat cleaver hack away at it. She could hear someone grunting with each strike that they delivered to the door. RJ's sobbing and hollering started back up again and he buried his face into his mother's chest.

"What the fuck do you want from us?" Antoinette bellowed, face turning red as hot tears slicked down her cheeks. The meat cleaver worked a hole inside of the door big enough for a hand to fit through, and one did. A meaty gloved hand came through the hole and a hefty arm snaked its way inside. The knob was turned and the door was pushed open. It banked off of the wall showcasing Malvo and Crunch littering the doorway. They glared at her as they clenched their teeth, their jaws pulsating with muscles.

Antoinette's heart raged inside of her chest, threatening to explode she was under so much stress. She was positive that nothing short of death would come next. Boy, did her mouth write a check that her ass couldn't cash.

"I got the bitch, you get the boy," Malvo said, tossing aside the meat cleaver and drawing his banger from his waistline. He stalked toward Antoinette and grabbed a fist full of her dookie braids.

"Please, don't hurt myyyyyyyy—" her voice raised several octaves as she was pulled up to her feet. Blood seeped from the roots of her braids and some of them even came loose. Malvo ushered Antoinette toward the door as Crunch pried RJ from her arms. Together he and Crunch escorted them down the hallway and into the living room.

Malvo shoved Antoinette onto the couch and plopped down beside her. He laid back and rested his banger on his thigh, staring at her with contempt. Antoinette locked eyes with Malvo, squirming under his gaze. She wondered what was going through his mind at that moment and what his intentions were. His forehead contracted and his eyes were ablaze with seriousness. To try him right now would be like head butting a knife. Stupid.

"Where the fuck is Ronny?"

"I swear to God I don't know, Malvo." She told the truth, sniffling and rubbing her eye. "I haven't seen him in nearly a month, hasn't answered my calls or nothing."

Malvo massaged his temple as he closed his eyes and exhaled. He was trying his best to keep from snapping on Antoinette's ass, but his temper got the best of him. Swiftly and without warning, the hand that gripped his banger swung across. *Crack*! Antoinette's head snapped back from the force of the impact from the side of the gun. A gash opened on her forehead and ran red, slicking the side of her face. She hollered and clutched her leaking forehead, blood running in between her fingers.

"Aghh!" Crunch howled in pain, taking his gloved hand away from RJ as he'd bitten him. The boy charged toward Malvo, screaming and ready to fight. "Leave my momma a—"

He froze in his tracks once Malvo pointed that banger at his little ass. Although he was young, he knew what real and toy guns looked like. And that one was the real McCoy. RJ stood where he was, tears rippling down his cheeks as his chest pumped back and forth. He was terrified of the big gun.

"Please don't hurt 'em!" Antoinette grabbed Malvo's arm and he snatched away. He shot her a dangerous look, then focused his attention back on RJ.

"Uh huh, I see you ain't stupid," Malvo smiled evilly. "You know if I pull this trigga it'll flip your lil' ass like a quarter brick, ummhmm. Back up, *back up!*" He shouted sharply, startling the boy. Crunch pulled the little nigga backwards by the collar of his shirt. He tucked that thang on his waistline and pulled a knife from out of his back pocket. With a twist of his wrist he snapped the knife open and placed it near the side of RJ's neck.

"Here," Malvo pulled a bandana from his back pocket and passed it to Antoinette. She used it to wipe the blood off of her face, grimacing every time she came into contact with the tender gash.

RJ's head was tilted down as he was glaring at Malvo with a wet face and twisted lips.

"You see this runt, Crunch?" Malvo looked from Crunch to the glaring RJ, amused. "He's on one right now. I bet if he had that gat he'd do me, wouldn't you lil' nigga?" He lay back on the couch, chuckling and saying, "Yeah, you would. I can see it in your eyes. You've got balls junior, real big balls.Don't you ever lose them."

"I can't believe this," she whined, looking between Malvo and Crunch, holding a hand to her chest. She was devastated that Ronny's closest comrades would switch up the game on him. "Y'all are doing this to us? You're supposed to be Ronny's best friends, the Godfathers to his son.

"Ho, I know you aren't tryna cop a plea after all of that shit you were popping a few minutes ago?" Malvo looked at her like, *Please tell me you're joking.* "I ain't tryna hear none of that family shit. Your nigga owe me, big time. He ran off with a lotta dope of mine and I plan on leaving here with my money or his life."

"I don't know where he is, Malvo, that's the honest to God truth." Antoinette swore. "I swear on my son's life I hadn't seen 'em in like three and a half to four weeks."

Malvo looked like he was weighing it for a time before he spoke again.

"Alright," he began, "Let's say I do believe you. I can't leave here empty handed."

"I got about twenty grand stashed here in the safe," she told him. "It's Ronny's money for a lawyer in case he gets caught up in the streets. I'll take you to it—" she moved to rise from the couch and he grabbed her arm, stopping her. Malvo closed his eyes and shook his head sadly. Antoinette looked at him with a furrowed brow, wondering what the problem was.

"Sweetheart, that lil' punk ass change ain't gon' be enough to pay back your man's debt, uh uh, you gon' have to give me something else."

Antoinette settled back down on the couch, holding the bandana to her gash and looking at it every so often. Malvo's eyes wandered down her body and settled on her exposed thigh. It was thick and succulent. He licked his top lip, hungry for what she had. Using his banger, he pushed up her skirt and revealed that she was wearing white cotton panties with pink polka dots. The imprint of her fat, shaved monkey caused the blood to rush up his flaccid dick, inflating it like a balloon at a little kid's party.

Antoinette scowled, smacking the cold steel away from her thigh and pulling down her skirt. "I don't get down like that," she protested. "My pussy isn't to be bartered for."

Malvo made a funny face and nodded. He looked to Crunch wearing a face of stone, saying, "Waste the midget."

Crunch tilted RJ's head back and he struggled against his grip, screaming and flailing his arms. Crunch ignored the tears and the pleas for his mother he uttered and placed the razor sharp blade to the little nigga's neck. His head snapped up to see Antoinette hopping up from the couch and getting down on her knees before Malvo. The grimy snake mothafucka seemed to be enjoying the mother pleading for her son.

"Oh, please, please, Malvooooo," Antoinette pleaded for her son's life, hands clasped together begging. "Don't kill my baby, don't take my only son! I'll do anything, anything you want me to!" Fresh tears misted her eyes and snot threatened to drip from her nose.

"Anything?" Malvo's ears perked up like a pair of silicone tits. He smiled deviously and leaned forward, combing his plump fingers through her braids.

He'd always wanted a crack at Antoinette, but kept his mouth shut since Ronny was sporting her on his arm. Now he had the perfect excuse to feel those walls of hers and all the thanks were owed to Ronny himself.

Malvo pulled his hand out of Antoinette's hair, circling the side of her face and gently pinching her chin. "Alright, darling," he laid back on the couch, staring down into her eyes. "I want slow neck and throwed sex." He unbuckled his jeans and slowly unzipped them. He moved to pull out his meat when…

"Malvo!" Crunch's voice snatched his attention in his direction. He shook his head and nodded down to RJ who was silently watching everything as it unfolded.

"Right," Malvo retorted. "Take our Godson in the bedroom while me and his momma get reacquainted with one another."

Once Crunch took RJ into the other bedroom and closed the door shut, Malvo pulled his limp dick from the rest haven that was his boxer-briefs. He tilted Antoinette's head up by her chin and stuck his finger inside of her mouth, first his index then his middle. He didn't have to say a word because she already knew what to do. Antoinette sucked Malvo's fingers, watching his fuck stick grow to stand at attention.

Once he'd gotten tired of her sucking on his fingers, he used that same hand to guide that wet mouth of hers down to his lap. As soon as she engorged his meat, a smile emerged on his face and he threw his head back. His eyes slowly narrowed into slits making him look like he had taken a couple of blunts to the dome.

He moaned and groaned as Antoinette got his mind right. He reached down and stuck his hand inside of her shirt, palming one of her perky breasts. His ass cheeks clenched together as he received her best asset, slow neck.

"That's right bitch," he rasped, "Suck my mothafucking dick, suck the skin off this mothafucka," he spat, looking down at her like she was the filthiest of whores. Antoinette gagged as she sucked on his meat, tears cascading down her face. "Come on now, you act like you scared of this dick, girl.Handle yo business."

He became agitated. Seeing that she wasn't trying to give him the blow job that he desired, he pressed his hand at the back of her head and began humping her mouth violently. She gagged and choked, squeezing her eyes tightly. She tried to pull away, but he held fast. He pulled her back into him and locked his legs around her neck, burying his cock in her mouth down to his hairy nut-sack. She pressed her hands against the couch and tried to pull back, but he had her locked firmly in place.

"Hold still, bitch, 'fore I blow yo noodles out!" He threatened her, pressing his gun to the side of her head. She submitted, sobbing hard, but her cries were muffled by a mouthful of dick. "Yeah, that's how daddy likes it."

Lying back on the couch, he humped between her lips wildly. His eyes rolled into the back of his head and he groaned as he furiously pumped without regard of how she felt. Tears flew down her face and snot oozed out of her nose, mixing with thick globs of saliva. The nasty marriage of goo threatened to hit the floor, but never fell.

Malvo paid it no mind as he continued with his merciless pummeling of her grill. "Uh, shit! Ahh, fuck! Here that shit comeeeee! Ohhhhh!" He croaked, thrusting the third hole in her face as he released every last drop of semen from his nut-sack.

He held her in place for a time, his body jerking, having gotten off. He smiled in delight, his sweaty face looking down at her. Her eyes were pink from crying and her golden brown complexion was now the color of rose pedals. She looked like someone had been choking her.

He took his legs from around her neck and scooted back on the couch, looking down at his dick. It was wet and dripping with her bodily fluids. A smile graced his face as he looked up at a sobbing Antoinette who was on the floor on all fours, gagging and coughing up his semen. An off white pool of goop was between her hands. It expanded the more she vomited and cried her heart out.

"Ohhhhh, God!Please, please, no more, no more!" She pleaded, scooting away from him, using her hands and the heels of her bare feet.

"Uh uh, I'm far from through with yo thick, pretty ass." He approached her, wiping his wang off with one of the couch pillows before discarding it. "I want some of that pussy, too." He licked his chops and pointed to her pussy with his gun. The thought of going up inside of her gave him an instant hard-on. Pre-cum oozed out of the head of his thick-veined cock like puss from an untreated infection.

Seeing him advancing, she crawled on her hands and knees as fast as she could. He wasn't about to chase her though. She had him fucked up. He had something in his ratchet that would reach her back before she went through that door. He lifted that thang up and took aim.

"Ho, you make another move and I'ma give Crunch the word to nod that lil' cum stain up in there." This halted her, she snapped back around to him, wide eyed and mouth hanging open.

"You wouldn't!" She looked upon him like the living nightmare that he was.

He smiled satanically and called out to his partner-in-crime, melodically. "Ooh, Cruunchh!"

"Okay, alright, I'll do…I do whatever you want me to."The tears kept coming, they wouldn't stop. She'd suffere through whatever his sick, twisted mind could conjure up for the sake of her son.

"I know you will, 'cause I'm *That Nigga*," he quipped, licking his top lip with his thick, long tongue as he feasted his eyes below her waist where that guerilla fist resided.

He called her over with a curl of his finger. Once she approached, he lowered her down to her knees before him. She was so scared that she trembled uncontrollably and goose bumps rolled up her skin. She closed her eyes tightly and tried to remind herself that she was doing this for her son.

"Do it for R.J, do it for R.J, do it for R.J," she repeatedly whispered over and over with her eyes closed.

The anticipation of sliding between her walls had Malvo's dick as hard as a diamond. He was so horny and stiff that his fuck muscle jumped slightly. Staring down at Antoinette, he rubbed his cock across her lips and smacked it against the side of her face. He grumbled under his breath, feeling his meat growing harder and harder.

He helped her to her feet and lifted her shirt up. He slipped her bra above her breasts and groped them, occasionally pinching her thick nipples. His hand slid down her pudgy stomach and found her second pair of lips, parting them with his middle finger. He worked her middle until they were somewhat damp. He already knew she wasn't about to get too wet because she was being forced to sex him against her will.

Malvo pulled his slick fingers from her southern lips and stuck them into her mouth, allowing her to suck her juices from them. He then turned her thick, Amazonian ass around and smacked her on one of her bodacious hams. Pointing a finger, he ordered her onto the couch on her knees with her back to him. She obliged, tooting her enormous ass up in the air and giving him a look at that inviting pink hole.

Malvo shook his head as he stared at that path to heaven, stroking his black baton. His dick head swelled further, running with a clear fluid. He stepped behind her on the couch, one leg propped up on the side of her. He spat in his hand and used his saliva to slick her lips for an easy entrance. He was just about to journey into the abyss when she drew her hole back, leaning forward and looking at him over her shoulder.

"Wa…wait…do you have a condom?"

"Nah, I'm straight though. You ain't got shit to worry about," Malvo told her. "Let me get this thang off."

"No, I don't wanna—"

Crack! Crack! Wop!

He punched her in the back of the head repeatedly and said, "Shut cho ass up and take this dick! You gon' do what I say, when I say it, or I'ma crush that lil' nigga of yours in the other room. You hear me?" He grabbed a handful of her hair and yanked her head back, drawing a shrill from her lips.

"Yes, yes, I hear you, I hear you!" She shouted.

"Alright then, I don't wanna hear no more back talk."

Antoinette really didn't want Malvo running up in her raw, but the way she saw it, she didn't have a choice in the matter. If she didn't give this nigga some pussy, chances were she and her son would be wearing toe-tags before the night was over. Reluctantly, she relaxed and got back into position.

Gripping the arm of the couch, she closed her eyes and exhaled, bracing herself. Malvo slid up inside of that thang slow and tilted his head back. He rolled his eyes and his mouth fell open. Antoinette's pussy felt like her mouth, warm and wet, only tighter. He started up at a slow, steady pace, but then it got good to him so he sped up, his belly smacking up against her rump.

He grunted as he lapped at her big, golden, red ass. Before he knew it his face was coated with sweat and he was rasping, out of breath. He held his banger in the hand of his injured arm while his hand was planted firmly on her ass. His thumb jabbed in and out of her asshole as he pumped her from the back. All you could hear in that mothafucka was his grunting and the slapping of wet flesh.

Antoinette cried silently, occasionally wiping tears from her cheeks as they fell. Her body lurched forward and backward as he slammed into that big, old ass of hers. Feeling himself about to erupt, Malvo slowed down his fast pace and slow stroke her. Beads of sweat formed on his forehead and dripped off on those humongous golden red orbs of hers. He watched as her snatch swallowed up his dick and then spat it back out.

Malvo bit down on his bottom lip and squeezed his eyes closed. He grabbed a fist full of Antoinette's braids and continued to hammer her from the back, making more sensual noises than she, sounding like a straight up bitch. You would have thought that it was him that was being fucked and not her.

"You ready for this cum, bitch, huh? Tell me you're ready, you fucking whore," he gritted as he punished her at the rear.

When she didn't answer him, he asked again, but she still didn't say anything. That's when he asked once more, yanking her head back by the braids and drawing a yelp from her lips. It wasn't until then that she answered him.

"Yes, yes, yes, I'm ready," She whimpered as the tears shot down her face.

"I can't hear you, hoe!" *Smack!* He smacked her on the ass and continued to slam his stroke up in her pink entrance. "Tell me to cum in your pussy."

"Cum…cum…cum in my pussy," her voice cracked emotionally.

"Ahhhhh, again," he tilted his head back and pulled her head all of the way back by her braids, firing his pelvis off at those two globes of golden, red meat. "Twice more, slut."

Smack! Smack! Smack! Smack!

She jumped forth as he laid into her backside, she stifled back a sob and wiped her tears away with a French tip manicured hand.

"Cum in my pussy, cum in my pussy!"

"Ahhhh, fuck yeah! I'm 'bout to give you what chu wan't!" He slammed into her ass cheeks three more times, then grinded hard into her as he shot all of his spunk into her glory hole. "Whew, that right there was the lick!" Taking his time, he pulled out his limp meat and stepped back, holding her ass cheeks apart from each other. He watched as his mayonnaise spilled out of her pink hole and dripped down on the couch cushion, staining it a darker color.

"Well, would you look at that?" He stuck his finger inside of her and when he pulled it out it was covered in his frosting.

He wiped his finger off on the arm of the couch. He then stood erect, tucking his black baton back inside of his jeans and zipping them back up. He was in the middle of buckling his belt when Antoinette turned over wiping her wet face with the back of her hand.

"Can I get a towel?"

He nodded yeah and watched as she stood up, dripping his spunk out of her slicked opening. He kept a close eye on her when she went into the hallway closet and retrieved a washcloth. She got it soapy and wet under the kitchen sink's faucet and propped her leg upon the chair at the kitchen table. He watched her as she scrubbed that pretty pussy of hers clean, licking his chops like a hungry dog.

He was just about to try for another crack at it when he heard the door opening at his rear. When he turned around he saw Crunch step halfway out of the bedroom holding RJ by the back of his shirt.

"Y'all through?" He inquired. Malvo nodded yes.

"Mommy?" RJ's head darted around in search of his mother.

At that moment Antoinette emerged from the kitchen. When RJ saw his mother, he broke free from Crunch's clutches and ran over to her. She scooped him up into her arms and hugged him tightly.

Malvo threw his arm around Crunch's shoulders and walked him off to the side, outside of earshot of Antoinette.

"Yo, you want a crack at that?" He held a thumb over in Antoinette's direction,

Crunch found her glaring at him and Malvo. He locked eyes with her, feeling really shitty about what he let go down between she and Malvo. He knew exactly what her eyes were communicating with him, but all he offered for an explanation was a shrug."You wanna stab that 'fore we get outta here?" Malvo asked again.

"Nahh, I'm straight," Crunch told him as he gazed across the living room at Antoinette. She wore a face that made him feel uneasy.

"You sho'? It's on me. As much as Ronny owes me, you'll be up busting nuts 'til the wee hours of the night."

"I'm straight, my nigga." Crunch turned his head from Antoinette to Malvo. "Let's make tracks."

"Alright, bet." Malvo picked up Antoinette's purse and dumped its contents on the coffee table. He then picked through it until he uncovered her driver's license and social security card. He held them both up so that she could see exactly what he had. "I got your L's and your social, so if you go running off at the mouth and figure you can just pick up and move, I'll come looking for you. And if I can't find you, I'll smash everyone that you love. You got that?"

Antoinette didn't say a word, she just sat there glaring at him through moist, bloodshot eyes. Her cheeks were sprawled with white lines which were dry tears. Her eyes told him that he would pay for what he'd done to her, but he didn't give a damn.

"Your silence is enough to let me know that you heard me." He tucked her license and social security card into his pocket. "I'm out, lil' man." He extended his fist toward RJ. The little boy moved back and buried his chest in mother's chest, hugging her tightly.

Malvo let his fist drop down to his side and tapped Crunch as he headed for the door. Crunch lingered behind, staring at Antoinette for a while, feeling a little bad for what he'd let go down. With a shrug of his shoulders, he turned and headed out of the door, thinking, *Fuck feeling bad, this ain't on me. This shit is on Ronny.*

Malvo slid into the front passenger seat just as Crunch was firing up the Tahoe. He pulled away from the curb and drove off down the street. He adjusted the rear-view mirror and stole a glance at Malvo who was fishing through the ashtray. Once he found a roach, he sparked that mothafucka up and tucked his Bic lighter into his jacket pocket. Smoke clouded the interior of the SUV making, it looked like a scene after an explosion.

"That shit was foul, Mal, that shit was real foul." Crunch shot him a look like, *You know that shit, too*.

"There's a method to my madness, Crunch," Malvo stated as he watched the dimly lit streets from the passenger window, holding the smoke in his lungs for a time. He blew that shit out and passed the roach to Crunch.

"What method is this exactly?" Crunch inquired as he blew smoke from his nostrils.

"After the shit I just laid down, Ronny is sure to come out of hiding," Malvo explained. "And when he does, I'm gonna pop 'em like the rubber band on a ten thousand dollar stack. Ya heard?"

"You're a genius," Crunch said, holding smoke in his lungs as he passed the roach back. "A pure, unadulterated genius."

Chapter Twelve

"So what's the address?" Fear asked as he slid in behind the wheel of his Dodge Charger R/T and fired it up.

Anton hopped into the backseat and slammed the door shut while Eureka was just sitting down on the front passenger seat. She flipped down the flap to adjust her burgundy lens shades in the small rectangular mirror. As she went about the task of fixing her shades on her face, she gave Fear the address. The lines on His forehead deepened as he thought about the address. He wasn't for sure, but he had an idea of where the address would lead him.

Taking it lightly, he pressed the address into the navigational system and backed out of the driveway. Thirty minutes into the drive the navigational system spoke, "Your destination is 200 feet and to the left."

"That's Inglewood Cemetery." Fear's brow furrowed. "You got fam that works in there?"

Eureka was staring out of the front passenger side window, watching the coming and going of the residents of South Central Los Angeles. She was so intertwinedin her thoughts that she didn't even hear Fear talking to her. It wasn't until he nudged her with his elbow that she finally sat up and gave him her undivided attention. "You good?" Fear asked.

"Uh huh," Eureka nodded. "I'm good, I'm straight."

"So, uh, does this *relative* work at the cemetery?" He asked as he coasted down Florence Avenue, looking for entrance gates of the Inglewood Cemetery.

"Something like that," Eureka spoke up.

"Fuck is up with all of the secrecy?" Fear questioned with a shrug.

"There isn't any secrecy," Eureka assured him. "You wanna meet my relative? Well, you're about to. Relax."

"Your destination is at ten feet, make a left," the navigational system spoke.

Fear pulled into the Inglewood Cemetery, taking directions from Eureka as she pointing her finger, leading him around the paved path.

"Stop, right here," Eureka told Fear as she peered through the window.

Once Fear stopped the car, she and Anton unbuckled their safety belts. They hopped out of the car and trekked over the mound, with Fear bringing up the rear. Fear took in the full scope of his surroundings. The area was long and wide. The lawn wasa pretty green and well kempt,while the headstoneswere in immaculatecondition. Fear looked around thinking about the lyrics B.G spat on Made Man.

And best believe I done took some niggas off the shelf/God forgive me I got a graveyard under my belt/I done walked in a killer shoes/ A drug dealer shoes/Done bad masked up and gave niggas blues...

The devil would be in possession of Fear's soul once his life finally came to an end, he was sure of it. There wasn't any question about it, he was definitely taking the elevator down when it was his time, and he was alright with that. Because if he was going to Hell when it was all said and done, then he was going to make sure that he had Heaven on earth.

"Fear?"

Fear looked up to see Anton waving him over from the top of the hill. He had lagged behind, having gotten so deep in his thoughts. He jogged up the hill and met up with

Anton. Together they walked over to Eureka who was on her knees before a blue marble headstone. Seeing Fear and Anton's shadows on the grass as they approached, she looked over to them as she was talking to Bootsy. Although he wasn't alive to reply, she imagined what his responses would be.

Eureka placed her shades at the top of her head and made the introductions. "Daddy, this is Fear. Fear this is my Daddy, Bootsy."

For a time Fear didn't say a word, he just stood there with a crinkled forehead, looking from the grave to Eureka.

Noticing Fear's delayed reaction, Anton nudged him and he nodded to his father's grave.

"Oh, uh, how are you doing, sir? Fear greeted, looking down at thegravestone. "Never mind Fear, it's an old childhood nickname. You can call me Al, or Alivin."

"Daddy, Fear was nice enough to take us in after what had gone down back in The Jordans," Eureka spoke to her father. "Without him, I don't know where Ant and I would be." She looked to Fear."My Daddy says thanks for looking after his kids, he really appreciates it."
 "No problem, sir. I'm glad that I could help." Eureka went on talking to her deceased father. Without taking his eyes off of her, Fear turned his head slightly and addressed Anton. "Is she, alright?" he asked.

"She's fine," Anton said. He had his eyes on Eureka too. "This is sis' way of coping. Everytime we come up here she has these conversations with our pops and imagines what he's saying back. Don't worry, she's straight."

"Alright, if you say so."

"Trust me."

"Ant." Eureka called out to her little brother.

"Watts up?"

"Let's have our customary drink with Daddy."

"Okay." Anton got down on his knees beside her.

When they were little, Bootsy used to sneak behind Giselle's back and let them get a taste of his favorite drink, apple Snapple and Belvedere, every now and again. He got a kick out of seeing their faces sour once they tasted the alcohol. What really got him was how they always wanted some more, right after. He understood that they loved him and wanted to be just like him.

Fear looked on as Eureka and Anton interacted with their father as if he was standing right there, alive and in the flesh. To him, it was strange how they carried on a conversation as if their father was standing dead smack in front of them.

"Look, Daddy, I brought your favorite drink." Eureka smiled, opening her hefty purse. "I bet chu thought that I wouldn't remember, huh?"

Eureka pulled out three glasses from her hefty purse and sat them around her father's gravestone. Next, she withdrew a bottle of Belvedere vodka. She sat it down on the lawn and dipped her hand back inside of the purse,pulling out an apple Snapple. After pouring up the glasses, she took out a stirrer and mixed the drinks.

Eureka snapped her fingers as she recalled something."I knew that I forgot something," she said. "Your flowers."

"You didn't forget, you told me to get 'em remember?" Anton spoke, causing Eureka's forehead to furrow. She didn't know what he was getting at because she was sure that she hadn't told him to do anything.

"I left 'em over there," Anton jogged across the lawn and snatched up a fresh bouquet of flowers from off someone else's grave. "Here you go, pops." He lay the bouquet of flowers down on Bootsy's gravestone.

Eureka eyes grew big and her mouth dropped open as she couldn't believe that Anton had done such a thing. Suddenly, she busted up laughing and he did too.

Seeing this caused a smirk to form on Fear's lips.

"What?" Anton grinned, pretending like he didn't know what he had done.

"Daddy, you see your son?" Eureka casted her eyes on the gravestone. She shook her head and smiled. "When you close your eyes for the last and final time, whoever's grave you stole those flowers from gone have a bone to pick with you."

Anton grinned and shrugged, saying, "I'll be ready. I'll have one of them thangs with me too, incase he wanna bang out." He spoke of a gun.

"Baby boy, you're too much for me," Eureka told him. Silence suddenly fell on the hour and nothing was heard except the chirping of the birds and the occasional passing car.

Eureka and Anton stared down at the blue headstone embedded on top of the ground that read: Michael Bootsy Jackson, Beloved Husband and Devoted Father. Eureka leaned forth and allowed her hand to sweep over the engraved letters of the marble stone. She couldn't believe her father was dead. She wanted so badly for the life she was living to be a dream so she could wake up and see his face again, but that would never happen. Bootsy had been stolen from her, ripped from her life like a sheet of spiral notebook paper.

Tears rimmed Eureka's eyes then spilled down her mahogany cheeks, dripping from her chin. The tears fell in abundance and splashed against the blue marble gravestone. Eureka sniffled and wiped her face with the back of her hand. Feeling a firm grip on her shoulder, she looked up and saw Fear's hand.

Closing her eyes, she rested her head against his arm and caressed his hand. Fear felt a little awkward with Eureka's display of affection, but held his ground. He wanted to let her know that he had love for her and felt for her situation.

"Can you two give me a minute, please?" Eureka looked up into Fear's eyes. He nodded and waved Anton on for him to follow.

Anton stopped behind Eureka and wrapped an arm around her chest. She grasped his arm with both hands and he kissed her temple. Eureka watched Fear and Anton trek back to the car for a time before lying down beside the grave. She allowed her hand to fondle the pretty green grass as she talked to her late father.

"Daddy, I miss you so much that it hurts. I really don't know what to do," Eureka admitted. "Every night I cry my eyes out thinking of you. It's been years now and I still haven't gotten over your death. The family keeps telling me that my heart will heal with each day that passes, but I honestly don't see that resolution anywhere in sight. I think I'll have to deal with this pain until my last days. It's like I'm almost never happy now," she confessed as tears casted down her face, dripping into the grass.

Eureka's shoulders shook as she sobbed. Her forehead and the skin surrounding her nose crinkled as she wailed, her voice going in and out. Her entire body trembled as if she was freezing cold. Her eyes narrowed into slits and her bottom lip shivered. She sniffled and wiped her wet face with the back of her fist. After getting herself together, she continued to talk with her father.

"If it weren't for Fear and Anton, I would have been done called it quits. I swear to God, Dad, Ant is the only thing that is standing between you and I reunited." Eureka sat up, staring down at the gravestone. "I have to go, I'll come back to see you soon, okay? I love you, always and forever." She kissed her fingers tips and touched them to the blue marble grave stone. She then picked herself up from the grass and headed back to the car. Pulling a Kleenex out of her purse, she patted her face dry and slid the shades back down over her eyes.

"You straight?" Fear asked from where he leaned against his Dodge Charger R/T beside Anton, chopping it up. He was took a drag from his cigarette and tapped it, dumping ashes onto the asphalt.

"I'm one hunnit," Eureka told him, saving face. She didn't want him to see her so vulnerable.

"You ready to roll?" Fear asked.

"Yeah, let's get out of here," Eureka replied.

Fear pulled his keys out of his pocket and pressed the red button on the black oval shaped remote. The locks popped up and Eureka opened the front passenger door, sliding into the seat.

Fear flicked the cigarette aside and he and Anton hopped in the car. He stuck his key into the ignition and was about to turn it when his business cell phone rang.

His brow furrowed because he thought that since the West Coast Connection had cut him loose, he'd have to go looking for work. He didn't expect his business cell to ring. In fact he'd only brought it along because his personal cell was acting up. Curious, he pulled his phone out of his pocket and looked at the screen, saying, "Y'all be quiet, I've gotta answer this." He held up a finger as he pressed 'answer' and brought the device to his ear. "Hello," before snatching an ink-pen from the sun-visor. He pressed the McDonald's napkin against the steering wheel and jotted something down. Eureka took a gander but she couldn't make out his chicken scratch. She couldn't understand a word of it.

Fear disconnected the call and laid the cell on the console. Taking hold of the napkin, he read over what he'd written down.

"What chu got there?" Eureka asked.

"Y'all's initiation into L.O.E," Fear smiled, happy to see another payday. He passed her the napkin and watched as she read over the information he'd written down. He could tell from the expression on her face that she was having trouble understanding it. So he snatched the napkin back and told her what she needed to know about her first hit.

"Father Damian Sullivan," Fear began. "You may have heard of him. He's internationally known. He has a huge following. He's does nationwide tours every two years. Now no one knows for sure, but it's said that he's worth an estimated forty million dollars."

"Forty million?" Eureka said with raised eyebrows, impressed by the priest's net worth. "We're in the wrong business. Religion is the hustle we need to get with. That's where the paper's at."

"Sis, you ain't never lied." Anton leaned over into the front seats.

"So what's up with this dude?" Eureka asked. "Why would someone want to have a priest whacked? What did he do? Fondle some lil' boy's fun parts?"

"He knocked up a thirteen year old girl," Fear told her. "This lil' girl's uncle happens to be politically connected. And he wants this sick bastard lying on a cold slab in the morgue."

"Damn. That's some wicked shit," Eureka shook her head. "There are some real wackos out in this world. Nine years old, that mothafucka needs to be castrated." Fear slowly turned his head in Eureka's direction. A one sided grin accented his face. "That's what the uncle wants?" Eureka asked.

"Yep, that's what he ordered," Fear nodded. "You take his ass out and bring back his prick. He also wants you to record the deed."

"How the hell am I supposed to do all of this by myself?"
"You won't have to," Fear assured her. He threw his head toward Anton, "Baby boy's going with you."

"Me?" Anton pointed a thumb to his chest.
"Yeah, family," Fear answered. "Ya see, not only does Father Sullivan have a fetish for girls, he has an acquired taste for young boys, too."

"A bisexual child molester," Anton shook his head as he sat back down in the backseat."Sick bastard deserves everything that he's about to get."

"And we're gonna be the ones to give it to 'em." Eureka swore. She couldn't wait to get down on this hit. It would earn her a spot in L.O.E and show Fear just how niggaz from The Jordan Downs projects got down. *He's about to see, that's on my Daddy's grave,* she thought, teary eyed, still reeling over the visit with her father. The sanctified child molester was about to feel her pain. Tenfold!

That night...

Eureka emerged from her bedroom dressed in a Catholic school girl uniform. Her ensemble consisted of a white blouse, plaid skirt, stockings, and flats. The makeup she had on made her look like a twelve year old girl trying her best to look like a grown woman. Anton stepped out of his bedroom and followed Eureka into the living room. He was dressed like a Catholic school boy. His attire was a navy blue blazer, which he wore over a white button-down, and candy striped tie, and khakis. He'd taken the liberty of giving himself an edge up and shaving to make himself look younger than his fifteen years.

When Eureka and Anton entered the living room, Fear and Constance were standing around the table. On the table-top there were several items laid out that they'd planned for the sister and brother duo to use in their mission.

"Ant, come here for a second, family." Fear motioned him over. When Anton stepped to Fear, he flipped up his collar and loosened his tie. The he slid some glasses on his face and handed him a tube of lip-gloss.

"Fuck you wan't me to do with this?" Anton's forehead creased with lines as he looked from the tube of lip-gloss to Fear.

"What chu think, lil' nigga, put it on," Fear told him.

"My nigga, I'm not putting this shit on," Anton protested."I'm notta booty bandit, you've got me tangled and twisted." He threw the lip-gloss to the floor.

Fear picked up the lip-gloss and placed a hand on his shoulder, gripping it. He looked him dead in his eyes and said, "Look, I'ma keep it a thousand with chu, lil' homie, I need this lick right now, my pockets short. The only way I know that it will go as planned is if we carry it out to the blueprint that I've laid. I need this one bad and I can't pull it off without my team. I looked out for you and yo sister. And I'm not one to do a nigga a favor and turn around and hit 'em back up for one, but shit I need it, and bad."

Anton thought about how the killer had looked out for them when he didn't know them from a hole in the wall and felt bad. How couldn't he do what he'd asked of him when he went out of his way to take care of him and his sister? That shit wasn't honorable, and it didn't sit right with him.

Anton stared down at the tube of lip-gloss pinched between his mentor's fingers and exhaled. *Fuck,* he thought, not really wanting to put on the lip-gloss. "Alright, man." He plucked the lip-gloss from his fingers and began applying it.

"My nigga." Fear smiled and playfully punched him in the shoulder. He gave him the once over after he'd finished applying the gloss to his lips. "Yeah, now you're ready," he said, pleased with Anton's appearance.

Anton took a picture of himself with Fear's cell phone and looked at it. "Man, I look like a real booty bandit in this getup," Anton declared as he stared at the picture he'd taken.

"That's the point baby, boy, you want to entice this nigga." Fear ran it down to him, "When he sees you, you want 'em to not be able to keep his hands off of you."

"Fuck that. I'm only letting that shit go so far," Anton deleted the picture and handed Fear back the cell phone.

"I hear you lil' one, a nigga can only ask for so much, right?"

"True dat."

Fear set the phone back down on the table-top and picked up a black, patent leather dress shoe about Anton's size. He twisted the heel of the shoe to the side and exposed a hollowed space.

"Constance, hand me that knife I told you to get." Fear took the knife from Constance and held it before Anton's eyes.

He pressed a button on the side of the weapon's handle and a five inch blade extended from it. The light in the ceiling bounced off of the blade and a small rainbow appeared. He pressed the button again and the blade shot back down into the handle. Fear dropped the knife into the hollowed space in the dress shoe and turned the heel closed. He grabbed the other shoe and handed them both to Anton, who sat down in a chair and began putting the shoes on.

Constance had just finished sewing a weave into Eureka's scalp and putting it into a bun. She took one last pull from her cigarette and mashed it out in the ashtray. She stepped ahead of Eureka and looked over the hairdo. Unsatisfied, she moved to adjust Eureka's bun. While Constance tended to Eureka's hair, she picked a Dillinger up from the table-top. Eureka gripped the compact weapon with one hand and closed an eye, as she pointed it around the living room at different furnishings.

"Don't play with that, it's not your pussy!" Constance snatched the Dillinger from Eureka's grasp. She then secured the weapon inside of Eureka's hairdo, making sure that it would hold in place. "This gun holds two shots, Sweetheart. If you can't get the job done with that then that's your ass. Remember, two shots," Constance held up two fingers.

"I got it," Eureka said with an attitude, rolling her eyes.

"Alright, do y'all have any questions?" Fear looked from Eureka to Anton, rubbing his hands together.

"Nah,"Anton shook his head.

"No," Eureka replied.

"Okay, look," Fear began, "the best way to go about this is to get this nigga to lower his guard. Eureka, play with his asshole, tickle his nut-sack if you have to, to get 'em to relax.You get 'em to chill out, make 'em feel like he's on that ride to Heaven. Then crush his bitch-ass!" He slammed his fist into his palm. "The hit will go much smoother if you can get 'em to feel comfortable." He motioned a finger around as he continued, "You whack this nigga, cut off his dick and get the fuck up from outta there."

"Got cha," Anton retorted.

"So if we do this, then we're officially apart of the crew?" Eureka asked.

"Y'all throw this nigga a party and y'all are official-ly apart of the family," Fear assured her. "My word is bond," he touched his fist to his chest.

"Okay," Eureka nodded.

"Alright, here's the cell phone." Fear gave Eureka the small flip phone. "Remember, y'all gotta film the deed. The uncle wants to see y'all hacking off his wang."

Eureka nodded and dropped the phone inside of her purse. She buttoned the purse closed and slung its strap over her shoulder.

Sensing nervousness etched upon Eureka's face, Fear tilted her chin up so that she'd be looking into his eyes. "Aye, everything is going to be okay, alright?" She nodded yes. "I have faith in you and Ant. I know y'all gon' crush this cock roach and bring it back home."

Seeing this, Constance narrowed her eyes into slits at the tender moment.

"You good?" He cracked a smile. She gave him a half-hearted smile and nodded."Here, y'all drink these." He passed Eureka and Anton a glass each of dark liquor.

"What's this?" Eureka inquired.

"That's Jack, straight, no chaser," Fear informed her. "I need y'all to relax, you're a lil' tense right now."

Eureka and Anton made sour faces as the dark liquor coated their bellies. The alcohol was so spicy that it felt like they were drinking glasses of Tabasco sauce.

"This shit is stronger than a mothafucka!" Anton made a face as he wiped his mouth with the back of his hand.

"Whew!" Eureka frowned, shaking her head from the strong liquor.

"Fucking amateurs," Constance took the Jack Daniels bottle to the head like a real lush.

"Constance, we got any of that gas left?" Fear asked.

"A lil' bit."

"Roll something up so they can get right."

Constance nodded and went to recover the last of the exotic weed they had on deck. While she was gone, Fear slipped on a pair of black leather gloves and screwed the muzzle on the barrel of his shotgun. He then went on to examine the weapon to make sure that it was in working order.

Constance returned and sat down at the table. She broke down the pretty green buds on the table-top as she watched Eureka and Anton indulge in their poisons. She smirked as if she knew something that no one else did, and truthfully she did.

After tonight, Eureka and Anton would be out of her hair and she'd have Fear all to herself.

Chapter Thirteen

A van pulled up to a red stop-light. Its driver was none the wiser to the looming danger hanging over his head. He tapped his wedding band finger on the steering wheel, sang along to the music playing on the radio, and observed his surroundings. His eyes met with the side-view mirror and bulged as he gasped and his mouth flew open. He nearly shitted on himself when he saw Fear's black ass creeping along the side of the van, masked up and strapped up

"What's popping, fam?" He asked, pointing the shotgun dead in the driver's face.

"Who the fuck are you?" The driver panicked and his hands shot up in surrender, meeting the hollow hole of the shotgun.

"The dentist, now, say ah," Fear commanded, his eyes projecting the murder on his brain.

"Ahhh," The driver opened his mouth and Fear jammed the shotgun into his grill, breaking his two front teeth and reddening his mouth. "Arghhh!" He mumbled in excruciating pain, feeling the long barrel pressed against the back of his throat.

Hot tears stung the man's eyes and cascaded down his face. His bloody mouth left crimson smears on the barrel. Fear took a quick scan of his surroundings to make sure there wasn't anyone present to see him doing his dirt. Once he saw that he was good, he looked back to the driver.

"Open the door and hop your bitch-ass up outta the van!" The driver did as he was ordered. Fear then grabbed him by the collar of his suit and pressed that long thang to the back of his dome. He led him to the backdoor of the van. "Open the door!"

The driver did as he was told and two Asian kids hopped out the back of the van. They were a boy and girl dressed something like Eureka and Anton. They didn't look any older than thirteen and fourteen years old. Seeing that enraged Fear. His eyebrows arched and he clenched his teeth. "They're kids, little fucking kids." His eyes glinted with insanity as spit clung to his bottom lip. The idea of children being sold as sex slaves infuriated him. He felt like his ears and neck were on fire he was so pissed off.

"It's not me, I just work for them," the driver managed to mumble around the barrel.

Fear slammed the butt of the shotgun into his stomach, doubling him over. He then slammed it across his jaw and spilled him to the street. He fell on his hands and knees, spitting bloody teeth on the asphalt.He rifled through his pocket and pulled a couple of dollars free, spilling loose change and gum.

He turned around to the boy and girl. "Are y'all alright? Are you okay?" They nodded yes. He gave the boy the money. "Take that and buy yourselves something to eat from that McDonald's up the street. After you order your food call the police and tell them you saw a dead body lying in the street."

"Alright," the boy replied.

"Okay," the girl said.

The kids took off down the block, leaving Fear and the driver alone. Fear set his sights on him, raised the shotgun, and then looked away so he wouldn't get any blood in his eyes when he pulled the trigger. The round sounded like a baseball going through the tube of a leaf blower when it exited the muzzle of the shotgun. The driver screamed and a hot-round sent the sound right back down his throat.

Splat!

Fear hopped into his Honda station wagon and pulled off.

****

Constance stole glances at Eureka and Anton through the rearview mirror as she pushed the Astro van. A slight smirk accented her face seeing that Eureka and Anton were faded. The entire ride to Father Sullivan's place they hadn't made as much as a peep. The liquor and the weed had them tipsy, but they weren't White Boy wasted. They'd had enough alcohol and weed to give them a little buzz. The siblings needed to be relaxed and their minds had to be at ease if they were going to execute tonight's mission. The last thing they needed was something going wrong and their plan getting botched. They had a lot riding on that hit and they couldn't afford for shit to go sour.

"You ever wonder what mommy's doing, right now?" Anton asked Eureka in a hushed tone.

"Yeah, I miss her," Eureka admitted.

"Me, too. We gotta try to find her and make her ass get some help," he told her. "She's our mother Reka, we can't just give up on her."

"I know, baby boy, we're gonna find Mommy and we're gonna get her right, too."

"Promise me."

"I promise," she interlocked her fingers with his.

Having overheard them talking, Constance stole a glance at them through the rearview mirror. About ten minutes later she was pulling through the gates of the mansion that the Father had rented during his stay in Los Angeles. She drove down the path and around the circular brick paved driveway. She killed the engine and looked out of the window. The holy man's personal bodyguards had just emerged through the door of the mansion. They were a couple of serious looking cats dressed in expensive suits.

Constance slipped a stick of Winter Fresh gum into her mouth. She then looked up into the rearview mirror at Eureka and Anton.

"Alright, here these mothafuckaz come," she told them. "Remember the mission: slice that cracka's joint off and stab out. I'ma be out here waiting for y'all to come down. Got it?"She looked over her shoulder into the backseat.

"Yeah, we got it, *boss*," Anton said sarcastically.

Eureka nudged her brother and then looked to Constance. "You don't have to worry about us," she assured her. "Me and baby boy got this."

"You sure?" Constance asked. "'Cause I gotta feeling you're gonna fuck it up."

"What the fuck is your beef with me, huh? I'm getting really sick and tired of your shit, you know that?" Eureka frowned.

"You really wanna know what my beef is?" Constance asked seriously.

"Yeah," she nodded. "I really wanna know."

"Bitches like you that are always tryna snatch another bitch's man." Constance spat heatedly. "That's what my beef is!"

"Well, maybe if your dog was held to a better leash he wouldn't be looking for another tree to bark up."

Constance was so hot that Eureka thought she saw steam rising from her head. Constance bit down on her bottom lip and her hand balled into a tight fist. She moved to fire on her, but tapping at the driver side window stopped her short. She uncoiled her fingers and allowed her anger to dissipate. She threw up her biggest smile as she turned to the window, holding down a button to let it down.

"How're you gentlemen doing tonight?" Constance's eyes shifted between the two bodyguards.

"Where's the entertainment?" The white guard with the buzz cut asked, ignoring her initial question. Fuck the pleasantries he wanted to get down to business. ASAP!

"Backseat," she threw her head toward the backseat.

The dark haired guard opened the backdoor of the Astro van. He peered inside at Eureka and Anton and his forehead wrinkled."This isn't the entertainment that Mr. Sullivan requested," he said.

"Yeah, I know. Sorry about that," Constance apologized. "But another client requested those two at the same time and day that Mr. Sullivan did. It was a lil' mix up with the schedule and my employer apologizes."

She watched the two suits exchange hushed dialogue with one another before the dark haired one called Father Sullivan. He wasn't on his cell phone a minute before he disconnected the call. He took a quick picture of Eureka and Anton and texted it to Father Sullivan. A second later his cell phone chimed with a text. He looked at the text, showed it to the buzz cut and he nodded.

"Alright, Mr. Sullivan says that he's okay with these two," Dark hair reported to Constance.

"Great," Constance turned to the backseat. "Y'all gon' and get out. I'll be waiting right here for you." Constance watched as Eureka and Anton were led into the mansion by the suits. Once they were gone, she focused her attention on sparking up a joint. She waited about fifteen minutes before she dialed 9-1-1 and brought the cell to her ear, clearing her throat. "Oh my God, you have to send someone down here quick!" She shouted into the cell phone. "This man just ran up on this old couple and cut them both down with an AK-47." Constance closed her eyes and took deep breaths as the dispatcher told her to calm down.

"Okay, alright, I'm calm now. The address is..." she gave the dispatcher the address then said, "Oh shit, he's coming after me! He has the rifle pointed at my faceeee! Helllppp!" she disconnected the call and tossed the cell onto the front passenger seat.

As soon as Eureka and Anton made their move to send the Father to meet his maker, they were going to be in for one hell of a surprise. Constance snickered, thinking that she was about to have Eureka and Anton out of her hair. She was as giddy as a teenage girl seeing her crush in the school's hallway.

****

The siblings followed the bodyguards up the long flight of steps. The first one crossed the threshold and held open the black door with the brass knocker for everyone else to enter. As soon as Eureka and Anton stepped foot onto the Spain imported tiled floor they were greeted by the classical music playing throughout the massive estate.

Damn, this place looks like Scarface's mansion. If Chester the Molester rented this thang out,his paper is as long as Fear said it is, Eureka thought.

This mothafucka plush...laid out, Anton looked around the enormous estate.

The suits lead brother and sister up an adjoining staircase. They stopped at twin,white double doors and one of them cleared his throat and knocked on it, saying, "Mr.

Sullivan, your entertainment has arrived, sir." He adjusted his tie and smoothed it out, re-buttoning his suit.

"Come in, Dorsey," he replied from the opposite side of the door.

Doresy turned the golden handle of the door and pushed his way inside. He then stepped aside and allowed Eureka and Anton access. They made their way across the threshold, taking in the scenery surrounding them. The master bedroom was made up like a Persian palace and was just as spacious.

Eureka and Anton tore their eyes away from the décor of the master bedroom and focused them on the man approaching them from the balcony. He strode forward, taking healthy pulls from a bong and allowing a fog to roll off of his tongue. He was five-feet-eight and sported a shaved head. His dark eyes and the jagged scar on his cheek gave him a menacing appearance. He looked more like an Irish gangster than the man of the cloth he was believed to be.

At that moment he was draped in a white bathrobe and sky blue pajama pants with white stripes. His feet nestled in the nappy carpet as he switched hands with the bong, stopping before the siblings. He blew the last of the smoke from his nostrils and cracked a slight smile, showcasing his off white teeth.

"Yes, yesss," he said, pleased with what he saw before him. His rough, wrinkly hand caressed the side of Eureka's face and she batted her eyes, smirking. "These are much, much betta than I what I wanted initially." Eureka licked the side of his hand and welcomed his thumb in her mouth. She sucked on it and drew a grunt from him. He licked his lips and felt his long, pink dick jump. "Yes, nice, nice."

He stepped over to Anton, took a step back, giving him the once over. "Oh my God. You, young man, are truly a gift from the Heavens. Ummummum," he shook his head, thinking of how lucky he was to have such a handsome young lad to do with as he pleased. "Do me a favor and turn around for me." He motioned with a finger then handed the bong off to Montana, the dark haired bodyguard.

Anton, reluctantly turned around, fearing what was about to happen next. He promised himself if things went too far that he was going to blow up the spot and take the Father out himself.

The old pervertstepped behind Anton, lifted the coattail of his blazer, and grabbed a handful of each of his ass cheeks. The youngster slightly bowed his head and gritted his teeth. He felt like a straight up batty boy letting that pervert cuff his cheeks. The old man closed his eyes and an elated expression crossed his face. He basked in heavenly glory, standing there groping the young boy's ass. He licked his earlobe and exhaled. Anton could feel his hot breath which made his neck hairs stand.

This nigga groping my ass man, Anton's face contracted. *This shit gay, on me. I can't take this shit no more.*

Just when he was about to set it off, the Father turned him around and took a step back, taking the bong back from his man. He rubbed his hand over his close fade, around the curve of his face, and stopped at his chin, flicking it gently with his thumb. He licked his lips. He was more than pleased with the vision standing before him. As a matter of fact, he was more attracted to him than he washis sister.

"Umm, my lucky day. What a treat," he shook his head like it was a crying shame, but truthfully he felt blessed. He was so fucked up mentally that he actually believed God Almighty had sent Anton to him for doing him such a good service for so many years.

"Mr. Sullivan, will there be anything else?" Montana asked, ready to leave because he didn't want to be around to see any more of the sick, twisted shit that Father Sullivan was about to do to those two kids. He had children of his own and what he'd seen made him want to puke. He didn't agree with the old man's practices, but the checks he wrote made him sleep better at night.

"No. That will be all, gentlemen. You can leave."

Sullivan led Dorsey and Montana to the door, opened it, and closed it shut behind him. He then locked it and turned around to his entertainment, firing up the bong. He took a deep pull and blew out smoke. He held the bong out to Eureka, silently asking her if she'd like to partake. She shook her head no and he gestured the bong toward her brother. Without hesitation, he snatched the bong and the lighter. He fired up the bong, taking long fulfilling pulls before expelling smoke. He needed the high desperately. There wasn't any way he could go through with some of the disgusting shit he knew was brewing in the old man's head if he wasn't high as giraffe pussy.

The Father stepped to Eureka and unbuttoned her blouse, he then undid her bra and granted her small breasts their freedom. Groping her chest, he kissed her hard and sloppily. Eureka rolled her eyes as their mouths massaged one another. He sucked on her tongue enjoying how sweet it tasted.

Oh, my God, I feel like I'ma 'bout to throw up. Hold this shit together girl, keep the mission in mind.

Before she knew it, one of his hands was undoing her plaid skirt while he kissed her and groped her other breast with the other.

"How old is this pussy?" He asked between kisses as his hand dipped inside of her panties, brushing against her baldness. His touch made her shudder, but she pressed on to get the job done.

"Fucking parasite," she said under her breath.

"What was that?"

She cleared her throat and said, "Thirteen."

"Umm," he moaned, thinking the younger the better. The sick mothafucka was turned on by illegal pussy. Hearing how young she was caused his dick to go from soft to hard like cooked coke. "Touch 'em baby, he won't bite. I promise." He spoke as he planted hickeys up her neck.

"What?" She was disgusted, scrunching her face. She looked over at Anton who wasn't trying to see what they had popping. His back was to them and he was still smoking on the bong. Eureka was thankful, she didn't want him to see her getting down like that.

"Gon' and grab 'em, reach in and give 'em a tug," he rasped.

Eureka hesitantly stuck her hand inside of his pajamas. She did it like she thought there was a needle in there that could poke her. Finally, she grasped the old man's joint. He had a full, eight inch lady killa with blue veins running throughout it. Its pink head was swollen and pulsating, looking like it was about ready to erupt and bless her with its cream filling. She went on to give him a tug job as he attended to her breasts, sucking on them like a thirsty kitten.

"Play with my ears," he told her, going back and forth between her breasts, stimulating them.

As he continued to pamper her breasts, she massaged and groped his ears, making counterfeit noises of pleasure. *Sick bastard,* she grimaced, *you deserve everything you're about to get.*

Sullivan had his eyes closed, licking, sucking, and gently biting on her erect nipples. When he drew his head back, there was a length of saliva that led from her nipple to his lips. When he rose to his feet, her breasts were glistening wet and her nipples were as hard as bullets. He took two steps back, keeping his eyes on Eureka as he peeled off his white bathrobe. When the bathrobe dropped behind him onto the floor, she got a good look at the graffiti that graced his form. He had a rosary beaded necklace around his neck, a four leaf clover on his left peck and his mother's face on his right, and a snake slithering through the hollowed eye sockets of a human skull on his abs.

He clapped his hands and Salt & Pepa's 'Push it' exploded from the speakers in the high corners of the master bedroom. He slipped off his striped pajama pants and was left in leopard print briefs. Eureka pushed him back on the bed and got down on her knees before him, pulling his briefs down around his thighs. She took his cock by the base and stroked it up and down, making sure it was rock hard. He looked down at her and licked his lips. He couldn't wait to feel those soft lips massaging his pole and gargling his balls.

While this was going on, Anton sat the bong down and set the cell phone to record on the dresser. He took off of his blazer and removed his shoes. He twisted the heel of the right one and pulled out the knife Fear had given him. He pressed a button on it and the fiveinch blade sprang up.

"Little one," hearing Sullivan startled him. He hid the knife behind his back and turned around. The old man was coiling his finger, signaling him over. Anton obliged him, he crawled into the bed and caressed his chest as he unbuckled his belt hastily. He couldn't wait to feel the young man's joint at the back of his throat.

Anton's face twisted into a scowl as he thought, *this nigga a straight up booty bandit, ugh.* He shook his head, growing frustrated. The pervert was too close to his wang for comfort. Anton and Eureka locked eyes. She turned the Gemstar razor over in her mouth and held it clenched between her teeth. He nodded when he saw the razor glare with a brightness.

Father Sullivan was so focused on springing the young man's joint from its hiding place that he hadn't notice what was going on. Seeing this, Eureka lifted his lady killa and dipped below its shaft to where his gray, hairy nut sack dangled. Twisting her head to the left, she pushed the Gemstar razor forward with her tongue and whipped her head to the right. Father Sullivan's eyes bulged and his mouth shot open, feeling a hot seething pain rip through his precious jewels. He screamed loud enough to wake the dead, but he wouldn't be heard over the loud music.

A look of confusion stole his face when he saw Anton about to stab him. His hand shot out and grabbed him about the throat. Father Sullivan's eyebrows arched and the skin on his forehead bunched together as he scowled menacingly. Gritting his teeth, he displayed the pulsating muscles in his jaws as he squeezed the young man's neck tighter. He watched the little nigga claw at his arm, struggling to break free from his death grip. Anton's eyes glazed over and he felt the veins in his head bulge as if they were attempting to explode. While he clawed at Father Sullivan's arm with one hand, he used the other to try to stab him.

Eureka yanked the Dillinger free from her pinned up bun and shot to her feet. Bringing it around, she gripped that little mothafucka with both hands and pulled the trigger. When nothing happened, she continued to pull the trigger. *Click! Click! Click!* She looked at the small gun and checked its magazine, it was empty. *Fucking Constance*, she thought, throwing the Dillinger aside.

Eureka pulled the crimson stained razor from between her teeth and dove on top of Father Sullivan, slicing away at his chest madly. Feeling the heat in his chest from the simmering slices, he released Anton he fell over the edge of the bed. Father Sullivan balled his fingers into a fist and swung his arm around, punching Eureka in the cheek. *Crack!*

Eureka flew over the bed, knocking over the lamp on the nightstand and crashing to the floor. She lay there as if she didn't know where in the hell she was, wincing and rubbing her aching cheek. Although Father Sullivan was an older cat, his punches packed one hell of a wallop. That came from intense workouts and a healthy diet. That put his strength on par with a man that was in shape and half of his age.

Father Sullivan got to his feet and looked down at the gash in his lady killa. He grimaced when he touched it and his fingers came away sticky with blood. The thought of someone doing that to him enraged him. He started in on Eureka, talking greasy like only an Irishman could. Along the way he picked up the lamp she'd knocked over and yanked the cord out of it. He then yanked the other end out of the wall, looped it into a belt, and got to whipping her like a master would one of his runaway slaves.

Eureka rolled around on the floor, guarding her face with her arms and holding up a leg. She hollered as the cord whistled through the air and bit into her skin, its sting equivalent to the leather whip she felt so many years ago. Anton looked up from where he'd gotten upon his bended knees, rubbing his neck. Through glassy, bloodshot eyes, he watched as Sullivan stopped whipping Eureka and began kicking and stomping her. Seeing his sister on the losing end of a brutal beating made his ears hot, he could literally feel his skin become flush as his blood rose to a boiling temperature.

Anton's top lip twitched with acrimony as he gripped his knife tighter. Pushing up off the floor, he charged the Father screaming like a banshee. By the time the old man turned around, it was too late to attack. All he could do was throw up an arm. When Anton brought the blade down, it stabbed into his forearm, bending and snapping in half.

A look of confusion crossed the old man's face as he was expecting more than his skin being broken. Anton frowned and looked at the broken blade, like, *What the fuck*? When he looked up, a hard overhanded right smashed into his face, sending him flying backwards. He slammed up against the post of the canopy bed and dropped to his ass, dazed. The Father went to turn back around to Eureka and she kicked him in his balls. An excruciating pain jolted through his southern region. He doubled over, holding his dick and balls in agony, his eyes looking like they were about to leap out of their sockets.

Eureka scrambled on the floor, looking for the razor. The hits from the beating left her arms, legs, and the side of her face with welts. Her skin felt inflamed it was so hot from the onslaught of the lamp's cord. Setting her sights on the razor, which was about two feet away from her, she crawled toward it as fast as she could on her hands and knees. Just as she reached out to grasp it, she felt a hand grab a fistful of her hair and yank her head back. With a madness glinting in his eyes, Father Sullivan pulled her up to her knees, causing her to yelp and wrap her hands around his wrist. He brought his other hand around and it locked onto her throat like a red nose pit bulls jaws, squeezing and shaking her neck violently. She grimaced and tried to break loose, but her attempts were of no avail.

Suddenly, a war cry ripped through the air as Anton ran, pounced off of the bed and landed upon Father Sullivan's shoulders. He looped his brown leather belt around his neck, slipped it through the buckle, and pulled it tight. The belt adjusted snugly around his neck with the strength of an anaconda, slowing the air from entering his lungs.

Father Sullivan's face turned beet red and his eyes became glassy. He spun around the bedroom, taking blind swings at Anton, knocking over lamps, a chair and a fifty-five inch flat-screen. Veins etched into Anton's forehead and he clenched his teeth as he looped both of his hands in the belt and pulled back on it with all of his weight. The buckle bit into Father Sullivan's neck, turning it burgundy and causing blood to seep in small trickles.

The priest hastily staggered backwards, still swinging on Anton, only this time he had become weaker and his fists were moving slowly. He accidentally bumped into the same chair that he'd knocked over and fell back against Anton. Anton's head slightly shook as he bit down on his bottom lip and pulled the belt tighter, watching Father Sullivan struggle for air.

"Reka," he called out as he strangled Sullivan.

Eureka grabbed the razor and straddled the Father, slicing away at his endowment. Each swing of the razor made his eyes and mouth grow wider and wider. The pain he experienced was paralyzing. He shrilled to the high heavens, his voice coming in and out of sync as she continued to assault his dick. Eureka continued her slicing until the thick white meat came loose and her blouse was stained with specks of blood. She looked up at her victim. He stared up at nothing as he released his last breath, arms and legs falling limp.

Anton fell flat on his back, breathing hard, his chest jumping up and down as he lay on the floor. When he sat up, he saw Eureka enter the bathroom with a pair of matching bloody hands. One carrying the razor and the other Sullivan's severed penis. He watched as she rinsed the blood off of her hands and flushed the razor down the toilet. She then yanked a washcloth from the rack and rolled the severed penis up inside of it.

"You okay?" Anton asked her as he unfastened the leather belt from Father Sullivan's neck. He rose to his feet, putting the belt back on.

"No. I'm fucked up, but—" Eureka was interrupted by a knock at the door. She and her brother's head snapped to the double doors of the bedroom.

"Mr. Sullivan, are you alright in there?" Doresy asked. "I thought I heard some loud noises in there." When he didn't get an answer he knocked again. "Mr. Sullivan?"

The door rattled and the knob jingled as the bodyguards rammed their bodies up against the door.

"Fuck! We've gotta get outta here." Eureka told Anton in a hush tone.

"No kidding," Anton answered back.

"I've got an idea," Eureka grabbed two pair of Father Sullivan's shoes, tying the laces together. She kept one pair for herself and gave the other to Anton. She threw her pair of shoes up at the light in the ceiling, shattering its bulb and cloaking them in darkness. While they were in the dark, Eureka told Anton what they were to do when suits entered the bedroom. As she was explaining the bedroom door continued to rattle under its punishment.

Ba-thoom!
Ba-thoom!
Ba-thoom!
Boom!

The door swung open, sending splinters flying everywhere. Dorsey and Montana entered, guns at the ready. Their heads snapped back and forth across the room, looking for someone, anyone. The bedroom would have been pitch-black if it wasn't for the ray of light that shined in through the opened door. Dorsey spotted Father Sullivan, lying stretched out on the floor.

"What the hell is— Jesus!" Montana said, seeing the old man lying about. He rushed over to him and touched two fingers to his neck, checking his pulse. "He's dead!"

With that said, the bedroom door slammed shut and the lock clicked. The en suite was bathed in complete darkness. They didn't hear anything but their own voices.

"What the fuck was that?" Montana asked.

"Hell should I know?" Dorsey replied,

"Probably the wind."

"There's no window open in here you imbecile, it's those goddamn kids," he barked. "Come on out you little shits!"

Swhack!

"Argh!" He hollered.

"You alright?"

"No," he bellowed in pain. "Bastards hit me in the face!"

"Oooof! My nuts," Buzz cut croaked, having been struck in the balls.

"Be quiet and don't move," Dark hair whispered to buzz cut. "We can probably hear 'em moving around in here."

"Got cha," he replied.

"Right here, bitch!" Anton's voice rang out.

"Kiss my pretty black ass!" Eureka's voice came right after his

Pop! Pop! Pop! Pop!

Bop! Bop! Bop! Bop!

Thud! Thud!

Silence fell in the bedroom. You could literally smell the fresh blood and gun smoke wafting around. Suddenly, a small light illuminated, carried about by Eureka. She was gripping the neck of one of the lamps. She stood beside Anton and waved the lamp's light over dark hair and buzz cut's strewn bodies. They lay upon the floor with their faces and chest riddled with holes. Eureka crept behind Montana and Anton crept behind buzz cut. They made noises to draw the guards' attention, duping them into shooting each other. Eureka's plan had worked like a charm.

"Here," Eureka passed Anton the lamp. "Grab the other lamp from off the dresser and turn it on. I'll be right back."

While Anton was doing as he was told, Eureka went to retrieve some things. She returned a couple of minutes later with a box of matches and a bottle of rubbing alcohol. She sat the box of matches down and opened the bottle of alcohol.

"What the hell do you plan on doing with that?" Anton asked curiously, lines forming on his forehead.

"I'ma light this bitch up!" she replied, soaking up the mattress and some of the curtains.

"For what?" As soon as the question left his lips he snapped his fingers, "Right, forensics."

"Exactly," Eureka nodded, "Could be a hair follicle or something in here that'll place us at the scene of the crime."

Eureka took a quick peek outside and saw Constance still waiting. Constance gave her a thumb up and she gave her one back, letting her know that they were straight. Eureka pulled her head back in and went about the task of splashing the floor with the alcohol. Once she was done she tossed the bottle of alcohol and struck a match at the back of the match box. There was a hiss and a faint trace of smoke then a flame came to life.

Eureka threw her head toward the bedroom door, signaling for Anton to follow her. They stopped at the doorway and she flicked the burning match. As soon as the match hit the floor lines and lines of fire raced throughout the bedroom until they all intersected and burned in unison. Eureka and Anton watched the flames eat away at the bedroom for a time before descending the stairs.

"I'm whipping that bitch's ass once we touch back down to Fear's." Eureka exclaimed as she and Anton hustled down the steps. "She gave me that dry gat and you that faulty ass knife. She was tryna set us up to get murdered."

"Filthy ass broad," Anton declared, gun dangling at his   side. Eureka opened the front door and stepped out. She and Anton's jaws dropped when they saw Constance pulling off, holding the middle-finger up out of the window. Hearing the police sirens invading the air, they chased after the van. They ran as hard as they could, but there wasn't any use because she had left them in the dust. Eureka and Anton slowed to a jog as they reached the closing gates of the mansion. They hunched over and placed their hands on their knees, breathing hard.

They darted back inside of the mansion. By this time the fire had begun to spread down stairs. They dashed inside of the kitchen and opened the door that lead to the garage. Anton opened the door and they peered inside. A black Mercedes Benz limousine was parked with a Kawasaki Ninja motorcycle's on the side of it. A smirk formed on his lips. He was sure that he could hotwire one of the Ninjas to get it started. Now he only had to keep the police off of their asses long enough for them to get away.

Anton looked to the banger in his hand and pressed the button on it, ejecting its magazine from out of the bottom of it. He caught the magazine before it could hit the floor and approached the microwave which was over the stove. He could hear the front door rattling as the police were trying to burst their way inside.

Ba-thoom!
Ba-thoom!

Ba-thoom!
Ba-thoom!

Anton pushed off bullet after bullet from the magazine into the palm of his hand. He bounced the bullets in his palm and took a good look at them. He had about six in all.

"What're you doing?" Eureka asked, lines spreading across her forehead.

"Creating a diversion," Anton tossed the bullets inside of the microwave and slammed the door shut.

He set the timer for five minutes. As soon as the timer started he heard the front door crashing down to the floor. He grabbed Eureka by the wrist and they ran out into the garage. She closed the door shut behind them and he got right to hotwiring one of the Kawasaki's. Once he got the motorcycle started, he slid on the helmet while Eureka slid on the helmet located on the other bike. She ran over to the switch that controlled the garage and looked to Anton, letting her hand hover over it.

Pop! Pop! Pop! Pop!

Eureka heard the semi-muffled gunshots coming from inside of the microwave in the kitchen. She then heard several more shots that she was sure came from the police. Shortly after, there was the stampeding feet of the police stationed outside as they came charging inside of the mansion.

Eureka flipped the switch and the garage door slowly began to rise. While it was in motion, she ran and hopped on the back of the motorcycle. The Ninja whined as Anton revved its engine. He mashed the gas-pedal and it shot out of the garage just as the door of the kitchen was being broken in.

The police flooded the garage and took aim at the speeding bike, popping shots at it. Hot rocks whizzed through the air missing their intended targets and hitting the lawn, dislodging chunks of the ground. Anton zipped through the gates. Bon Voyage.

Chapter Fourteen

Fear made his way down the sidewalk with a backpack slung over his shoulder, trying his best to blend into the nightlife with the rest of the shady characters. Adjusting his black LA snapback, he took cautious ganders over his shoulder to make sure no one was following him. About an hour ago he'd contacted Constance through his Blu-Tooth headset to give her his location.

He was making his way across the intersection on a green-light amongst a crowd when he made the van she was driving. Clutching the strap of the backpack tightly and glancing over his shoulder once more, he jogged over to the van and hopped into the front passenger seat. He sat the backpack on the floor between his legs and looked to the backseat, worry lines quickly formed across his forehead. He looked to Constance and she was looking straight ahead, smoking a joint.

"Where are Eureka and Ant?" He asked, concerned.

Constance shook her head and blew out smoke.

"What the fuck is this supposed to mean?" He shook his head like she did. "Gimmie some fucking answers, what happened?" He demanded.

"Shit went left," Constance told him. "The Ones turned out and I got the fuck outta dodge.

Homegirl and her brother got yoked up."

"Fuck, fuck, fuck!" Fear threw his fitted cap at the dashboard and slammed his head back against the headrest, heatedly. Once he finished his tantrum, he sat up in the seat breathing heavily, and rode the rest of the way home with his face in his palm.

Thirty minutes later

Fear flopped down on the sofa and ordered Constance to roll up some more gas. A couple of minutes later, an odor equivalent to a wet, stinky asshole tainted the air. He lay back where he was perched,trying to suck the life out of the blunt. He was stressing like a nigga with a life sentence looming over his head. So much so, that Constance thought she saw him grow ten years older right before her very eyes.

He took a couple of more tokes and passed it to Constance. She sat back on the sofa watching him as she took casual pulls, allowing the smoke to fog her lungs. He poured up a glass of Hennessy and took a sip. He then lay back on the sofa, thinking as he set the glass on his thigh, twisting it around. He had a decision to make that was weighing heavily on his mind. Seeing that he was debating, Constance decided to give him a little push in the direction that she wanted him to go.

"Look, we don't have much time," Constance began, sitting up on the sofa. "You need to put in a call to our people so they can extinguish this fire before it spreads back to us, you know what I'm saying? I know this shit is hard 'cause you like them and all, but don't let your love for them destroy us. L.O.E." She threw up her hand, boasting the ink there. "Nobody comes before this, and they ain't this."

She passed him back the L and picked up her glass of Hennessy. Fear tossed his decision back and forth across his mental. He took a couple of puffs and looked at the blunt,thinking of how fiyah it was. He then looked to Constance and nodded his head.

"Alright, hand me the throwaway,"he told her.

Constance struggled to contain a manipulative smile from surfacing on her face as she rose to her feet. She passed him the burnout cell phone to place a call to their connect down at the precinct. Their connect would see to it that Eureka and Anton were murdered before they were finished being processed through the system. It would cost Fear a pretty penny, but at least he wouldn't have to worry about fighting a case if Eureka and Anton had plans of ratting him out for their freedom.

Fear didn't really want to drive the last nail through the younglings' coffins, but due to the circumstances, he didn't see any other options. He loved his freedom and he wasn't about to gamble on a couple of kids with it.

Fear was just about to press the speed-dial button when someone knocked at the door. He and Constance exchanged glances. He grabbed his .9mm off of the coffee table and approached the door, cautiously. He looked through the peephole and frowned once he saw who it was on the other side. He then looked at Constance wearing a face of confusion.

Fear opened the front door and in filed Eureka and Anton. The expressions on their faces told the tale of how pissed off they were. Shit, they were hotter than a trap spot under police surveillance. Their fists were clenched and their mad dog stares were focused on Constance.

"I thought y'all got caught up,"Fear stated, seeing the two of them there was the equivalent of seeing two dead people rise and walk again.

Eureka frowned. "Almost did," Anton said, eyes stuck on Constance as she made to get to her feet."No thanks to this slimy snake."

"What chu mean?" Fear asked.

"This ho sabotaged the mission," Eureka spoke up. "The knife was defective and the gun wasn't loaded. She sent us there to die, but we survived."

"We barely made it outta there alive." Anton added.

"Are these accusations true?" Fear inquired.

"Yeah, so what?" Constance shrugged, eyes glued on Eureka. "I told you that I didn't want these lil' mothafuckaz here, but chu didn't listen.So I had to get rid of 'em the best way I knew how."

The dips of Fear's forehead deepened as a revelation struck him like an open palm. He looked upon Constance with an eerie expression as his lips peeled apart. His eyes took on a transfixed looked.

"It was you," he stepped into Constance's face and clenched his jaws so tight that they throbbed. "You killed Italia."

"What?" Constance raised an eyebrow, looking at him as if the accusation was farfetched.

"Don't play stupid, bitch, you killed the love of my life." His eyes became glassy and rage danced in them as a thick vein bulged at his temple.

Eureka and Anton exchanged glances, wondering what the fuck was going on.

"Yeah," Fear nodded, tears threatened to spill over the rims of his eyes. "You took her out."

Italia was one of those ghetto fabulous, bourgeois bitches, straight out of Compton. You couldn't tell her that her shit didn't smell of potpourri. Constance couldn't front though, her little ghetto ass was well put together. Her body was the truth and the reason. She pushed a 7 series Beemer and owned a Malibu beach house overlooking the ocean. Her neck and wrists were always dripping in diamonds and she stayed dipped in designer labels.

Constance believed that she was either some high class escort or she had some baller type niggaz breaking her off grips, because she sure enough wasn't bringing home any check stubs. When Constance asked Fear how she stacked hers he hadn't a clue. Nor did he care.

Fear had taken a real liking to Italia, which surprised Constance because she didn't peg her as being his type. Things between them had gotten pretty serious though. One night, Constance had even overheard Italia on the telephone telling her girlfriend that she was thinking about proposing to him. And although Fear had sworn to never get seriously involved with anyone, Constance had a feeling that he would have accepted if Italia proposed. Constance knew that she had to do something quick if she ever hoped to salvage Fear's love for herself. So naturally, she utilized the very talent that she was good at: killing.

Musiq Soulchild's 'Love' played in the background as Italia moved around the room gracefully, setting the table for her and Fear's dinner that night. There was a roast with potatoes and carrots and homemade mashed potatoes smothered in gravy. To drink, she had an expensive bottle of white wine and for desert they were having blueberry cobbler. Once Italia had finished setting the table, she dimmed the lights and lit the vanilla scented candles. She picked up a glass and poured a little white wine. When she sat the bottle of wine down and took a sip from her glass, the doorbell chimed.

"Oh, that's my baby!" Italia beamed brightly.

She headed toward the door, stopping to straighten herself up in the oval shaped mirror along the way.She unlocked the door and pulled it open, smiling from ear to ear. The smile declined from her face once she discovered Constance standing before her. She looked over both of her shoulders and over her head, hoping to see Fear, but he wasn't anywhere in sight.

"Constance, what're you doing here?" She asked, displeased with her presence.

"Fear...I mean, Alvin, wanted you to know that he was going to be a little late and that he was sorry, so he sent me over with these." She presented her with a dozen long stemmed red roses and that smile of hers made an encore.

Italia closed her eyes as she inhaled the scent of the roses, her smile expanding even wider. "Well, thanks, I'll throw these in some water." She went to close the door and Constance stuck her foot in, stopping the door from closing shut. Italia looked down at the Timberland that blocked the path of the door and scrunched her face, looking back up at Constance irritated.

"You mind if I use your bathroom right quick?" Constance smirked.

Italia threw up a counterfeit smile and said, "Sure, why not?" She stepped aside, granting Constance entrance inside of her home. She took inventory of Constance's attire as she crossed the threshold and rolled her eyes. "You know, sweetie, there's no wonder why you never had a shot with Alvin. I mean, don't get me wrong, you're a pretty girl and all, but look at that nightmare you're wrapped up in. Black fatigues and Timberland boots. I swear, if I didn't know any better, I'd think there was cock and balls behind that zipper and not a vahjayjay."

Constance stood with her back to Italia, looking around the living room. She rolled her eyes and mumbled something under her breath, agitated by the sound of Italia's voice. Her vocals were the equivalent of simmering, hot sewing needles being jabbed in and out of her eardrums over and over again. She wished she would just shut her fucking pie-hole.

"We're the only ones here?" She asked innocently.

"Girl, this is my place. I don't rock with roommates," Italia spat with attitude, one manicured hand on her hip as she rolled her neck. That sharp tongue and that 'Hood' mentality seeped out every now and again, exposing who she truly was underneath all of those diamonds and designer labels. "The bathroom is down the hall and to your right," she motioned with a manicured finger. She then headed into the kitchen.

While her back was turned, Constance picked up the butcher's knife from the table where it lay beside the roast. Italia filled a clear, see-through, glass vase with water and dropped the long stemmed roses into it, spreading them out. She inhaled the fresh, sweet scent of the roses and picked up the vase, smiling. She'd just turned around when something sharp slammed through her chest, hitting bone. Her eyes looked like they were about to pop out of their sockets and her mouth shot open. She croaked and released the vase, it exploded when it hit the floor, sending broken shards flying everywhere.

Italia looked down at the butcher's knife buried into her chest down to the handle. Her thick blood traveled the length of the blade and dripped onto the floor. Red droplets splattered as they hit her Manolo Blahnik high heel pumps. Her white, Narciso Rodriguez, low-high gown quickly soaked up the blood like a maxi pad.

Italia looked up from the handle and into the malicious orbs that were Constance's pupils. Her facial features seemed to transform right before her eyes as she took on the appearance of a horned creature, a monster, a demon. A Devil. Italia tried to say something, but the pain in her chest paralyzed her vocal cords.

Constance placed a finger to her lips. Keeping eye contact with her she said, "Shhh, I want you to understand something, he belongs to me. He's mine," she pushed the knife upward, lifting Italia to the tips of her Manolo's, "and he always will be. I'm not gon'—" Italia tried to say something again, but only succeeded in coughing up blood. Constance hushed her and said, "No, listen. I'm not gon' let you or 'nan other bitch take him away from me, okay? Before I let that happen, I'll kill you and a hunnit more hoes that look just like you."

A devilish smile curled Constance's lips as she combed her gloved hand through Italia's long expensive weave, watching the tears pool in her eyes and spill down her cheeks. Blood flooded Italia'sgrill and spilled down her chin, dripping on the floor. Constance broke the knife off in her chestbone and shoved her back, causing her to fall up against the wall. She then dropped the other half of the weapon and sat down at the table. She stuffed a napkin cloth into her shirt and prepared herself a plate.

Eating, she watched Italia attentively. Her eyes became lazy and she struggled for breath. Her white gown was covered in so much blood that you would have thought she'd purchased it in that color. Once Italia's body went slack and she unleashed her last breath, Constance ate, washed her dishes and left.

"It wasn't just my baby you killed," Fear continued,"Desiree, Trishelle, Gloria, Chyna, Taraji, Unique…You put the love on all of 'em."

"Fear, I didn't—" She was cut short by him suddenly grabbing her by the throat, causing her to gag. He pressed her up against the wall and stuck his .9mm into her mouth.

"Lie to me again!" Spittle flew from his lips and clung to her face. "I dare you!"All was silent as he looked into her face with dangerous eyes, clenching his teeth. He looked like he wanted her to try him just so he could send some heat into her cum catcher. "You saw Eureka taking a possible interest in me and you sought to get her outta the picture too." Fear told her the plans she'd laid out. "Just like you gave Italia and the rest of 'em that work.Right?"

Constance stared him dead in his eyes as she nodded her head and confessed. "I killed them, I killed them all. They were going to take you away from me."

"You're a selfish bitch," he shook his head. "All this time I thought it was Gustavo's people that had done away with them, but it turned out that the snake was in my own backyard." He relieved her throat and took his .9mm out of her grill. "What chu did then is in the past. I'ma let that shit go, but you will answer for your negligence. You went against my orders and put the lives of our recruits in danger. You know the punishment for disobedience."

"Fear, I'm sorry." Her voice cracked under raw emotion, knowing that she'd hurt the very man that she'd claimed to love.

He looked down, shaking his head and then back up. "I'm not even tryna hear that shit. Go!" He pointed with the hand that gripped his banger.

Constance stood there, locked within Fear's gaze. Slowly, her eyes began to mist and obscure her vision. She could hear her heart shattering into pieces like a store's window glass during the '65 Watts riot. She swallowed hard and digested the hurt that clogged up her throat. She dared to blink her eyes and hot tears shot down her cheeks. She didn't bother to wipe them away though. For the first time in her life, she didn't care if anyone saw her cry. She ambled forth, bumping shoulders with Fear as she walked passed him, heading up the stairs. She knew the punishment that awaited her and she was going to face it with her head held high.

Ten minutes later

Constance hung bond from the ceiling inside of the garage, titties loose and back naked. Eureka and Anton stood off to the side, wearing expressions of confusion as they wondered what would happen next. Just then, the door that separated the garage from the kitchen opened and Fear stepped out. He had a solemn face as he pulled the door shut behind him, a black leather whip wrapped around his knuckles.

He'd traded in his garbs for a wife beater and jean shorts. He strode past Eureka giving her a glimpse of the scars that his wife beater partially hid. She could tell that the scars were from a lashing, much like the one that he was about to give Constance. Although the scars weren't nearly as bad as the keloid welts on Eureka's back, she had a profound respect for Fear. Seeing the scars let her know that he wasn't above having himself punished for breaking the rules. Eureka admired him for that because he meant it when he said that no one was above their union.

Not even him.

Fear stopped before Constance and looked her directly in the eyes. He pulled a red bandana from his right back pocket and held it up to her mouth. "Bite down on this," he told her. "It'll help."

"Fuck you!" Constance screamed on him, then harped up a glob of phlegm and spit in his face.

Fear squeezed his eyes closed as the goo splattered against in his face. The nasty white glob rolled down his face and curved at the shape of his nose. He wiped his face clean of the goo and tucked the bandana into his right back pocket. He then stepped behind Constance. Drawing his arm back, he took a deep breath, and swung his arm forward. The black leather whip uncoiled, whistling through the air en route to Constance's naked back.

Whack!

Constance's eyes rolled to their whites and her jaw went slack feeling the sting of the leather whip across her flesh. She was about to unleash a scream, but quickly clenched her teeth and squeezed her eyes closed. She wouldn't give them the satisfaction of hearing her wallowing in pain. Never, she'd take her whipping like a straight up G. Fear had molded her in his image and she was going to show him that she was built like he was.

Whack! Whack! Whack!

The whips came just as fast as they left, splitting the skin of her back and causing blood to seep. Constance's eyes fluttered and her mouth quivered. She went slack on the chain, hanging as if she'd fallen dead.

Fear continued the whipping. Initially, he was only supposed to give her ten lashings, but the more he thought about how she had stolen the love of his life away from him the more lashings he dealt her. The whip licked at her rear, back to back. He laid into her with all of his might. While this was going on, a worried Eureka looked back and forth between them both. Even though Constance had done her scandalous, she didn't want to see her beaten to death.

"Fearrrr, stop! You're gonna kill her!"

The wailing of her voice snapped him back to reality. Nostrils flaring, chest thumping, he looked around like he was just realizing where he was. He looked up at Constance's bloody back and then down to the whip in his palm, dropping it. He checked the pulse in her neck to make sure she was still alive. Once he concluded that she was still with them, he picked up the bottle of Jack Daniels from the floor and screwed off the cap.

"Drink this," he told her as he held the bottle up to her lips. Her eyes were slightly peeled apart and he could see her pupils moving around lazily. Her mouth moved as if it had a mind of its own. She was teetering between consciousness and unconsciousness, but that didn't stop her from being defiant still.

"Fu—fu—fuuuuck—youuu," she stammered. "Fucking fuck you!" She screamed on him.

"Alright," he nodded his head and said, "fuck you, too, then."

He unsheathed his bowie knife, pulled up a chair and stepped upon it. He grabbed her by the wrist and carved the L.O.E tattoo from her hand, causing her to scream out at the top of her lungs. He let the square piece of skin fall to the floor and jumped down. He grabbed her by the jaw and squeezed hard, looking up into her eyes.

"Constance Payne, I hereby banish you from Loyalty Over Everything," he spoke sternly. "Tonight you are to pack your things and leave. I—no we, don't ever want to see your face around her again." He undid her bondages and took her into his arms. He carried her out of the garage, not bothering to speak to Eureka and Anton.

****

An hour later

Anton stood off to the side with his arms folded across his chest. His head was at an angle and his eyes were slightly narrowed as he watched Fear attend to his sister's injuries. Fear's face was a mask of concentration as his latex gloved hands stitched up Eureka's cheek as she sat on the sofa. From the expression on his face, you would have thought that he was a surgeon performing the most difficult surgery of his life the way he carried on with the needle.

Eureka narrowed her eyes as she winced, taking the bottle of Jack Daniel's to the head to sooth her pain. Her body tensed and she scrunched her face tightly, the sting of the needle felt like a sewing machine needle jabbing the side of her face rapidly. The process was long and tedious, but only because Fear wanted it done perfectly. He was sort of an expert, having stitched himself up on several occasions.

His body had been through a lot in his line of work. He had been shot, stabbed, tazered, beaten, bitten by dogs, burned, and tortured. Hell, the nigga had even been hung once. His clients had christened him *The Man That Would Not Die* due to all of the shit he'd been through. You name it and it had happened to him. A lesser person would have been lying six feet in the dirt, but Fear was in a class all his own. He was in the top physical shape of a human being. He had literally trained his body to be a weapon. He was proficient with both knife and gun, but even without them, he was still one of the deadliest men to have walked the earth.

"Fear," Eureka uttered.

"Yeah," he answered, concentrating on the task at hand.

"Are you okay?"

"I'm straight," he responded. "Now hold still."

"Ssssss," Eureka gritted her teeth, feeling the needle being woven in and out of the flesh of her soft cheek.

"Relax, I'm almost done," he assured her, tongue hanging out of the side of his mouth as he went about stitching her up. "Alright," he said, finishing up the stitches. He picked the scissors up from the arm of the sofa and cut the stitch. He then handed Eureka the portable mirror like he was a barber that had just finishing hooking her up with a fresh fade. Eureka took the mirror and gave her reflection the once over. Feeling on her stitches, she couldn't help thinking how they felt like the ones on a baseball."What chu think?"

Eureka nodded her approval and said, "They're official," as she took a swig from the Jack Daniel's bottle.

"Thanks."

"Don't mention it."

Hearing someone coming down the steps, they turned around to find Constance coming down the staircase. She had a duffle bag slung over her shoulder and one in   her   hand. She staggered forward and fell with her bags, the beating had left her weak. They all watched as she struggled to get back on her feet.

Her eyes were swollen so bad from crying that it looked like she had an allergic reaction to something. She managed to get back up and look around at everybody before asking, "What the fuck are y'all looking at?"

No one said a word.

She tossed Fear her keys to the house and he caught them. She continued for the door, locking eyes with Eureka as she went along. Without uttering a word she let her know that the beef was far from over. Reading exactly what her heinous look was telling her, Eureka gave her a slight nod letting her know that she would be ready and waiting whenever she decided to bring it.

Constance looked back around, grimacing from the pain in her back. Fear looked and saw the blood staining the back of her white tank top. He took on a hard face as he didn't feel any remorse for her. She had it coming. Just as she disappeared through the front door, Fear stepped into the doorway holding the door open. He stood there watching her as she walked out of his life forever.

She was sure that he was watching her from the door because she could feel his eyes on her back. She dumped her bags into the backseat and hopped behind the wheel of her ride. Behind the black tinted windows of her BMW, where she was for sure that he couldn't see her, she broke down crying. Her shoulders jumped as she sobbed, tears pouring down her face in buckets. She grabbed a couple of napkins out of the glove-box and wiped her face.

She then pulled a picture out of her pocket. It was a picture of Eureka, Anton, and Giselle, taken some time ago after Bootsy's death. You could tell that Giselle was high when they'd taken it. Constance had snatched the picture on her way out of the door. She didn't know why she'd taken it, she just did. Sitting the picture down on the front passenger seat, she fired up the engine and threw her car into drive, pulling off.

****

"I'm sorry Fear, I..." Fear lifted his hand, cutting Eureka short.

"Don't be sorry, Constance knew the rules," he told her. "Now it's time you and Anton get familiar with them."

Fear left the living room and came back with a haggard, thick, cherry brown book with a unique design engraved on its cover. The cover had a human skull with snakes coming out of its eye sockets and swords forming an X behind it. There were rusted gold hinges at both ends of it and a rusted latch with a pad lock attached. The book had information about killing that dated way back to the 1800s, during the medieval era, until present day.

Every assassin that the book had been passed to placed new information inside of it, including its latest owner. Its information was priceless to a killer. Fear took a necklace from around his neck that was held onto a golden skeleton key. He used the key to unlock the pad-lock and flipped the latch open. He opened the book and turned it to Eureka and Anton. On the first beige, tattered page was a long list of rules dating back centuries ago, the latest of them had been updated in the year 2011.

"These are the rules of L.O.E," Fear began. "You will learn them for they are your gospel. And you shall adhere to them like they are the words of the Lord. Do we understand one another?" The siblings nodded, looking over the set of rules as Fear went on. "Great," he nodded. "The penalties for breaking said rules are as follows." He slid a finger down the lines of penalties for breaking the codes aligning the page. Eureka and Anton's eyes scrolled down the raggedy page. The punishments for violations ranged from whip lashings, to beatings, to executions (the most extreme measure). "No one is above L.O.E, not even me." Fear said. "You follow the rules and we will live in peace and harmony, violate them and you will get the underlying punishments. Got it?"

"Got it," Eureka nodded.

"I hear you," Anton replied.

"You will learn this book from cover to cover, just as I did." Fear closed the book and set it on the arm of the sofa. He left the living room and returned with a white towel slung over his shoulder and a Zippo lighter. He ducked off inside of the kitchen and pulled open the cupboard above the stove. Reaching inside, he took down a bottle of Jack Daniel's and headed back toward the living room, grabbing up a chair that was sitting at the kitchen table.

He set the chair at the sofa and sat down, laying the towel over his leg. He then tossed Anton the bottle of Jack Daniels and opened up the lighter with a flick of his wrist. "You're first youngling. Gon' and take it to the head," he told Anton.

Anton looked from the Jack bottle to Fear, wearing lines across his forehead. "What's all of this?"

"I'm gonna singe off the tips of your fingers and toes." When he said that Eureka frowned.

"For what?" Anton inquired.

"If you ever get snatched up by The Ones, it'll make you harder to identify."

"Listen, if you don't wanna go through with this you don't have to."

"I've came too far to turn back now."

Anton twisted the cap of the Jack Daniel's bottle and took it to the head like an ugly chick would a compliment. He hissed, feeling the dark liquor burn his esophagus as it went down, making a face like he'd gotten a whiff of some rank pussy. He then took the bottle to the head again until he felt himself becoming tainted by the alcohol. He wiped his mouth with the back of his hand and passed the Jack bottle to Eureka. She didn't waste any time getting shit-faced. She wanted to be good and faded when her time came around.

"Alright, let's get it," Anton placed his palm on the towel and lifted his fingers.

A flame jumped from the lighter once Fear struck the round metal ball in a downward motion. He held

Anton's fingers while he went about the task of burning the tips of them. Anton's face balled up and he clenched his teeth, feeling the blue flame licking up his finger tip. Eureka grabbed his freehand and squeezed it tight. Anton's foot was tapping the floor slowly at first, but sped up the longer he felt the hot flame.

An hour later

Fear wrapped Eureka and Anton's fingertips and toe tips in band-aids. He watched them put in work on the last of the Jack until they were pissy drunk and could barely feel the pain in their hands and feet. Fear snapped the Zippo closed and snatched the blood splotched towel from his leg. He stood erect and carried the chair back inside of the kitchen.

Returning to the living room, he saw Eureka cradling the bottle, lying on one side of the sofa asleep. On the opposite side was Anton, laying his head against the armrest, knocked the fuck out. Fear stuffed the Zippo into the pocket of his jeans and tossed the towel on the armrest of the sofa. He scooped Anton up in his arms and carried him up the stairs into their bedroom.

He came back down stairs and murdered the light in the living room. He took the Jack bottle form Eureka's hand and sat it down on the floor by the sofa. He then picked up Eureka from the sofa and headed for the stairs. Along the way she shifted around, smacking her lips and wrapping her arms around his neck. He looked down at her, watching the slight movements of her nostrils as she breathed. She looked at peace lying there in his arms. She was beautiful. Hands down the most stunning woman he had ever laid eyes on.

"Reka," he addressed her after lying her down in the bed beside Anton.

Eureka's head snapped up and she looked at Fear with hooded eyes and a wobbly neck. She was lit off that Jack and it was written all over her face.

"Huh?"

"Tomorrow, after I pick up this loot, training begins." Fear told her. "We're moving out in the A.M. Alright?"

"Alright," she nodded, turning on her side and closing her eyes.

Fear left the bedroom and closed the door shut behind him. Come tomorrow evening, he was going to play God and create two of the coldest killers the world had ever seen.

Chapter Fifteen

Malvo stood at the center of his living room, punishing the punching bag with DMX's *WhoWe Be* serenading him. He attacked the bag with all of his might, laying into it with a vengeance and showing no remorse. All he could think about was Eureka and what had went down at 7-Eleven that night. He had gotten caught slipping.

She could have easily left him on the curb bleeding and stinking something awful. He knew that she would have, too, if it weren't for The Boys showing up. He hadn't been so happy to see the police in all of his life. Before then, they had only been good for harassing niggaz and handing them ass whippings. But boy did they do his black ass a service that night. He could have groveled at their feet and kissed their shoes for saving his life.

Malvo had placed a call to Ernie to require the services of a hit-man he knew. He paid him the finder's fee and he set up the meeting with the contract killer. He showed up at the location that they were initially supposed to meet, but the cat never showed up. It wasn't until sometime later that he'd gotten a call from Ernie telling him that the assassin was picked up on a couple of murder charges. With that added to the equation, it was back to the drawing board for the dope peddler. He was back on the prowl, looking for another hitter to bring him Eureka's head.

Each blow that connected caused the chain that the punching bag was hoisted on to jerk violently and rattle. Malvo was covered in beads of sweat and his face was a mask of intensity.Once the song faded out, he dropped to the matt on the floor, breathing heavily. He screwed the cap off a bottle of water and took it to the head, guzzling it until there wasn't a drop left. When he was done, he tossed the bottle aside and wiped his mouth with the back of his hand.

His thoughts shifted to Ronny. It never occurred to him that he hadn't run off with his drugs and that he had been busted with the counterfeit money. If someone told him that right now, he wouldn't believe him. He had started off buying from Vladimir with real money. But once he linked up with Ernie, who could provide him with counterfeit bills, he decided to do a little experiment.

The first time he copped from Vladimir using the fake bills and got away with it, he got greedy and kept using them to buy from the Russian. He had been getting away with his fuckery for so long that he thought that he would never be found out but, he was wrong. And his treachery would leave Ronny to pay for his lengthy tab.

"Nah," Malvo made a face and shook his head, unwrapping his hands. "Ain't no way Vladimir found out. Ronny's punk ass just skipped town with my shit. That's what it is," he tried to convince himself. But at the back of his head he knew that it was a great possibility.

The coldest part about it was that he had violated his man's woman and child. They were innocent in everything, but he didn't give two fucks. The way he saw it through his eyes, what he did was for a purpose. It didn't matter that he had known Antoinette since she was fourteen and had been RJ's Godfather. None of that meant anything to him. Only his selfish needs mattered.

Hearing a knock at the door, his forehead creased with lines. He got to his feet and snatched his banger off the floor before heading to the door. He stole a peek through the peephole then unlocked and unchained the door. He snatched it open and stepped aside. Crunch stormed in, pissed off. He closed the door and headed back into the living room. The dark skinned goon was pacing the floor, punching his fist into his palm. Malvo angled his head and narrowed his eyes. Crunch's right eye had a welt under it and his lip was busted. The boy was heated, so heated that he could feel the temperature in the room go from sixty-five to seventy-five.

"Niggaz gotta die, fam. Straight up, them boys gotta go! On me!" Crunch ranted, pacing the floor faster and punching his palm harder. Someone had given him an ass whopping that had him on one.

"Slow down, C. What happened?" Malvo asked concerned.

"Lil' Tut and Spider, that's what happened. Look at my fucking face, man," he pointed to the shiner he was wearing, it had already started blackening.

Malvo grabbed him by the chin, turning his head from side to side. The other side of his face was bruised red. Seeing this enraged him. He felt like his crew was untouchable. Having this happen to Crunch was a slight at their reputation. The violators had to be prosecuted to the fullest extent of his banger.

"Run down to me exactly what occurred, don't leave shit out," Malvo struck a match and lit up a cigarette. He fanned the flame of the match out and tossed it into the trash can. He leaned up against the counter and gave Crunch his undivided attention.

"I had just come out of Louisiana Fried Chicken on Rosecrans…

Crunch emerged through the exit of Louisiana Fried Chicken, taking a bite out of a chicken wing. En route to his car, he found two young men sitting on the hood. One was taking a 40 oz of Olde English malt liquor to the head while the other was just posted up, watching his every move.

Crunch ran the young men's faces through his mental rolodex and quickly came up with names to match. The one with the .40 oz was Spider and the one posted up went by the name Lil' Tut. These were a couple of the Baby Locs that were outside of Eureka's apartment when he, Ronny, and Malvo had gone seeking revenge that day. He would never forget that day. The drama had escalated and they were lucky to have left with their lives.

Fuck man, I left my shit in the car, Crunch thought, remembering that he'd stashed his gun underneath the driver seat. Nonetheless, whatever was to be his fate, he was going to face it head-on.

He finished his wing and tossed it aside, sucking the crumbs off of his fingers. His face transformed into the meanest scowl that he could muster as he stepped to the young thugs. Spider slid off of the hood of the car, screwing the cap back on his 40 while Lil' Tut approached the cornrow rocking hoodlum.

"What's cracking, cuz?" Lil' Tut started in on him.

Crunch looked Lil' Tut up and down, disgusted, and said, "Your fucking head if you don't get the away from my car."

"I think you need to watch your mouth, homeboy," Spider stepped up, mad dogging.

"Nigga, suck my dick!"

"Suck yo dick?" Spider puffed up his chest. "Suck on this!"

He slammed the 40oz bottle into Crunch's head and it exploded on impact. Beer suds washed over Crunch's face as he folded like a futon, falling to his hands and knees. The young niggaz didn't waste any time descending upon him like a couple of hungry hyenas. They rained kicks and punches on him until they were content. Once they were done, Spider gave him one last kick in the ribs and spat on him for good measure.

"Bitch-boy," Spider looked upon him with arched eyebrows and a scrunched nose. He spat on Crunch as he lay on the side of his face on the ground, he was barely conscious and groaning in pain. "Yo Lil' Tut, hand me that thang-thang, I'm 'bout to push this nigga."

Lil' Tut brandished his burner and cocked it, passing it to his homeboy. Spider pointed the banger down at Crunch's melon. He was about to leave him with his thoughts plastered to the ground when Lil' Tut grabbed him by the wrist and nodded ahead. When the ruffian looked up, the patrons of Louisiana Fried Chicken had their faces pressed up against the glass, watching the whole scenario unfold.

"Homie must gotta guardian angel or something, 'cause this hour was for damn sho' 'pose to be his last." Spider passed the burner back to Lil' Tut and he tucked it. He then tapped his arm and they started back for their car. Coming in and out of conscientiousness, the last thing Crunch heard was tires screeching as they peeled off.

"I told you, man, when that shit cracked off in the Jordan's we were supposed to been at that nigga that same night," Crunch spat angrily. "Niggaz are thinking we're soft out here, we gotta answer back! If you ain't riding, fuck it! I'm gathering the wolves and we're getting active with these fuck-boys!"

If this nigga says no I know something, and once I'm done with Lil' Tut and Spider, I'm coming back here to let 'em hold something hot too. Crunch thought.

"Alright, we're at them boys tonight.Let me get dressed," Malvo turned around and headed toward his bedroom.

Crunch watched as he disappeared through his bedroom door. He then ducked off inside of the kitchen and sifted through the refrigerator until he produced a cold Heineken. He held the cool bottle to the bruised side of his face before cracking it open and taking a drink. Malvo returned wearing a bulletproof vest and handing him one of his own. Once he strapped the vest on, they were out of the door. Someone was going to die that night.

****

"Is that him over there?" Malvo asked Crunch as they sat slumped in the Tahoe truck underneath the shadow of a tree.

"Yeah, that's that faggot," Crunch nodded with a scowl, gritting his teeth, thinking about how Lil' Tut had played him. Involuntarily, his hand tightened around the handled of his banger. He could hear his gun begging him to kill something, *Come on, fam, let's air these pussies out and show 'em we're the wrong nigga to fuck with!*

Malvo continued to take casual pulls of his square as he watched Lil' Tut through narrowed eyes. He was on fire inside and his blood felt like molten lava. He couldn't believe that the little nigga had come at his crew like they were as soft as baby shit. He and his goons had dropped plenty of bodies down by the way. Niggaz and bitches knew that they were willing to take it to the extreme if need be, there was no questions about it. They didn't think twice about making an example out of a nigga that violated.

Malvo found it funny that all of the work he had put in over the years could be so quickly forgotten about because of one incident. He knew that the beef with Loc Dog back in The Jordan Downs projects would have to be handled and he had planned on addressing it, just not as soon. He'd first planned on flipping the dope to run up his bands and knocking off Eureka and Anton. Those plans would be put on the backburner, though, because tonight, Loc Dog's minions had to get acquainted with a couple of hollow tipped bullets.

Tonight Spider and Lil' Tut would be fed lead sandwiches for dinner.

Malvo mashed out his cigarette as he blew smoke out the corner of his mouth. He looked to Crunch, extended his hand and wiggled his fingers, signaling for him to give him something. Crunch opened the console and pulled out an extra banger. He went to pass it to Malvo, but he frowned and shook his head. He didn't want that thang, he had something else in mind.

"Nah, fuck that banger. Let me get that poker, my nigga," Malvo told him.

Crunch nodded and deposited the banger back inside of the console. He then felt underneath the driver seat and brandished what looked like a ten inch ice pick with a handle wrapped up in a torn white bed sheet. Malvo inspected the ice pick, admiring the length of its blade. He could have easily pushed Lil' Tut into the next life with one through the temple, but he wanted to get up close on him. He wanted him to see his face and the whites of his eyes when he did him, so he'd know that he made a grave mistake when he decided to cross him.

Malvo stashed the ice pick on his person and turned to Crunch. "I'll be right back," he threw open the door and oozed out of the truck, his Timberland boots touching the sidewalk without making a sound. He gently closed the door back shut and pulled his hoodie from off his head, he wanted Lil' Tut's bitch ass to know who was giving him that work.

For a big nigga Malvo moved swift and silently, almost with the stealth of a ninja. With each step he took he could hear the conversation Lil' Tut was having with his homeboy growing louder and louder. He adopted the shadows, using them as his aid so that he could get close enough to dispatch his target. He moved with the technique of a lioness waiting for the perfect moment to pounce on its prey.

"Aye, you think that nigga Crunch might roll back?" Spider asked.

Lil' Tut shrugged and spat on the curb. "I don't know, I'm strapped up though. You holding?"

"Oh, I stay with that thang, thang," he patted the bulge on his hip.

"That's what I'm talking about. Fuck that nigga."

"Fuck 'em," Spider slapped hands with Lil' Tut.

At that moment, Malvo grunted and then a shrill cut through the night that could wake the deaf.

"Aghhhhhhhhhhh!" Lil' Tut threw his head back as his eyes shot open and his jaw dropped, in a bone chilling scream.

His head turned slightly and his eyes met with a vindictive Malvo, hacking that ass up with that homemade shank. The sharp metal sounded like small fists punching thick flesh as it stabbed in and out of Lil'Tut's puny body. Spider went to draw his banger. Malvo didn't even bother to turn around when he felt movement at his back. A gust of wind brushed past his cheek, disturbing the stubble on his face. And then he heard it. The gunshots.

Bloc! Bloc! Bloc! Bloc!

Spider went down in a hail of bullets, blood, and gun smoke. He fell like a tree that had been hacked down in the forest and landed just as hard. Even after he had expired, Crunch kept letting that thang go on him. Crunch kicked the lifeless body and turned to Malvo. He was still wailing on Lil' Tut's stiff corpse. The boy's eyes were rolled back in his head and his body jerked with each stab that punctured his form.

Malvo slowly stood erect, looking like a madman with flaring nostrils and specks of blood covering his face.

"Come on, man. Let's get the fuck outta here!" Crunch ran past Malvo and he took off moments later, right behind him.

The next night

Loc Dog sat back on the couch with his rosary beads around his knuckles, caressing them with his thumb. He looked to be in deep thought as two of his Baby Locs stood before him. Goose and One-Punch were the youngest of the litter, but just as vicious as any of the dogs in the kennel.

"Loc, did you hear what I just said?" This was Goose. He was sporting a Vikings jersey and a purple bandana on his dome, Tupac style. His neck and wrists were covered in light jewels that he'd purchased from the Slauson Super Mall.

One-Punch snapped his fingers before Loc Dog's eyes and waved his hand, looking for some sort of reaction. He frowned when he didn't get one and said, "Cuz, we just told you that Lil' Tut and Spider got hit tonight and you ain't got shit to say about it?" He was wearing a wave-cap and a long sleeve white T-shirt.

Loc Dog's face twitched with disdain as he gripped the rosary even tighter in his hand, grinding his teeth. Suddenly he shot to his feet, startling the two soldiers.

"Lil' nigga, don't chu ever come telling me that some of the homies got peeled!" He spat with malice in his eyes, spit leaping from his lips. "If anything, you tell me that you just put in work!" His head snapped from One-Punch to Goose with wide nostrils and heavy breathing. Hearing that his cousin and his homeboy had gotten laid down had his blood boiling. He could literally feel the flushness around his ears and neck.

"That's what we saying, cuz, we know who did that," Goose said. "We got one pistol between us and that's that nigga Tah Tah's piece of shit .9mm with the broken handle. We need some heat, my nigga. Trust and believe we're ready to get active with these dudes."

"You lil' niggaz stay fresh to death, but ain't gotta decent burner between y'all?" He shook his head shamefully. "Alright, I got that, but who're these fools that cut the homies lifelines?"

Goose and One-Punch exchanged glances. One-Punch shrugged and said, "Malvo and that black ass nigga, Crunch. Least that's what the streets saying."

"Malvo," Loc Dog's face tightened with the skin pulling toward the center of his face. He looped the rosary necklace over his head and adjusted the kufi on his head. His eyes caught a roach moving along the arm of the tattered couch he was sitting on. "I knew I should have crushed that cock roach a long time ago." His fist slammed down on the arm of the couch, squashing the bug and causing yellowish-green puss to ooze out of it. He flicked the mashed roach off the arm of the couch, brushed his hand off on his form fitting black V-neck, and turned around to the young men. "Y'all niggaz follow me downstairs, man," he waved them on as he left the living room.

Entering the kitchen, he approached the pad-locked basement door and unlocked it with a copper key from his pocket. He opened the door and slapped up the light-switch on the inside wall, bringing life to a staircase. He motioned for the men to enter and came in behind them, closing the door to as he led them down into the basement. They stayed behind, trying to peer through a sea of darkness as he moved about. Seconds later they heard a drawstring being pulled and a bright light illuminated the entire basement.

Loc Dog walked over to a floor rug and drew it back, revealing a combination locked wooden door. He kneeled down, and after making sure that the youngsters couldn't see him, he twisted the dial. The lock snapped open and he removed it. He sat the lock down and flipped opened the latch, throwing the wooden door open.

"Y'all niggaz come here," Loc Dog motioned them over. They came to stand behind him and he started pulling some military issued type of shit out of the floor, passing them off to his pups. Goose whistled as his hands grasped the machinegun, examining it and pointing at the furnishings down in the basement just as One-Punch was doing.

The OG slammed the wooden door closed and re-locked it. When he rose to his feet, he was clutching an M-16 assault rifle. He chambered a round into the lethal weapon and turned around to his Baby Locs. "Let's go see this nigga," he said with twin raging fires in his pupils.

Twenty minutes later

Malvo came from around the back of his trap, puffing on a Black & Mild as he watched the traffic coming to and from his business. He'd just left from checking in on his workers, making sure that they were doing what they needed to be doing and that everyone was there and accounted for. Normally, he would have Crunch doing shit like that, but he had him staking out Antoinette's house in case Ronny showed up. Blowing smoke from his nose and mouth, he dropped the thin cigar on the ground and mashed it out under his Timberland boot.

"Yeah, that's that nigga Malvo, kicking it out there like he don't know what time it is." Loc Dog leaned over between the front seats, peering through the windshield as he made to tie a purple bandana around the lower half of his face. He finished tying the bandana over his nose and mouth and picked up his M-16.

"That's alright 'cause The Dog about to remind his pudgy ass."

"That's what I'm talking about.Let's let these dudes know that it's real in the field," Goose said, gripping his MP-5 with both gloved hands. His face was fixed with a scowl and his eyes were bloodshot from weed smoke. He wore black sunglasses over his eyes and a black bandana over the lower half of his face.

"Punch, murder them lights and creep on them fools," Loc Dog ordered, unlocking and cracking open the sliding door of the van, allowing the night's cool air inside.

"Ai'ight," One-Punch responded, bodying the headlights like his big homie commanded.

The van crawled up the street toward the unsuspecting dope fiends zig zagging back and forth across the street, trying to get or already having gotten their medicine. As soon as the van stopped, the sliding door was thrown open. Loc Dog and Goose unleashed fire into the droves of addicts, trying to lay Malvo down. Blood, bone fragments, and severed body parts went flying every which way as the horrified cries of men and women invaded the air.

The van came to a screeching halt. Loc Dog and Goose hopped out, heads snapping in every direction as the creatures of the night scattered around them. The OG's eyes scanned the area frantically until they ID'd his intended target. He smiled manically when he spotted him running alongside a fiend, occasionally glancing back over his shoulder. He took off after him like a race hound, covering ground just as fast as one with that long black thang firmly in his grasp.

As hard as he ran, he couldn't keep up with the pace of the junky or Malvo which was surprising being that he was a big, burly mothafucka. Loc Dog's chest was on fire and he was panting out of breath. Figuring that slugs would catch up to him before he could, he braced the M-16 against his shoulder blade, aimed, and hugged the trigger, cutting loose with a burst of flames.

Rat! Tat! Tat! Tat! Tat! Tat!

"Argghh!"

"Argghh!"

Malvo and the fiend fell awkwardly to the sidewalk, littering it with specs of blood. Loc Dog lowered his rifle, smiling wickedly as he licked his lips.

"Got 'em, coach!"

Rat! Tat! Tat! Tat! Tat! Tat! Tat! Tat!

The sudden burst of gunfire brought him around, ready to retort with his own. He lowered his weapon once he saw Goose hanging out of the van with his machinegun pointed in the air, firing it, raving like a lunatic as the vehicle rolled up the block.

"Yeahhh, mothafuckaz, yeah, niggaz! Mafia!"

Rat! Tat! Tat! Tat! Tat!

The shrill of police sirens contaminated the night as Loc Dog ran and hopped into the van. The van slowly coasted by where he'd laid the fiend and Malvo down. His eyes took in them both. The dope head had half of his lemon missing and horror stitched upon his face. Malvo on the other hand, eyes were stretched open and mouth was agape. He looked like he experienced some excruciating pain before he left this life for the next. Sensing that, Loc Dog pulled his bandana down from the lower half of his face and laughed sinisterly, hoping his spirit would hear his taunting one last time. He then ducked back inside of the van and pulled the door closed.

"You get 'em, cuz?" One-Punch asked excitedly, looking from the windshield to Loc Dog.
"Does a bear shit in the woods and wipe his ass with a rabbit?" He retorted.

"Smashed that cock sucka, that's what I'm talking about," Goose gave the OG and his partner-in-crime three high fives.

"You've gotta be shitting me?" Loc Dog frowned, seeing Malvo get up from the sidewalk and run into a neighboring yard. "Nigga still alive!"

"What? I thought you said you got 'em?" Goose spat sharply.

"Played possum," Loc Dog gave his theory. "Punch, turn this bitch around, cuz."

One-Punch glanced at the side-view mirror and saw a fleet of police cruisers invading the block. "No way, The Rollers are on the rise."

"Sheiiit! Fuckk!" Loc Dog elbowed the seat and punched the ceiling in a rage. Calming down, he ran a hand down his face and said, "It's okay. It's alright. We'll get 'em next time."

Best believe that, Loc Dog thought as he watched an abundance of red and blue lights merge in the side-view mirror.

Chapter Sixteen
The next morning

Fear spotted the man he was looking for at the bar, hunched over a glass of something dark, swirling it around inside of his glass. He was a plain looking white dude dressed in a very expensive suit. Out of all of the people inside of the establishment, he stuck out like a sore thumb. It didn't take a rocket scientist to tell that he didn't belong there which made Fear wonder why he'd chosen the place for the meeting at all.

Fear studied the man for a time before starting in his direction. He took a seat right beside him, but before he could say anything the man spoke. "Fear, right?" He had a long face and thinning dark hair that he brushed to the front to cover up a balding spot.

Fear's forehead furrowed as he stared at the man for a minute and nodded his head.

"I spoke with you over the phone, I'm Mr. Cousins," the man extended his hand in introduction and Fear shook it. "You got something that's gonna make me smile?" Keeping his eyes on Fear, he took a sip of his drink.

Fear nodded his head, pulled a cell phone from inside of his jacket, and placed it on the bar top. He took a cautious look around before pushing it before Cousins.

Cousins picked the cell up and turned down its volume. His lips birthed a smirk as he watched the footage of Father Sullivan getting castrated. Having seen enough, he flipped the cell phone closed and slipped it inside of his jacket.

Fear gave another cautious look around the bar and sat the silver briefcase on the bar top. Cousin's frowned. He looked up and Fear nodded.

Cousin's shrugged and pulled the briefcase closer and popped its locks. When he opened the lid, a cold fog emanated, spilling into the air. Inside, was the Father's severed dick in a large glass vial held up by metal rods. "Nice." He smirked, studying the severed penis frozen in animation behind the glass vial. He closed the case and locked it back. "Really nice, my employer will be very pleased with this. Good job." He shook Fear's hand, pleased with his work. Using his foot, he pushed a briefcase beside his leg.

Fear picked it up, popped the locks, and was pleased with what he saw. Someone cleared their throat. Fear looked up to meet the eyes of the bartender who was cleaning out a mug. He knew that grunt all too well, the old man wanted his taste of the action for the illegal transaction that had taken place inside of his business.

Fear pulled a couple of hundred dollar bills from out of one of the stacks of money inside of the briefcase and dropped it on the bar top, sitting a half empty beer bottle on it.

"Thank you," Nigel said, lifting the beer bottle and snatching the loose bills.

"Alright, I guess that concludes our business." Fear locked the briefcase and rose to his feet. He extended his hand and Cousins shook it. "You know, I was thinking, if you need my services again. You can—"

"No, we won't."

"Excuse me."

"You've been blackballed, Fear," he told him. "Mr. Arturo is a very powerful man with friends in some very high places. The only reason why you got this job was because we couldn't find anybody else. Frankly, we were desperate, so Mr. Auturo gave us the okay to contact you for your services. But hey, I'm sure ol' Nigel could use some help around this place. What do you say, Nigel?" He threw his head back like, *What's up?*

"Yeah, man, I could always use a hand around here," Nigel spoke sincerely.

"Well, I'd better be going," Cousins downed the last of the drink and dropped a couple of bills on the bar top. "Take it easy." He patted Fear on the shoulder and headed for the exit.

Fears' eyes followed Cousins as he walked toward the exit door, toting the briefcase. He was scorching hot; he could actually feel his ears and chest heating up. He had it in mind to chase Cousins down and baptize him with his .9mm, wet his mothafucking ass up. But he knew better than to let his emotions get the best of him. That's what women did and he was all man. He ran his hand down his face and took a couple of deep breaths to calm himself. Once he'd gotten himself together he made for the door, but Nigel called him back.

"Aye, buddy, here you go," He sat an application on the bar top.

Fear shot him a look that startled him, causing the bartender to think about grabbing that pistol grip shotgun behind the bar. With that, he left the bar with his briefcase. His next stop would be home to dump the cash into his safe until they got back to divide it up.

An hour later.

Fear drove the van out to the mountains to a cabin he owned up there. It had been quite some time since he'd visited the place, but every now and again he'd send Constance up there to make sure the place hadn't been broken into. He had many places to lay his head, but this was hands down his favorite. He never felt more at peace than when he was up there away from civilization.

He didn't bring along a TV, a cell phone, computer, or any of the latest technology when he journeyed up to the southern side of the mountains. Mother Nature was enough to keep him company. It was the perfect place for him to train Eureka and Anton because there weren't any interruptions or distractions.

Fear pulled up to the cabin and hopped out, with Eureka and Anton following suit. The black, wood cabin was about two stories tall and sat alone at the top of the mountain. All around the cabin for miles there wasn't anything in sight but trees and dead leaves on the ground. Fear closed his eyes and a smile stretched across his face as he inhaled the air. He then turned around to Eureka and Anton who were just looking around.

"You smell that?" He asked them.

"Yeah, it smells like a bear took a shit up here."

Fear snickered and shook his head saying, "Come on. Let's get this stuff out of the van and get settle in."

Fear, Eureka, and Anton gathered their things and headed into the cabin. They dropped their stuff in the living room and took in the scope of the cabin. The place was sparsely furnished with a shag floor rug, a sofa, and a love seat, and a big flat-screen TV that hug over the fireplace.

"I'm starving like a hostage," Anton said, turning to Fear. "Where's the kitchen?"

"Straight ahead," he nodded.

Anton disappeared through the doorway of the kitchen, moments later he was marched back with a perturbed expression on his face.

"Man, it ain't nothing in there but a box of bacon soda and some shit to make coffee." Anton complained.

"I know," Fear admitted. "You'll eat what we hunt and capture."

"What?"

"You heard me lil' nigga," Fear said. "Now get dressed." He tossed Anton his backpack and handed Eureka hers. "Your first lesson begins in five minutes. Don't be late."

Four minutes later…The first week.

Fear threw the noose over the tree's branch and tied the other end around a nearby tree. He stood upon the chair and pulled the noose down, tugging on it. Once he was sure that it was secure, he hopped off of the chair. He stepped before Eureka and Anton, rubbing his hands together.

"Alright, whose going first?" His eyes shifted from Eureka to Anton.

Anton raised an eyebrow as he looked from the idling noose to Fear. He gave him the side eye and twisted his lips.

"My dude, I know you don't think I'ma 'bout to hang myself from no mothafucking tree?" Anton folded his arms across his chest, looking at Fear like, *Nigga, you can't be serious*. "No way, no how, that ain't happening."

"If you're gonna be in this game, then you can't be afraid to die," Fear told them. "You gotta be able to look death in its eyes and laugh, crack a smile, tell that cock sucker to suck your dick. You feel me?"

"This ain't the nineteen-twenties and I ain't looking to be lynched."

Fear took a deep breath and exhaled. Hands to together, he stepped before Anton.

"Baby boy, this is the first step in your training, if you can't do this then step off," Fear pointed a crooked finger beyond him. "You try your luck out there with the boy Malvo and see how you come out."

"Fuck it. That's what it is then," Anton shrugged and was about to walk off until Eureka stepped in his path, outstretching an arm across his chest.

"We'll do it and I got first."

"Reka," Anton frowned.

She whipped around, eyebrows arched.

"Don't Reka me. You wanted in this life? Well, here it is," she told him. "I'm not going back to the streets, baby boy. There ain't nothing there for you or me. You with me?" She held out her hand.

He looked down at her hand, thinking for a moment.   And   then,   "Yeah." They gave one another a complex handshake and she stepped over to Fear. He directed her toward the chair and she stepped upon it, both feet planted firmly on the seat. Grabbing the chair about the back, he stepped upon it and brought the noose down, looping it around her neck. He then jumped down.

He and Anton looked up at her as if she was the Empire state building. Eureka stared straight ahead, taking deep breaths to prepare herself for what she'd gotten into. Using his red bandana, Fear tied her hands behind her back and stood off to the side of her.

"You sure you wanna go through with this?" Anton questioned, he got a bad feeling about her being hung up like that from a tree.

The whole idea was stupid to him, but he loved her without a fault. She was his sister and his best friend and he'd follow her to the end of the earth. They were down for one another. They were like Ryu and Ken, Batman & Robin, Goku and Krillin.

Eureka continued to stare straight ahead as she nodded. She listened to Fear as he talked, his voice coming from the left of her.

"Alright, on the count of three I'm going to kick this chair from under you, okay?" He asked. She nodded and took two deep breaths, blinking her eyes. "Okay. One. Two," he kicked the chair from underneath her feet before the count of three, taking her and Anton completely off guard.

Her body hurled toward the ground, but the rope yoked that mothafucka right back up. She dangled from side to side, eyes growing moist and legs thrashing the air wildly. Her face quickly reddened and veins formed on her temples.

"What the fuck man? You said three!" Anton barked on Fear, ready to whip his ass. "That was unexpected."

"Death is unexpected." Fear looked up at Eureka, struggling upon the rope. He stayed focused on her as he talked to Anton. "You wanna be a killer, then you need to accept the fact that death will come for you any day. You don't get to make an appointment, that bastard just shows up and it's time for you to go. She doesn't come down until her lips curl."

Anton and Fear stood side by side, watching Eureka dance upon the rope. Her eyes looked like they were about to burst out of their sockets. White stuff accumulated at the corners of her mouth and her tongue hung out, drool dribbling from it. She looked like a mentally challenged person having a seizure.

"Come on, Reka. You can do it, ma," Fear said under his breath, hoping that she'd pass the first test.

"You got it, sis," Anton balled both of his hands into fists. "Show'em how niggaz out the 'jects are built."

Eureka felt light headed and saw stars dancing before her eyes. With them came a black shroud zipping back and forth across the sky with warp speed. It was moving so fast that her eyes registered it as a blur. An eerie shriek came from the shroud and it shot up into the air taking Eureka's eyes along with it. She looked down and dead people started to appear before her eyes one by one. Her father, Bootsy, Bugsy, Ms. Charlene, Red, Coal, who she'd murdered back at The Snooty Fox, and a host of dead relatives and friends she'd lost over the years.

Tears slowly pooled in her eyes and trickled down her cheeks when she saw her father. He was staring dead at her, wearing a smile on his face as he waved. She tried to utter his name, but the rope around her neck was so tight that it stifled her, causing only an awkward noise to escape her lips.

"Come on," she'd seen him mouth and then he motioned for her to follow him as a blinding florescent light appeared beside him. It started off as a ball and then expanded into a portal that rays shined out of, kissing off of her face. The dead people filed in line behind each other, heading inside of the portal of intense light.

"No, no. Anton. I'm all—I'm all—he's—he's got left. I'm sorry," she managed to get out, blackness flicking before her eyes.

The flame of the burning candle that was her life shrank and began to flicker out. She watched the look of disappointment emerge on her father's face. He glanced at the ground and adjusted his tie, exhaling. He then looked up at her and smiled.

"That's enough!Cut her down!" Anton ordered Fear, seeing his sister's dancing legs slowing down. Their movements had become sluggish. Her eyes were hooded and moving around lazily, she was on the ledge of death.

"Not yet, she can do it," Fear slightly turned his head as he spoke, but kept his focus on Eureka. "Come on, lil' momma. You can do this! I know you can!"

"I said cut her loose!" Anton demanded, but Fear ignored him.

He continued with his encouraging of Eureka, acting as if the boy wasn't there. Anton licked his lips and nodded his head, realizing what he had to do. Hastily, he scanned the grounds until he located a broken branch submerged in a pallet of brittle leaves and twigs. He fished the branch out of the brittle leaves and twigs, taking it into both hands.

Feeling movement at his rear and seeing a shadow on the ground, Fear's forehead rippled with lines and he whipped around. Anton was bringing the branch around his back, about to knock the killer's head from his shoulders, when he heard a funny gag that stopped him mid-swing. He and Fear's face contracted with surprise and their lips slightly parted. Their heads snapped in Eureka's direction and she was wearing a smirk. Fear's face broke out in a wide smile and so did Anton's.

Fear ran over to Eureka and hugged her legs, holding her up and loosening the strain that the rope had on her neck. Over his shoulder he called out for Anton, telling him to untie the rope from around the other tree. While Anton went to relieve the rope from around the tree, Eureka coughed and gasped for air. Once Anton took the rope from around the tree, Fear sat Eureka on the ground and untied her wrist. She lay there coughing and gasping for air. Fear and Anton were at her side, attending to her.

"Sis, are you alright?" Anton asked, worried, a hand on her shoulder.

She coughed and rubbed her neck, saying, "Yeah. Yeah."

Anton hugged her and kissed her on the cheek. She held onto his arm, patting it. Abruptly, Fear snatched her up and spun around in circles holding her up.

"You did it! You did it, lil' momma," he said jovially, hugging her with one arm. Eureka was able to look death in the eye and smile at it as if it were a joke. She'd passed the test. She wasn't afraid to die. Fear screwed the top off of a canteen and held it out to her. "Here, take this. It'll help."

She snatched the canteen and took it to the head, turning it up. The water spilled down her chin as she drank thirstily. She took the canteen from her mouth, gasping for air and wiping her mouth with the back of her hand. Once she felt she'd gotten enough air, she took another long drink from the canteen while Fear kneeled beside her, rubbing her back.

"You sure that you're alright?"

"Yeah, I'll be fine," she nodded, passing him back the canteen. He screwed the cap back on it and secured it on his waist. He then grabbed both of her hands and pulled her to her feet. He rubbed her back as she continued to cough uncontrollably.

"Come on, man, it's my turn. Let's get this shit over with," Anton said, looping the noose around his neck, and stepping upon the chair.

Fear headed back over to the tree to tie the rope around it. Once he secured the rope and made sure the noose was firm around Anton's neck, he took a step back.

Looking up at him he began, "Alright, on the count of three…"

On the count of three he kicked the chair out from underneath Anton's feet just like he'd done to Eureka. The rope yanked his little ass back up and he performed the same dance that his sister had. Anton hit the ground like a sack of potatoes when Fear released the rope from around the other tree. The boy gagged and couched uncontrollably as Eureka attended to him, pulling the noose loose around his neck. Fear passed her the canteen as he kneeled down and she took it,holding it to Anton's mouth as he drank from it. Eureka and Fear looked upon him happily. He had passed the test and now it was on to the next.

"I'm proud of you, lil' bruh," Fear shook his shoulder.

Once Anton had gotten right, Fear pulled him upon his feet and picked up a very expensive arrow and bow-gun. He threw his arm over Anton's shoulders and led him out into the woods with Eureka following beside them.

Three hours later.

Night draped a cloak of darkness over the sky, bringing to life all of the sounds in the woods of the mountains. Fear sat on a log across from Eureka and Anton. They all were eating on the chunks of deer that slowly roasted over the fire cooking the animal. The fire crackled and popped, illuminating a golden orange glow that shone on all of their faces as they munched on their respective pieces of meat.

With Fear's tutelage, Anton was able to track down the dear and kill it with the bow-gun. He then dragged him back to the camp where Fear showed him the proper way to gut the animal's carcass. Afterwards, he showed him how to butcher and cook the meat. Eureka and Anton were shown a lot and learned a lot that day. Fear was teaching them how to live off the grid, a skill that would come in handy in the future.

Once Fear stripped his piece of meat down to the bone, he discarded it over his shoulder and wiped his mouth with a rag. He then reached behind the log and grabbed a bottle of Ace of Spade, pouring up three flutes. He passed two of the flutes to Eureka and Anton and kept one for himself. After wiping their mouths off with rags, Eureka and Anton switched hands with the flute.

"I'd like to propose a toast to my lil' homie Ant, for coming through on dinner tonight. Salute," Fear smiled, leaning forward and clinking flutes with Eureka and Anton. They all then took a sip from the flute, "Good job today, man. You're a natural with that bow-gun. You ever shot one before?"

Anton shook his head no as he picked particles of meat from between his teeth with his finger nail. Once he wedged it from between his teeth, he spat it out to the side. "Nah, today was my first try," he admitted. "Was kind of fun though."

Fear nodded and said, "You're gonna succeed in this game, you're just like me when I first made my bones. I took to the murder game like a duck takes to water, real life."

"So, bro bro's your protégé, huh?" Eureka grinned and playfully elbowed Anton. He smirked and shrugged, like, *Aye, what can I say?* "Regular chip off the old block."

Eureka and Anton grew silent, wearing grins on their faces as they took sips from their flutes. Eureka looked over to Fear. He looked to be in deep thought as he swirled the champagne around in the flute, staring straight ahead at nothing particular.

"You're thinking about her, huh?" Eureka asked, causing Fear to throw his head back like, *What's up?*

"Who?' He asked frowning.

"You know who, her! Constance." She saw that he wasn't trying to answer so she pressed him. "Come on now, keep it a stack."

"Yeah, big homie, keep that shit a thousand," Anton threw in his two cents. "And toss me that bottle."

Fear grabbed the Ace of Spade bottle and tossed it to Anton. He didn't waste any time cracking the bottle open and refilling his flute.

"What Constance did was unforgivable," Fear told her. "She betrayed this family by putting you two at risk. I banished her from L.O.E., but truthfully, I was supposed to have killed her, you read the rules. For the first time in my life I allowed my feelings to get the best of me. I'll tell you one thing though, it will never happen again. 'Cause next time, I'ma do right by the book."

"She murdered the love of your life, how does that make you feel?" She inquired.

"I can't even begin to explain the pain that I felt in that moment when I found out,"he admitted. "I'ma street nigga.So for me, betrayal is worse than death, you feel me?"

Her eyes darted to the ground, then looked back up at him.She nodded her understanding."I know she worshipped the ground that you walked on, but did you ever love her?"

"No. I could have, but I already saw that she was becoming clingy," Fear confessed. "Constance didn't want me, she *needed* me.And for me that was a turn off. I suppose I couldn't blame her though, especially with all of the shit that she's been through."

"Do tell." Eureka refilled her flute.

Hearing rustling over by the trees, Fear shot to his feet, gripping his .9mm. His brow furrowed as he looked about.

"What was that?" Anton panicked. His body whipped around when he heard it.

Eureka was on her feet beside him, clutching a crooked branch, ready knock something smooth the fuck out.

"Probably a mountain lion."

"There are lions up here?" Eureka frowned.

"Yep, the smell of blood is probably drawing them." Fear tucked his banger on his waistline. "Come on. Let's kill this fire and mask the blood with this dirt."

Chapter Seventeen

With the introduction to Murder 101 having been over, it was time to get down to the meat and potatoes of this murder shit. Fear was going to teach Eureka and Anton every single thing he knew about killing, filling them in on even the smallest details. He would be their professor and they would be his students.

He had his work cut out for him being that he had to squeeze a year's worth of training into a year. After the confronting death in the lynching, Eureka and Anton's bravery had already been tested. They passed that obstacle with flying colors. He had them studying the thick brown book that he'd showed them back at the house. The book had information on the human anatomy, the human psyche, war tactics and strategies, amongst several other things.

With the reading out of the way, Fear taught them how to defend themselves and breathe in a fight. He even showed them how to calm themselves when critically wounded to slow their heart rate and blood flow so that they wouldn't bleed to death. Next, he demonstrated, with a knife, the points of the human body to attack to kill a man quick and proficiently. He also showed them the proper way to yield the knife and use it as a weapon. Once the third week had approached and he was sure that they had devoured every lesson, he moved them on to guns.

Third week.

Empty cans and glass bottles lined the log that lay on the ground. The siblings stood, watching as Fear placed the last empty glass bottle at the end of the log. He then balled up the brown paper bag the recyclables were in and tossed it aside. He snatched the .9mm from off of his waistline and paced the ground, like a drill sergeant would, addressing his men.

"What we have here is two of the most powerful weapons in the world," Fear began, clutching the meat in his cargo pants and holding up his .9mm. "That's your gun and your dick."

Eureka and Anton's forehead wrinkled.

"Why are they the most powerful weapons in the world?" Anton asked.

"Your dick gives life and your gun takes it," Fear told them. "The third and most deadly though… Well, that would be pussy." His eyes cut to Eureka and he smirked. She smirked too. "Oh, yes. Pussy can be a dangerous weapon when in the right hands. I'm not just talking about any ol' pussy, I'm talking about good pussy. Oh yeah, good pussy is just as lethal as the atomic bomb, so in turn, that makes females some of the most dangerous people on the planet." He fell silent as he paced the ground, looking from Anton to Eureka. "Now if a man was to take control of that pussy, he'd be the…" he trailed off and shook his head. "Never mind. Today's lesson is all about guns. Guns, guns, guns."

Fear gave Anton his .9mm and produced a second one from the holster at his back. He placed this banger in Eureka's hands and stepped behind her.She smirked, feeling his meat up against her ass. His face was one masked by seriousness as he told her and Anton how to hold their bangers.

"Alright, hold it like this," he positioned Eureka's hands on the .9mm and extended her arms. He glanced over to Anton who was holding his gun to the side with one eye closed, aiming. "My young nigga, you done watched too many gangsta movies. You hold that bitch like this here, with your legs spread apart," he ordered, and Anton did as he said. He then focused on Eureka. "Spread your legs open like this, Reka." He spread his legs apart and she followed his instructions. "Okay, now aim her at whichever one of those cans or bottles on the log."

"Gotcha."

Fear stepped from behind Eureka and went to stand off to the side. He looked from brother and sister to the cans and bottles lined up on the log. "Alright, Reka, show me what cha got, ma." There was a moment of silence as she was making sure her sighting was lined up with her target. Then the explosions came.

Ping! Shatter! Shatter! Ping! Shatter!

The empty cans fell while the glass bottles exploded as bullets whizzed through them. Eureka lowered her smoking gun and cracked a smile. She looked to Fear who was smiling and clapping his hands.

"Alright, baby boy.It's your turn," he told Anton.

Anton aimed his banger and executed the cans and bottles flawlessly. Fear smacked him on his ass like a basketball player would his team mate after making a basket.

"I'm impressed, y'all are fast learners."

"My daddy taught us how to shoot some time ago," Eureka informed him. "He used to take us duck hunting down south."

Fear nodded his head in approval and said, "Good, it stuck with you. I wanna show y'all a couple of more things, then we'll move on to the rifle training."

Eureka and Anton practiced shooting the cans and bottles two more times. They then went on to practicing on moving targets. From there he showed them how to kill someone up close.

"When executing a mark, if you can't reach the nigga from a far, you wanna get right upon 'em," he told them. "But not too close, 'cause you don't want his blood and/or hair follicles clinging to your clothes. Believe me when I say that forensics are a mothafucka. Alright," he pointed his banger at a dummy hanging from the same tree that Eureka and Anton were almost lynched on. The adult sized doll had a plastic head and a cotton, stuffed cloth body. The body had a diagram of the human beings, mostly vital organs which were located on the left side. If any of these organs were to be severely damaged, death would be the result.

"Once you're close enough, give 'em one to the head," he pointed the .9mm at the dummy's head. "When he falls, you stand over 'em and give 'em two to the sternum to finish 'em off. Y'all got that?" Eureka and Anton nodded. "Okay, then let's move along."

Later that evening.

Fear, Eureka, and Anton lay on their stomachs beneath the shade of a tree. Fear peered down below with an expensive pair of sleek, black, electronic binoculars. He worked the buttons and knob on the side of binoculars and the front of it extended. Neon blue lights flashed on and off around its lenses. A green light stayed lit at the center of the binoculars and its antenna stood tall.

"Alright, there he is. Right on time." Fear sat the binoculars down and picked his silenced sniper rifle up from its opened case. He slid on the last attachments and chambered a round into the deadly weapon. After making sure the weapon was good to go, he passed it along to

Anton, telling him how to hold and fire it. Anton took the assault rifle and rested his eye against the scope. His face slightly scrunched with his concentration. "Okay, line it up with either his chest or his head, whichever you please. You got it." He looked from the scope to the sighting of the rifle, trying to see if Anton was getting the hang of it. Through the scope there was a tall, hunk of a man walking down a path, having just come from climbing a mountain. "You got it?"

"Yep, right on his chest."

"Great. Now watch his chest as it slowly rises and falls with each beat of his heart," Fear coached him. "Watch closely, because I want you to become one with the beating of his heart. Fall in sync with it, become one with it. You are it and it is you." He fell back for a few moments, allowing Anton to merge with the beat of the man's heart. Once he felt like they had become one, he continued with his coaching of him. "Now, very gently place your finger on the trigger, don't pull it just yet. Wait until that moment."

"What moment?"

"*That* moment," Fear answered. "I can't describe it, but you'll feel it. It's kindred to a Spidey sense. It'll let chu know when it's time to squeeze the trigger."

Eureka's head snapped back and forth from the man Anton was aiming at to Anton behind the rifle. Her face became masked with worry as she hoped that he hadn't planned on doing what she'd thought.

"You aren't going to kill 'em, are you?" She panicked.

"Shhhh," Fear held a finger to his lips. "Can you feel it, lil'homie."

"Nuh uh, not just yet," Anton answered, his sole attention was focused through the scope of the deadly weapon on the man that was his target.

Eureka's heart pounded inside of her chest as if it were trying to break through its bone casing. The last thing she wanted was to see an innocent man dead. To kill someone who was in the game was one thing, but someone who wasn't a willing participant was wrong in her eyes.

"Fear, he's innocent," Eureka reasoned, looking at him with pleading eyes.

Fear's head snapped in Eureka's direction and he said, "No one's innocent. I'm sure the Jolly Green Giant here has more than his share of dirt caked up under his fingernails."

Seeing that she wasn't going to get anywhere with Fear, she tried reasoning with Anton.

"Baby boy, that's an innocent man down there. He hasn't done anything to warrant his life being taken."

"Oh yeah?" He asked, eye still focused through the scope. "How you know that?"

Eureka's head recoiled, surprised to hear that from her little brother.

"Anton—"

"Reka," Fear looked at her as if he was a mad dog tainted by rabies, eyebrows arched and jaws clenched. "If you don't like what's about to happen here, I suggest you take a walk."

Eureka gave him a look that matched his intensity, clenching her jaws like an angry Pit Bull. "Fuck what chu talking about, I'm not letting my brother steal an innocent man's life."

At that moment they heard someone yelling from a far. Their heads snapped in the direction from which the voice came and they saw the burly man in mid fall with red splattering on his forehead and chest. Eureka's heart thumped behind her chest plate. Her eyes snapped open and her mouth shot open. She looked to Anton who was just taking his eye from out of the scope, wearing a more than pleased expression.

Anton and Fear smacked hands and patted each other on the back. The killer was proud of the boy's flawless execution. Eureka sat on the ground on her hands and ass, stunned, like she'd found out that the family dog had been hit by a car. She was stunned for a moment, but her face quickly transformed to one poisoned by anger.

"What the fuck did you just do, Anton?" Eureka shot to her feet, grabbing Anton by the front of his shirt and forcing him up against the tree.

"What the hell is your problem?" Anton shoved her away. She stumbled backwards and nearly fell, but quickly righted herself.

"You killed him! He didn't do anything wrong!" Her eyes became glassy as she jabbed the air with a finger. "Anything! What if that had been Daddy?"

Anton and Fear looked to each other and busted up laughing, doubling over. A look of confusion fell over Eureka's face like a veil. She looked from Anton to Fear like, *What the fuck is wrong with these niggaz*?

"What the hell is so funny?" She asked, wanting in on the joke.

"Take a look," Fear handed her the binoculars. Operating the buttons and knob on the binoculars so that the lens would zoom in on the fellow that Anton had shot below.

Through the lens of the binoculars she saw him standing to his feet. He wore red paint on his forehead and on his chest. Anton had shot him with red paint balls. The angry man looked up at her and held up two middle fingers. Seeing this caused Eureka to start busting up laughing. She dropped the binoculars and rushed Anton, playfully punching on him. Fear and Anton were cracking up, having pulled a joke on Eureka.

"You dick! That wasn't funny!" She laughed as she playfully strangled his neck.

Fear came up behind Eureka and grabbed her about the waist, lifting her up off of her feet. She laughed and giggled, begging for mercy as Anton tickled her unmercifully. They all fell out on the ground, lying beside each other and laughing their heads off.

"You should have seen your face!" Anton said. "He was an innocent man! What if that had been Daddy?" He wiped a tear from his eye with a curled finger as it went to drip.

"You thought we were really finna do ol' boy, huh?" Fear chuckled.

"The way y'all were acting, yes." Eureka looked to him over her shoulder, grabbing him by his jaw and pulling him closer. Their lips danced and their tongues played with each other as they met with a kiss.

"That was nice," Fear told her.

"Nice?" Eureka looked at him with raised eyebrows like, *You better have something better to say about my kissing than nice.*

"Amazing, spectacular, astonishing, all of that shit," Fear smirked.

"That's more like it," she told him and kissed his lips.

"Come on, it's your turn." Fear got to his feet and pulled Eureka up to hers. He moved to dismantle the rifle and pack it back up. Guncase in hand, Fear walked off with Eureka and Anton beside him.

"We've gotta find us another mark for target practice before sunset, you game?" Fear hung his arm over Eureka' shoulders and looked to her.

"If you thought baby bro was somebody to watch out for, well, wait 'til you get a load of me." She draped her arm over Anton's shoulders and pulled him close.

Chapter Eighteen
The fourth week and last night

Fear was confident that Eureka and Anton were ready for the game now. He had given them vast amounts of knowledge in a short time and he was sure that they would utilize it. Their course wasn't over, though. Class would always be in session because the best teacher in life was experience. He could teach them all he wanted, but they had to go through it to be prepared for it on the next go around. Even so, he was without a reasonable doubt that his newest recruits were more than prepped to rise to their greatest challenge. And that was the dismantling of The West Coast Connection.

He'd provided them with years of service and loyalty and in the end they gave him their asses to kiss. It was a smack in the face to him and he'd be damned if he turned the other cheek. Nuh uh, they had him fucked up. Once it was all said and done, it would be he who had the last laugh while they lay bleeding in pools of their own blood.

The sun had partially settled and had given the sky a golden orange complexion. Fear had gone to rustle up dinner for the night while Eureka and Anton chopped logs for a fire. Eureka had done her part and was sitting off to the side on a stump. She wiped her sweaty forehead with a rag and took a long drink from her canteen as she watched her baby brother hack away at a lengthy log. Beat, Anton delivered one last strike to the log and rested the axe across the back of his shoulders. Gripping it at both ends, he leaned back as far as he could, face wrinkling and lips tightening. Once he heard his back cracking, he stood upright and took the canteen his sister was offering. He took a drink and passed it back to her. He then whipped a rag from out of his back pocket and wiped the streaks of sweat from his face.

"Man, I never knew that chopping wood could be this hard," Anton said, stuffing the rag into his back pocket.

"Yep, me and Daddy used to chop wood all of the time for a fireplace back in Arkansas when we visited Granny's house," Eureka told him. "My hands used to cramp and my back used to be yelling at me. Mannn, it was good times, though, ones I'll always hold onto."

Anton lifted the axe above his head, he was about to take another hack at the log when he saw a flicker of moment at the corner of his eye. He nearly shitted his jeans when he whipped around. His eyes bulged and his jaw dropped open as he took a step back. Eureka turned around wondering what he had seen. Frightened, she fell off of the stump and quickly scrambled to her feet.

The creature slowly emerged from the darkness of the mountains, moving slowly and stealthily. Its eyes seemed to glow in the night as it looked upon Eureka and Anton. Its belly grumbled with a low growl that was anxious to escape its powerful jaws. It licked its chops as it was hungry for its next meal. Anton stepped before Eureka and pulled her to the back of him. If he had to, he'd sacrifice himself in order for her to live. It was his duty. His father had always taught him that a man provided for and protected his family.

"Where did it come from?" Eureka asked, gripping the arm of Anton's jacket.

"I don't know, but we've gotta get up outta here," Anton told her, his eyes stuck on the mountain lion as it stalked forth. "On the count of three, we're gonna haul ass to the house, okay?"

"Yeah." Eureka nodded.

"Alright," Anton said. "One. Two. Three!"

The lion picked up on their sudden movement and went after them. He ran forward, leaping into the air. Its brows arched, its nose scrunched, and its jaws contracted, showcasing a set of bone crushing fangs. The feline's claws shot out of its paws ready to tear flesh from bone from its intended preys. Still airborne, the cat was about to come right down upon Eureka and Anton when…

Thud!

Ooomf!

Fear tackled the big cat and went rolling across the ground with it. He scrambled upon his feet and whipped around. The lion approached, swinging its razor sharp claws at his torso and slicing his clothes into ribbons. One swipe would have split his stomach open if it weren't for his jumping back. Still, the swipe was close enough to open up a gash on his side and make him grimace.

Fear closed his eyes as he grimaced, doubling over. The beast jumped on him and both of them rolled to the edge of the mountain top, tussling. The lion was in a weakened state, having been wounded by a gunshot from a hunter. On top of that, its ribs were showing so it was apparent that it hadn't eaten for a number of days. If it wasn't for that and the fact that Fear was in top physical shape, he wouldn't have stood the slightest chance in fending off the beast.

"Fearrrr!" Eureka shouted. "Oh my God, Anton, get the rifle!"

Anton darted for the assault rifle while Eureka looked on. Fear ended up on his back, gripping the wrists of the mountain lion with it snapping at his face. He turned his face to the side, squeezing his eyes shut and gritting his teeth. A second later and the animal would have bitten a chunk out of his head.

Fear peered over the edge and saw that it was a long fall down. All he could see were a crowd of trees and never ending darkness. Looking back at the mountain lion, he struggled against the stronger mammal and knew that he'd better react fast or he'd be a slab in the morgue. He pressed his boots into the lion's chest and kicked him off. While it was in midair, he scrambled over to a large stone. When he turned back around, the lion was running toward him. When it jumped, he slammed the stone into the side of its head, drawing a howl of pain from the beast. He knew that he'd hurt it pretty good, but it wouldn't be enough to keep it off of his ass.

While that was going on, Anton was hustling down the steps with the rifle. He'd just chambered a round into the weapon when he heard the lion howl out. He looked up to see it staggering to the side.

"Anton, shoot it!" Eureka yelled to him.

Anton lifted the lethal weapon. Looking through its scope, he saw the lion running after Fear. He tried to get the beast in his sight, but he couldn't because Fear was in the way.

"I can't get a clear shot!" Anton announced.

"What?"

"I said, I can't get a clear fucking shot!" Anton ran to the opposite side for a better angle. He cracked a grin once he saw that he could pick the creature off from his angle. He was about to take aim until he saw the lion leap into the air with a frightening roar. The grin fell from Anton's face when he saw the lion's shadow shade Fear. The killer had just picked up the axe from the ground when the beast came down upon him.

Aghhhhhhhhh!

Ahhhhhhhhhh!

"Noooooooooooo!" Eureka screamed, cupping her face as hot tears shot down her face back to back.

Fear and the lion lay face to face screaming into one another's faces. The lion's snapping at his face slowed as its eyes moved around lazily and it spewed warm blood from its mouth. The warm red river coated Fear's face. His brow furrowed and his nose wrinkled in hatred. He looked upon the savage animal with animosity, pulling the axe further up its belly. Its stomach split open and its entrails came spilling out in a heap, soaking Fear's torso. The lion went still and its eyes closed for what would be an eternity.

Eureka took her hands away from her face. She was in awe by what she'd seen. She had written the assassin off, thinking that tonight was to be his end. Anton came to stand beside her. Together they watched as Fear got to his feet, holding the lion by the neck of its pretty golden coat. He looked at his crimson stained axe and tossed it aside. Hunching down, he grabbed his kill by both ends. With a grunt, he lifted the creature high into the air, releasing a battle cry that echoed throughout the mountains. His challenger had been defeated and he was the victor. He was triumphant. Alvin Simpson was without a doubt, *Fearless*.

Fear threw the limp mountain lion aside and walked toward Eureka and Anton. He was completely drenched in blood. From his head to his waist was red and dripping into the dirt. He looked like some shit you'd see in a gory horror film. He ambled forward. His knees buckled along the way, but somehow he managed to keep from falling. Eureka and Anton took a step back. Anton stepped in front of her and was ready to put one through his brain. He looked crazy as hell with all of that blood covering him, his appearance was off-putting.

Fear stood before them breathing heavily with limp arms. Exhausted, his eyes rolled off into their corners and he collapsed to the ground. Eureka and Anton scrambled to his aid.

An hour later.

Using the First-Aid kit under the bathroom sink, Eureka packed Fear's wound until they were able to get back to the city and go to the hospital.

"My road dawg in there asleep?" Fear asked from where he sat on the floor sipping apple cider tea with a blanket draped over his shoulders. He was wearing a wife beater and cut off sweat pants. Once he'd come to, he took a shower and got dressed in something a little more comfortable. The tussle with the mountain lion had left him drained. Being appreciative of him saving their lives, Eureka cooked up the fish he'd caught along with some homemade garlic bread and a spinach salad. After the meal, Fear took up the space beside the fireplace and savored his apple cider tea.

"Yeah," Eureka said, closing the door shut behind her as she left the bedroom that Anton was asleep in. Her head was wrapped in a silk scarf and she was decorated in a Pistons basketball jersey and pajama pants. "He kept going on and on about you and that lion. He's never seen anything like that before. Hell, neither have I for that matter." She sat on the sofa across from him and picked up her cup of tea, taking a sip. "You're something else you know that?"

Fear grinned and said, "Nah, not something else, I'm *something better*."

"Talk that shit," Eureka grinned. She looked over to the crackling and popping of the burning fire inside of the fireplace. Its golden orange hue shined on her and Fear, casting their shadows on the wall behind them. She thought of something and looked in his direction. "You know what? I just thought of something. I don't really know anything about you. I mean, you're so secretive. You hardly ever say anything about yourself, tell me. Tell me about this dark, mysterious man with a heart of gold."

"What would you like to know, Ms. Jackson?" He took another sip of tea and sat the cup aside.

"I don't know, just tell me about you." Eureka said. "From the time you were a kid 'til now. I wanna know everything, so start at the beginning."

Fear stared into Eureka's eyes for a time before running his hands down his face and exhaling. He looked down between his legs and then back up at her.

"Alright, Ms. Jackson, I'ma give you Alvin Simpson in his entirety, raw and uncut." Fear went on to recount his life story to her. He didn't leave out anything. He gave her the truth, every layer of it. From his rich kid upbringing to his stint as a kingpin to his escapades as a hit-man. When he finished he was relieved. It was like he had confessed his sins to a Catholic priest.

"Wow," Eureka said, digesting his story.

It was an epic tale that would surely go down in the history books should it ever be written. She'd even gotten a glimpse of Constance's life through his eyes. Although she felt for her, she still didn't like her. You couldn't blame her though, the crazy bitch had tried to kill her. "I bet chu think I'm some kind of monster, huh?" Fear looked up at her, hoping he hadn't ruined the way she pictured him.

The look in his eyes was one of a child hoping to be accepted by his peers. She had never seen him like that before. She knew that he had a heart, but he didn't show it often. Now she could see it clearly, like it was sitting behind glass. At that moment she didn't see him as the ruthless hit-man that he was. There was a chink in his armor, a vulnerability that no one had seen, not even Constance. He wasn't just some killing machine. He was a person, with feelings and a heart. This was Alvin 'Fearless' Simpson in his rawest form.

Seeing him look away, Eureka knew that something had gotten to him, so she crawled over to him. She got down on her knees and cupped his face. When she turned his face to hers, she could see that his eyes had moistened. For the first time she saw that his soulless eyes had some signs of life to them.

"If you're a monster than we all are monsters," Eureka spoke sincerely. "Me, Ant, and Constance included. We've all done things that we'll have to live with for the rest of our lives." He turned his head and attempted to take her hand from his face, but she turned him back so he'd be facing her. "Look at me, Alvin," she called him by the name written on his driver's license. "You're the most beautiful person that I have ever had the fortune of getting to know. I wouldn't trade the time I've spent with you for a ticket to heaven. You hear me?" He nodded slightly.

They stared into one another's eyes for what seemed like forever and a day. Then it happened, the inevitable, they kissed. And even though it wasn't the first time, it definitely was the sweetest. While their lips and tongues did their rituals, their hands were occupied removing clothing. Once the last article of clothing was discarded, they stood on their knees, admiring one another's bodies. Although his was marred, it was still chiseled with rock hard abs, unique and marvelous in its own way. Scars and all, she still found him as desirable as he found her.

Her eyes traveled down his washboard stomach to his dick. His wang looked like a baby's arm trying to show off its bicep. She came toward him on her knees, licking and sucking on his perky nipples. Once she'd had her way with them, she paid extra special attention to the old bullet holes and stab wounds on his body, licking and sucking on them as well.

He closed his eyes and threw his head back as she pleasured him. Her actions made his stroke even harder, causing pre-cum to ooze out of its head. When she came back up, they kissed again, their lips lapping at one another. Their tongues slithered out and mingled as their mouths got to know each other on a personal level. He moved to turn her back to him, but she wouldn't budge. He looked into her eyes and she slightly shook her head no. She didn't want him to see what Kilo had done to her back for fear that it would appall him. He knew the story so he gave her a nod, letting her know that it was okay. Reluctantly, she gave in and gave him her back.

He allowed his palm to travel down the length of her back, over the keloid welts that would be there forever. Her scars were ugly, just as ugly as the world that they both lived in. But how could he not love and embrace them when they belonged to someone so beautiful, inside and out. Taking her by the shoulders, he placed kisses as soft as rose petals on her back. His delicate touch brought tears to her eyes and they fell from their corners, encircling her face. Their hearts, minds, and souls collided, becoming as one. At the same time they heard Maxwell's *This Woman's Work* playing as they had passionate sex.

I should be crying but I just can't let it show/ I should be hoping but I can't stop thinking

All the things we should've said that I never said/ All the things we should've done but we never did/All the things we should've given but I didn't/ Oh, darling, make it go, make it go away give me these moments/ Give them back to me/ Give me your little kiss.

Fear lay between Eureka's legs in the missionary position, propped up on his fists. They were locked in a deep kiss as he dug her out, plunging deeper and deeper with each stroke. He sucked on her neck as if it were a succulent tit, his rotation and rhythm never breaking as he grinded into her. She closed her eyes and her mouth shot open, unleashing a sensual shrill that he cut short when he sped up.

Tears flowed down her cheeks and she locked her ankles around his lower back. He pulled his head back, chin pointed toward the ceiling as he chased his orgasm. His head tilted down and his eyes peeled apart. The creases in his forehead deepened as he peered into Eureka's face. Seeing that she was crying he abruptly stopped.

"Are you okay? Do you wanna stop?" He asked, concerned, hoping that he hadn't hurt her.

She looked up at him, grinning and caressing the side of his face, tears still rolling. She mouthed no and shook her head. He tenderly kissed her lips, going about his stroking of her wet pussy, making it run hot with her juices. She whimpered his name softly and clawed at his back, breaking the skin, as he stirred against her mound. Feeling the sting of her scratches, he gritted his teeth and veins shown on his temples. His mouth fell open as he felt semen surging up his shaft and swelling his mushroom tip.

Her eyes were rolled and her mouth was hanging open, this was the face of a woman on the plane of ecstasy. Maxwell's *This Woman's Work* was still playing in their heads when he lifted up out of her and roared. The veins disappeared from his temples as he plastered her stomach with his babies. She squirted on the carpet soon after and turned her head, panting out of breath. She motioned for him to lie against her and he did. Both of their eyes closed, they listened to Maxwell's song as she stroked his head and they finally fell asleep.

The next day, in the evening

Fear stood in the lake facing Eureka and Anton. His hand was on the top of Anton's head while the other was holding his arm. Today was the day that the ceremony was taking place for them to be inducted into L.O.E. At that moment the baptism was taking place.

Fear gave a sermon that ended with, "Anton Leron Jackson, I hereby baptize you in unholy water," he dunked Anton into the water, quickly pulling him back up.

Excited about being born again, Anton embraced him and stepped aside. He watched as he placed his hand on top of Eureka's head and repeated the same sermon. A minute later, he was dunking her into the water and pulling her back up. It was official now. They were L.O.E. Killers. Assassins. From that day forth their worlds would never be the same.

Chapter Nineteen
That night.

The four weeks that Ronny spent locked up inside of that homemade prison felt more like eight weeks to him. The only thing that kept him sane was the thought of being able to hold his son again and tell his lady how much he loved them. If it weren't for his family he would have thrown in the towel and let Vladimir go ahead with his lynching.

It was the thought of leaving his family behind with no income and no one to protect them that kept him in the fight, otherwise he'd be hanging idly inside of a basement in some undisclosed part of the city. To him, for a man to give up on life knowing he had a family that depended on him was one of the most cowardly acts that he could commit. Ronny believed that was just as bad as taking the stand and ratting on your right-hand man. He couldn't let it go down like that, because if he did, he wouldn't be any better than his old man that ran out on his mom's when he was a kid.

Ronny passed his time working out, thinking, eating, and most importantly, thinking of a way to get the fuck from up out of there. He'd grown a wig of short dreads and nappy facial hair that looked like a shag carpet. If any of his friends or family were to see him now, there wasn't any way they would have been able to tell that it was him. He was sure of it.

Tonight was the night that Ronny planned on breaking out of his domicile. He had spent most of the night lying on the mattress with his hands clasped behind his head, staring up at the ceiling and listening to the Russians in the opposite room. They were smoking, drinking, and playing cards. They had been at it for a good four hours, behaving like a couple of college kids at a frat party. Once everything had fallen silent and he heard snores and snorts, old Ronny sprang into action. Tiptoeing to the door, he hunched over and listened closely for any sounds of movement. When he didn't hear anything, he slowly lifted the doorknob and twisted it. This was how he had heard Mikhail tell Nicolay to open the door.

The door would lock, but it could be easily opened by applying that slick little technique. Ronny mouthed *yes* when he heard the door click open. He pulled the door open as quietly as he could and stepped out. Standing in the doorway, he scanned over the bodies sprawled about in the room. Every last one of the Russians was fast asleep, sitting slumped in chairs or lying on mattresses on the floor with either handguns or assault rifles.

Ronny moved as silent as a grave, sneaking past the bodies on the floor and the ones on the chairs. He froze in place when he saw Nicolay switch to a comfortable position on the mattress on the floor and smack his lips. He froze where he was and closed his eyes and mouthed a prayer to the Lord that the man didn't wake up. Once Nicolay became still and started back snoring, he moved along, hearing snorts and farts coming from the sleeping men.

Ronny would speed walk and then creep across the room every so often. When he saw the front door was just fifteen feet away from him, he had to restrain a smile. His salvation was behind that very door. Excited, Ronny moved just a little too fast and ended up kicking over an empty Vodka bottle. The noise it made was loud enough to wake everybody up in the room, so he figured he would be busted.

He squeezed his eyes closed, waiting for the Russians to pounce on him. A time passed of nothing happening and he opened one eye and then the other. Both eyes open, he gave the room another sweep and found the Russians still fast asleep. He had just turned his head back around from scanning over the room when he heard a dog at his rear. He closed his eyes and swallowed hard, hoping that it was his imagination that was deceiving him, and that it wasn't some flea bag at his back. He slowly twisted his neck and looked over his shoulder. His eyes became as big as saucers when he found a Doberman there. The hostile hound was mad dogging him with its mouth in a sneer, showcasing it fangs.

Grrrrrrrrrrrrr!

It growled, ready to tear Ronny's narrow ass limb from limb. The dog had eaten the flesh of many different races of men, women, and even children, but he had never sampled any dark meat. Ronny knew that his movements had better be as careful as possible, otherwise that ass was going to be on the pooch's menu for a midnight snack. Cautiously, he turned around to the dog, speaking in a low tranquil voice.

"Easy, easy boy, Uncle Ron Ron's got a little something for ya." Ronny's hand eased inside of his pocket and pulled loose two old chicken bones he had saved from his last meal. He tossed the chicken at the dog's feet and it went to work on it. His growling had stopped, being that he was busy with the consumption of the chicken. Ronny sighed with relief and wiped the sweat from his forehead with the back of his hand. He turned around and met the eyes of Mikhail who was wide awake and staring dead at him. His finger was resting on the trigger of his Desert

Eagle and he looked like he was about ready to gift him a three round burst.

As soon as Mikhail made to move, Ronny kicked him hard across the face. The swift blow sent him spilling to the floor and woke up the rest of the Russians. They all grabbed their tools and looked around with hooded, sleepy eyes. When they saw Ronny, they looked alive and made to leave him lying still forever.

Ronny broke for the front door, running so fast that his heels were kicking his ass. Nearing the door, he threw all of his weight against the right side of it. The door broke free of its hinges and sent wood splinters hurling every-where. Ronny crashed to the ground, lying on top of the ruined door. Eye's narrowed and jaws clenched, he looked up from where he lay and took in the full scope of his surroundings. A barbwire gate surrounded the warehouse and beyond it, in all directions, there were miles and miles of paved ground. Ronny didn't know where he was going to run, but he knew that he'd better get out of there, espe-cially when he looked over his shoulder and saw the Russians and the Doberman closing the distance on him.

Ronny leaped to his bare feet and bolted toward the barbwire gate. He jumped forward and clung to it like Spider Man, climbing his way up. Making his way over, he got tangled up in the barbwire and fell, hitting the ground like a sack of potatoes.

"Arghhh! Ssssshit." He gritted, feeling the pricked metal ripping into his flesh. It hurt like a son of a bitch, but he had to get out of dodge if he wanted to live to tell someone this story. He looked up as he struggled to get free of the barbwire which was still cutting into his skin. He saw the hound barking at him and the Russians lifting their weapons to shoot him. They were about to turn him into a fresh cadaver, but Mikhail stopped them with a wave of his hand.

"No, Vladimir wants him alive," he told the others.

With that said, Mikhail moved to unlock the barbwire gate so that they could pursue Ronny. By the time Ronny got untangled from the barbwire he was sliced up and bleeding. He scrambled to his feet and took off running as fast as he could and as far as his feet would carry him. He didn't even bother to look back, he just kept running until he couldn't hear the voices of the Russians or the Doberman's barking.

Ronny's running slowed to a jog until he eventually stopped. He hunched over with his palms on his knees, breathing hard. He looked over his shoulder and the Russians weren't anywhere in sight. Figuring that he should put as much distance between himself and his foreign kidnappers as he could, he took off running again. He made it a half mile before he came to a stop, holding a hand above his brow and looking ahead at a pair of florescent orbs heading in his direction. He smiled and giggled seeing that it was a limousine that was approaching.

Ronny jumped up and down, flailing his arms and shouting for the driver of the limousine to stop as he drove past. The vehicle came to a stop on the side of the road and the driver side window came down. The driver stuck his hand out and waved Ronny over. Ronny jumped up and swung on the air he was so happy. He jogged over to the car, opened up the backdoor and slid in on the plush leather seat. Pulling the door shut, he turned around to thank the driver and met the backseat passenger. He could have died on the spot when he saw who was sitting next to him.

Thunk! Thunk! The door locks locked with child protection when Ronny tried to open the passenger side door.

"Well, look what the wind blew in, what a coincidence. I was just on my way to come get you," Vladimir smiled as he swirled the dark liquor around in his glass. "We're gonna go looking for a fat back stabbing piece of shit, and guess who's going to be our guide." He continued, not waiting for him to respond. "That's right, *you.*" He pointed with the index finger of the hand he held the glass in.

"I—I—" Ronny stammered. He was so choked up that he couldn't get it out.

"Please, shhhhhh," he said with a finger to his lips. "Don't say another word. My daughter just graduated from college today and I'm overwhelmed with joy. See," he looked him dead in the eyes with a creased forehead and scrunched nose.That was hardly an expression a man claiming to be overwhelmed with joy would have. Although his daughter's graduation was of the utmost importance to him, so was his dealing with Ronny. His reputation meant everything to him so the infraction that Malvo committed had to be addressed.

"So the last thing I want is whatever bullshit that's about to roll off of your tongue to do is succeed in tainting my happiness. Now. while I may be okay as at the moment, if you continue talking, I'm gonna draw this knife from my back pocket and jimmy your fucking eyeballs out of your skull. Do we understand each other?" Ronny nodded his head rapidly. "Good."

Vladimir's eyes darted to something silver and shiny on his waistline. He snatched it free and closely examined it, wonder lines forming across his forehead.

Ronny had made a shank out of the tin pan he was given to eat out of back at the homemade prison. It was long and just as thick as a butcher's knife.

"It's—It's—"

"Its history," Vladimir let down the window and threw the shank outside before letting it back up again.

Seeing a van speeding down the street, the Russian shot-caller alerted his chauffer and told him to garner the approaching vehicle's attention. The driver did as his boss ordered and blinked his headlights twice. The van slowed down and pulled upon the side of the limousine. Its driver side window descended and Mikhail came into view.

"Where are you going?" Vladimir inquired.

"Our prisoner got away; we've got to find him," he answered.

"Your prisoner is right here, shithead," he grabbed Ronny by the back of the neck and pulled him into view of the back window so that Mikhail could see him. A smile spread across Mikhail's face once he saw Ronny. Vladimir released Ronny's neck and he sat back in the seat. The Russian gangster then focused his attention on Mikhail saying, "We're going to find Malvo and give him his just due."

"Yes," Mikhail smiled fiendishly, rubbing his hands together.

"Retrieve the other vehicles and follow me."

"You got it, boss."

The van turned around and headed back in the direction of the warehouse with the limousine following closely behind. Vladimir threw back the last of the dark liquor in his glass and poured up another. Setting the Louie XIII down, he held up the glass and admired the liquor that it held.

"The time has come for you to meet with Death, Mr. Malvo, and guess who's made the appointment." He smirked and took a sip from the glass.

****

Vladimir's limousine pulled upon the dimly lit block, followed by two black Mercedes Benzes. The doors of the Benz's opened and his men spilled out, taking in their surroundings and keeping their hands near the weapons stashed on their waistlines. They surrounded the limousine to make sure their boss was well guarded. The backdoor was thrown open and Ronny stepped out first. The men pulled him in close to them so that he couldn't just take off running. Vladimir stepped out next, sticking the cigar back in his mouth and re-buttoning his suit. Nicolay closed thedoor shut behind him then joined the rest of the men.

"Alright, lead the way," Vladimir told Ronny.

Ronny started off toward his house with Nicolay and Mikhail on each side of him, and the rest of the lot bringing up the rear. Ronny had a small black leather book at every trap house and address under Malvo's name. The plan was to raid every spot and residence until they found the drug dealer or create enough chaos to draw him out. Ronny would act as their ghetto tour guide. He would gain them easy access to the traps and help them raise enough hell to flush his ex-boss out into the open so that they could eradicate him.

"If he tries to run, cut 'em down," Vladimir said in a hushed tone to one of his men as they collectively moved up the sidewalk. The man nodded his head and stared at the back of Ronny's head, hoping that he tried something so he could put something in his back.

Ronny stepped to the front door and cleared his throat before he knocked.

This may be a nigga's last hurrah 'cause I know these mothafuckaz are gonna kill me once they find out that I'm not giving the homie up. I just wanna kiss my girl and hold my son one last time and tell 'em I love 'em.

"It's Ronny, boo, open up!"

"Ronny? Oh my God, thank you God!"

Hearing the locks being undone and the chain coming loose from across the door caused Ronny's heart to thump. A smile stretched across his face as he was anxious to see the woman of his dreams, live and in the flesh, even if it was for one last time. The door swung open and Antoinette stood before him cradling a shotgun. The side of her head bore stitches and she looked stressed, despite the smile she wore. She was so happy to see her man that she hadn't even thought about lying the shotgun down. She had completely forgotten it was in her clutches.

Ronny and Antoinette stood there, staring at each other for what seemed like forever. Suddenly, her eyes pooled with tears and her bottom lip shook. He caught her as she jumped into his arms. He carried her into the house as she lovingly embraced him, planting like a million kisses all over his face. He let her down and she kissed him hard like he was a soldier that had been drafted for the war and she didn't know whether he was coming back or not. She then pulled away and hugged him tightly. Her face pressed against his chest and she cried until her heart was content.

"You miss a nigga, huh?" Ronny cracked a smile, staring down at the top of her head.

"Yes. We thought we weren't ever going to see you again," she spoke with a shaky voice, tears steadily pouring. She pulled her head back and for the first time she noticed Vladimir and his men at the door. Worry lines went across her forehead as she wondered what was going on. "Ronny, who are they? Are you in some sort of trouble?"

"No. Baby, I'm okay," a grinning Ronny combed his hands through her thick braids. "These actually saved my life and just wanted to make sure I got home alright."

"Really? Well, what happened?" she asked concerned.

"I'll explained it all later, lover." He frowned, remembering the stitches on the side of her head and the shotgun she'd came to the door with. "But, uh, you mind explaining to me what happened with you." She noticed him staring at the stitches on the side of her head. She placed a hand over it and turned her back on him as if she was embarrassed.

"It's nothing, I'm alright," she lied. "Just got into a lil' scuffle is all."

Ronny grabbed her by the arm and turned her around to him. He looked into her eyes and he could see that what had happened was more serious than she was letting on. "You opening the door with a shotgun looking like hell, I know there's something more to it than a little scuffle," Ronny told her with a dead serious face. "Tell me what's wrong, boo, let cho man know what's cracking with you."

Suddenly, Antoinette dropped the shotgun as she began trembling all over. She broke down crying and falling into Ronny's arms. She released all of the hurt, the turmoil, the aggression and heartache she'd held inside since the rape had happened. Seeing the love of his life like this fucked Ronny up, at that moment he hated himself for not having been there to protect her from whatever had happen. He wished he could zap all of her pain away so she wouldn't have to bare it. Instead, he hugged her into him with the tightness of an anaconda, rubbing her back and kissing her head.

"It's okay, baby, I'm here now. Everything is going to be all right." He assured her. "Now tell hubby what happened."

"You don't wanna know."

"I do wanna know, boo, you're my rib," he told her some real shit. "Somebody hurts what's mine they gotta answer to me, okay?"

"Uh huh."

"Good. Now what happened?"

"I—I—I was raped."

The revelation made his eyes snap wide open and his jaw drop. He looked like a hot piece of coal had been jammed up his asshole. Anger quickly procured his face and he held her at arm's length. Staring into her face he could see that she was in total disarray. He had never seen her like this before. What had happened had fucked her up royally and she may never be the same again.

"What? When? Who did it?" He rattled off question after question.

"It was— It was—Malvo, baby." He was stunned.

Hearing that the man he had praised as if he could walk on water had violated his soul mate shook his world to the core. He felt like someone had ripped out his heart, threw it down, and allowed a soccer team to use it in their game.

"I wanna know what happened, from start to fin-ish." He began pacing the floor, running a hand down his face. He couldn't believe it was true. Not his homie, not his dawg, not his round, his mothafucka nigga if he didn't get no bigger. It was the truth and the truth hurt.

Antoinette wiped her face dry and balled up the Kleenex. She swallowed hard and took the time to gather her wits before she recounted the story to Ronny. Ronny bummed a cigarette from off of one of Vladimir's men and continued his pacing of the floor, taking tokes of the square. He listened contently and once she was done, he mashed out his cigarette. He then picked up a chair and threw it at the 42' flat-screen, shattering the black tinted glass. From there he went on a rampage tearing the living room apart until he was down on his hands and knees, exhausted. He looked up from where he was, bloodshot eyes spilling tears down his cheeks.

RJ came running from the back having heard all of the crashing going on in the living room. Antoinette had told him to hide somewhere in the house when she heard someone at the door. She was in fear that it was Malvo again and she'd planned to blow his ass away.

"Daddyyyy!" RJ ran toward his father, but his mother snatched him up before he could reach him. She knew that Ronny wasn't in the mood to handle his son right then.

"Not now baby, give your daddy a minute, okay?" She kissed him on the cheek.

"Okay," RJ replied, staring at his father eerily. From the look on his face he could tell that he was going through something.

"See, this is what I have been trying to tell you, Ronny," Vladimir mashed out his cigar in an ashtray on the coffee table. "Malvo is a snake." He grabbed him under his arm and pulled him to his feet. He cupped his face with his hands and looked deep into his eyes. "Look what he's done to your family, look how he played me. When will it stop, my friend, huh? I'll tell you, when that filthy varmint is gone and buried."

Ronny nodded in agreement. He hadn't believed Vladimir when he told him that Malvo had sent him to cop with counterfeit money. He honestly thought that he was lying and that he wanted his to kill his big homie for another reason. Whatever that reason was, he didn't give a shit because he wasn't about to rat his man out, under any circumstances. It was hard for him to believe that the man that had been a father to him had sent him on a mission that he may not come back from. If Vladimir killed him his girl would have been left to raise their son alone. The more he thought about the situation that he was put in, the angrier it made him, Malvo was one black hearted mothafucka.

Ronny had been a stalwart soldier in Malvo's army and he would have laid down his life in his honor without a second thought. So to find out that he had squatted and taken a shit on him cut him deeper than the sharpest sword. Malvo had to pay, there wasn't any ifs, ands, or buts about it. He was going to be lying face up in a coffin soon. Real soon.

Ronny stepped around Vladimir and kneeled down to his son. He pulled him close for a warm embrace and kissed him on the side of his head as he held him. When he tried to break their embrace the little boy wouldn't let go. He held him tightly as he silently sobbed, the tears trickling from his eyes, hitting the nape of his father's neck. He'd missed the hell out of him and was glad that he was home. It was just too bad that their little reunion was about to be broken up. Ronny broke his son's embrace and looked into his tear streaked face.

"Aye, what I tell you about crying? You a big boy now, junior, and what big boy's don't do?"

"Big boys don't cry," he answered, wiping his face with the back of his hand.

"That's right," Ronny told him. "Now I'm gonna be gone for a lil' while and I want chu to take care of your momma while I'm gone. Can you do that for me, son?" RJ nodded yes as he continued to wipe his face. "Okay. While I'm gone, you're the man and you're in charge. You hear me?" He nodded. "Let me hear you say it, then."

"While you're gone, I'm the man and I'm in charge."

"That's right." He pulled RJ in and hugged him again, kissing the top of his head. "I'm the king and you're the prince, take care of the queen and protect the castle, alright?"

"Alright, Daddy."

"Good boy." He playfully patted him on the ass and stood erect, approached his girl. He kissed her deep and passionately before breaking there embrace. "I gotta go baby, take care of our son. If I don't make it back, you raise him right and teach 'em to be a better man than his daddy."

"Wait a minute, Ronny. Where are you going?" She grabbed his arm, stopping him.

He turned around, looking her dead in her eyes. "Where do you think?"

When he said that, tears came back in full force, drenching her cheeks and running over her lips. She wished she would have kept her mouth shut. She knew how he was built and where he was willing to take it behind his loved ones. If the next time she saw him was on a cold metal table in the morgue, she'd never forgive herself.

Seeing Ronny bending down to pick up the shotgun, Vladimir's men drew down on him. They were about to pollute the living room with gun smoke until the Top Dawg halted them with a wave of his hand. Ronny curled the shotgun into his hands and turned around to Vladimir, racking that bitch. Fires were ablaze in his pupils and murder had tainted his heart, infecting his blood stream.

His eyes took in all of the men standing before him and he said, "You want Malvo? Fine, I'm gonna help you find him, but I want to do the honors of killing 'em." Vladimir nodded. "Alright, let's go find this cock sucker." He made his way out of the door with the Russians bringing up his rear.

Wherever Malvo was in the world, he'd better be prepared for Ronny because he was coming, and all of hell was coming with him.

Chapter Twenty

Fuck bein' on some chill shit/ We go 0 to 100 nigga, real quick/They be on that rap to pay the bills shit/ And I don't feel that shit, not even a little bit/Oh, Lord know yourself, know your worth, nigga/ My actions been louder than my words, nigga/How you sold out, but still so down to earth, nigga/Niggas wanna do it, we can do it on they turf, nigga.

Fear, Eureka, and Anton rode in the van, spitting Drake's lyrics as if they'd written them themselves. They grooved around in their respective seats, pointing fingers in one another's faces as they recited the words to each other. Once the song slowed down and switched to the next beat, they settled down, slightly bobbing their heads as they listened to the Canadian rapper's vocals.

Anton leaned back in his seat and stared out of the window, watching the streets fly past him. Something caught his eye and he sat up, looking alive as he peered closely. A grin etched across his face just as the van stopped at a red stop-light.

"Ohhh, shit, look!" He pressed his finger against the glass. Eureka and Fear looked to where he was pointing. A shabbily dressed lady was hauling ass down the street with cash register in her hands. An older Mexican man was on her trail, holding a baseball bat above his head, ready to beat the brakes off of her.

"Man, if he catches ol' girl it's over," Fear predicted.

"If so, then that's what her ass get for stealing," Eureka added her two cents. "There's some scandalous, trifling mothafuckaz out in L.A, I'll tell you."She shook her head and plucked the roach end of the blunt out of the ashtray. She'd stuck it between her lips and was about to light it when…

"Reka, that's mommy!"Anton blurted.

Eureka snatched the roach out of her mouth and whipped around in her seat, thinking that she'd heard her baby brother wrong."That's mommy!" Anton said again, reaching into the hatch. When he came back around he was holding the silenced rifle.

"Ant, hold on." Fear turned around, trying to grab him before he could get out, but he was already on his way. Fear threw the van in park and Eureka slid into the driver's seatto take over. While she was bringing the van around, Fear was in hot pursuit on Anton's heels.

Giselle fell to the ground and dropped the cash register. It made a ding sound and the drawer shot out, spilling its dollar bills and coins. The Mexican man, who was dressed in a T-shirt and apron, had just caught up with her. He kicked her hard in her side and spat something at her in Spanish as he lifted his baseball bat to exact out his own justice.

Evil lurked in Anton's eyes as he sped walked toward the Mexican man, chambering a copper missile shaped bullet into the weapon. His nose was scrunched up and his lips were peeled back into a sneer like he was about to spit juice from chewing tobacco. He was so focused on the Mexican man that was about to beat his mother with the baseball bat that everything failed to exist to him. He couldn't hear the traffic or Fear running up behind him screaming and waving his arms.

Anton stopped where he was and took aim at the Mexican man; his sight was set dead on his chest. His heart beat in slow motion and he heard it thumping at the pace of a snail inside of his ears. *Thump, thump, thump, thump.* He could even hear his breathing. *Haa, haa, haa, haa*! He heard the click of the metal trigger as he pulled back on it. It sounded like the long metal latch that you lifted from a large wooden door inside of a castle.

As soon as he pulled the trigger back, the barrel of the rifle was lifting up in the air, letting off a burst of fire. Anton was zapped back to reality right there on the spot. When he looked up he saw Fear pulling the rifle from his hands.

"Slow your roll, family, we got an audience." He swept a crooked around there area. Anton turned in a circle, looking. People had stopped their cars to see what he was about to do. There were even some that had stopped walking and were now focused on him. "Come on," he tapped Anton and they started for the Mexican man. He'd dropped his baseball bat when the bullet went off and backed up against the building. He looked scared as shit with his bug eyes and slackened jaw, head whipping back and forth, wondering what was about to happen to him.

"I suggest you beat it, hombre, unless you wanna ass full of some hot shit." Fear spat with a hard-face. With that said, the Mexican man broke ass back to his liquor store. Eureka pulled to a screeching stop behind Fear and he tossed the rifle inside of the van through the window. With Anton's help, he pulled Giselle to her feet. His brow furrowed once he saw her face. She looked a hot mess and she smelled of vomit. Her hair was matted to her sweaty face, her lips were chapped and white stuff had formed at the corners of her mouth. "*This* your moms?" Fear frowned, wanting to be sure. He knew that their mother was strung out, but not that bad. "Alright, let's get her to the van and take her to the house."

Anton hopped into the backseat of the van and slammed the door shut. His face balled up once he got a whiff of the dried vomit clinging to his mother like the scent of a perfume. The stench was overwhelming, but he'd brave through it for the love of his mother.

"I'm sick, I need to get right," Giselle cried and complained, holding her stomach.

"We've gotta get some dope for her," Eureka looked to Anton.

"Dope?" Anton pulled his shirt off of his nose. "Reka, we can't give mommy no dope, that's enabling her."

"Ant, she's sick, she could die," she told him over her shoulder. "I don't wanna give it to her either, but we don't have a choice right now."

"I know where we can get some," Fear told her as he pulled off.

"Okay," Eureka responded. "I'm not tryna get her high, just tryna make sure that she's all right."

Anton settled back in the seat and pulled his shirt over his nose. He scooted beside his mother and tried his best to comfort her on their ride back to Fear's house.

Thirty minutes later

Giselle was feeling relaxed, having gotten her 'medication'. Eureka released the tourniquet from around her arm and pulled the syringe from her vein. She then capped it and passed it to Anton to throw away.

"Thank you, baby, you've become quite the expert at this," Giselle proclaimed. Her eyes were closed and a smile was plastered on her face.

Eureka placed the items Giselle used to shoot up with inside of a worn, brown leather case. She was disgusted after having given her mother a shot of dope. Although she did it to save her life, it didn't stop her from feeling bad about it.

"Mommy, *please*," she zipped up the worn, leather case and laid it upon the coffee table. "And what happened with you and Aunt Debbie? Why are you living out on the streets?"

"Bitch kicked me outta the house," Giselle shook her head as her eyes misted. She turned her head not wanted her kids to see her crying.

"What was it about, Ma?" Eureka asked, concerned.

"Here you go, Ma," Anton gave her a ball of paper towels when he returned from the kitchen.

Giselle wiped her eyes and nose. Sniffling, she addressed her daughter. "Over some dick, that no good nigga of hers, Keith. He tried to sex me, but I said no, and he told Debbie that I was tryna fuck on 'em."

"It's alright, Ma, don't worry about it. We're here now," Eureka rubbed her mother's back.

Anton kneeled down to his mother and placed a hand on her knee. Looking up into her eyes he said, "Ma, gimmie Debbie's address and tell me what this Keith looks like."

"Ant, let that shit go," Eureka laid a hand on his shoulder.

"Fuck that," he stood erect. "That nigga made Mommy feel some type of way, now I gotta show 'em where it's real at."

"Ant, let. It. Go." She gave him a stern look that he read as, *Just drop it*. "Come on, Ma. Let's get chu outta these clothes and into the tub."

She pulled her to her feet and helped her up the staircase. Turning at the corner of the hallway, Giselle looked over her shoulder into Fear's bedroom. She saw him down on his knees inside of the closet. She didn't know exactly what he was doing, but she knew he was sifting through an in-floor digital safe.

Fear's cell phone rang. He pulled it out of his pocket, pressed answer, and brought it to his ear.

"Hello?" He said itas he closed the safe, letting the flap of carpet fall over it. A smile formed on his lips as he listened to what the caller was saying.

****

Water so dirty that it looked like it belonged inside of a sewer swirled down the drain. Eureka helped her half sleep mother out of the bathtub and draped a towel over her head and body.

"Come on, Mommy," Eureka grabbed her mother's hand. She was about to lead her to the bedroom to get dressed when Fear darkened the doorway. Eureka gave him a smirk and he shot her one back.

"What's got chu with all thirty-twos?"

"I got that call I've been looking for," he answered. "Come on. We've gotta roll."

"Wait a minute, let me put Mommy in bed."

"Bed?" Fear gave her a disapproving look.

"Yeah, is there a problem?" Her forehead succumbed to wrinkles.

He pulled her out of the bathroom and into the hallway, speaking in a hushed tone.

"No disrespect, but your mother is a dope fiend," Fear told her. "I don't want her up and wandering around my house."

"Look at her," Eureka began. "She's as tired as a runaway slave. She not gonna be wandering around here, how long do you expect to be gone?"

"30 minutes to an hour."

"Shit. We'll be back way before she wakes back up," she told him. "I mean, look at her. She's been out in the streets for God knows how long and she's been fighting that monkey for at least a couple of days. She's too exhausted to be moving about up in here."

Fear looked to Giselle with the towels draped over her head and body, she was nodding off to sleep on her feet.

Fear exhaled as he ran a hand down his face. He looked to the side and then back up at Eureka. "Alright, but Ant's gonna stay here with her. Get her dressed and in bed, then meet me down stairs in the car."

She beamed brightly, holding his face as she kissed him twice on the lips. Fear headed back down the hallway while Eureka took her mother inside of the bedroom to get dressed.

****

"Me and your sister are about to make this run to meet this dude," Fear said as he entered the living room.

A peeved expression crossed Anton's face. He wasn't trying to kick it with Mom's, he wanted to roll with the crew.

"Mannn, why I gotta stay?" Anton complained.

"'Cause I said so, lil' nigga," Fear told him. "I'ma chief and you are an Indian. Now let me hit that." He took the blunt that was pinched between his fingers. He'd taken a couple of drags when he saw Eureka coming down the staircase.

"You ready?" She asked.

"Yeah, let's roll." He passed the blunt back to Anton and headed for the door.

"Don't wait up," Eureka pecked Anton on the side of the face and made her exit.

With Eureka and Fear gone, a disappointed Anton mashed out the blunt and headed up stairs to take a leak.

Anton had just pulled out his meat to relieve himself when he saw a shadow approaching. Before he could turn around something went crashing into the back of his head. Everything went black and the tiled floor came slamming into his face. Giselle dropped the broken half of the lamp to the floor. She stood over her son, looking over him. She hadn't seen him so peaceful since he was a baby.

"Sorry, baby boy," she kneeled down to him and kissed his head, caressing the side of his face.

She left the bathroom, pulling the door closed behind her and darted into Fear's bedroom. She flipped on the light switch and took a quick scan of the bedroom. Spotting the dresser, she darted over to it and sifted through it until she found her prizes, a wad of money and a zip-loc of heroin. Giselle smiled and jumped for joy, like she'd been asked to the prom by her crush.

She closed the drawer shut using her hip. Turning around and stuffing the money and zip-loc into her bra, she froze where she was, seeing the closet door. She licked her lips like a lizard, knowing that there was something precious behind it. What would be her prize? Maybe it was jewelry, or maybe cash. She didn't know for sure, but she was about to find out.

****

Giselle walked down the street pushing a shopping cart, occasionally taking a gander under the blanket that Fear's digital safe was hidden under. Although it had taken her sometime she had successfully pried it out of its prison in the floor. It had taken her a little over an hour to get it down stairs and loaded into the shopping cart, but she was sure she'd be handsomely rewarded for all of her troubles.

Giselle was convinced that there was something as sweet as a mother's love inside of the safe and she couldn't wait to get her unkempt hands on it. She felt like it was her birthday that day, being that she had found $2, 500 dollars in the hit-man's sock drawer and a small zip-loc of heroin. She had thought about cutting Debbie in on her come up, but quickly tossed the thought out of her mind once she thought about her throwing her out on her ass because she thought that she was sex playing her dude.

Left out in the cold, she was forced to suck and fuck most nights to feed her habit and keep a roof over her head. Even though that was something she'd done on a regular to feed her need, she felt like she shouldn't have had to go back to doing it on the account that she had a friend with a perfectly good place for her to lay her head and get high. Debbie had slighted her and hurt her feelings, so the only way she was getting anything from her was if she pried it from her cold dead hands.

Nahhh, she shook her head as she gave it some thought, *to hell with Debbie and that nigga Butch.* She was going to take the safe over to her Aunt Trisha's, who didn't live too far from Fear's house in the city of Downey, and roll it up inside of her garage. She had an assortment of tools that her husband had left behind in his wake that she could use to try to open the safe up. If it turned out that the safe didn't bear fruit like she thought, she was sure her aunt would let her hole up at her place for a time. All she would want was her company and a six pack of cold-ones. Hell, she could swing that and have mad money left to support her habit.

I wonder how much is inside of this mothafucka, she stole another peek under the blanket that the safe was hiding beneath. *It could be thousands, millions, billions even. Cool it bitch, you're getting beside yourself. It couldn't be that much money in there.* Giselle shook her head and cackled, thinking of how she was letting her imagination run wild. Whatever it is in here, his ass won't miss it. I'm sure of that, especially with how fancy that place was furnished.

One thing is for sure, that lil' buff ass nigga is gon' be mad as shit when he comes home and finds this baby missing, she patted the safe and licked her lips.*From the lil' time I spent with them I could tell that he's gotta thang for Eureka so I won't have to worry about him retaliating for fear of falling out of her favor. My baby girl will soothe the sting of his loss though, she'll wanna look out for her momma. That's my baby, my Reka.*

Giselle pulled the folded up $2,500 dollars out of her dingy, linty bra and kissed it lovingly. She couldn't believe her luck. The Lord of the heroin Fiends saw it fit to smile on her cruddy ass again. Although his blessings were few and far between, this one was unexpected and welcome. Giselle stashed the money back inside of her bra and pulled the zip-loc from her tattered jean pocket. A smile spread across her face as she stared down at her ashy palm at what she deemed as the Heavenly Father's greatest creation. Giselle shoved the zip-lock inside of her pocket and continued to push the shopping cart up the block.

Feeling a cool breeze brush against her cheek and disturb her loose strands of synthetic hair, she pulled the drawstrings of her hoodie and enclosed the hood around her head. Giselle made her way down the sidewalk, speed walking up the street in a rush to get to her aunt's house so she could crack the safe open and see what fortune it possessed. She was as eager as a kid was to open his gifts on Christmas morning.

Giselle felt a presence at her rear and snuck a glance over her shoulder. To her dismay a car with limo tinted windows was creeping up behind her. Sensing trouble arising, she made hurried steps, pushing the shopping cart faster up the street. When she picked up speed so did the creeping vehicle. Before she'd realized it, she was racing down the block with the shopping cart ahead of her. Although she was covering her fair share of ground, swiftness couldn't beat a car's acceleration.

Giselle was hastily approaching an alley, she was just about to turn inside when the car swung into her line of vision, cutting off her path. Giselle abandoned the shopping cart and hauled ass up the street like her heels were ablaze. The driver side door of the vehicle swung open and the driver stepped out, dressed in all black attire. The driver held up a long bamboo stick, aimed, and blew hard into it.

Once the hot air hit the object inside, it sounded like a spitball going through a straw. A tainted dart whizzed through the air and stabbed Giselle in the back of her neck. Her running slowed to a trot as she began to feel sluggish and light headed. She stopped and leaned against a building, pulling the dart from the back of her neck. She looked at the dart and saw that it was tranquilized.

Giselle let the dart fall to the sidewalk and turned around. She saw three separate images of the driver approaching her with the bamboo stick in his hand. Giselle turned around to run and it felt like she was moving in place. She fell to the sidewalk and crawled ahead, blacking in and out of consciousness as she climbed on the ground.

Suddenly, her eyes involuntarily shut and her head fell against the concrete. She was out cold.

The driver tucked the bamboo stick into the small of his back and scooped an unconscious Giselle into his arms. He then stuck her into the backseat of the car he'd stalked her in, hopped into the driver seat and pulled away from the scene.

Chapter Twenty One

Fear and Eureka came waltzing out of Starz strip club in the city of Gardena off of Rosecrans Avenue. Following behind them was a short box head nigga by the name of Lavonte. Lavonte was a light skinned kid with a pencil thin mustache and a receding hairline that lead to small corn-rows that barely reached his neck. He was dressed in gold glasses with maroon lenses and matching silk button-down shirt. His hand was curled around a glass of something that had him as tipsy as a one legged horse. Lavonte walked Fear and Eureka over to their car. He hunched down to the driver side window just as Fear closed the door shut and fired up the car.

"That info is good, big dog, trust." Lavonte tapped his fist to his chest.

"We'll see." Fear replied.

"Alright then." He patted the roof of the car and made to walk away when he was called back. He turned around and raised his eyebrows like *What's up?* Looking as serious as a gunshot wound to the head, Fear looked into his eyes and said, "If this fruit you gave me rottens before I'm able to eat it…expect to bury your entire family." The grin melted from Lavonte's face as he watched Fear drive off.

****

Meanwhile in Watts

Loc Dog played the shadows across the courtyard of the Jordan Downs projects watching the crack heads copping and bopping amusingly. He smiled like a proud father seeing his kid walk across the stage at his college graduation. He took a .40 oz of Olde English malt liquor to the head, guzzling it. Bringing the bottle down from his lips, he wiped his mouth with the back of his hand and thought back to what had driven him to slinging out of the projects in the first place.

He and Malvo had been locked into a war over the past few weeks. The streets had become so hot that both parties had to shut down their traps. He had taken his workers to the Jordan Downs projects and used the tenements there as home-base for his operation, turning them into The Carter building out of the New Jack City movie. It wasn't long before he fell out of favor of the residents but he didn't give a rat's ass as long as he could make a dollar. The only thing that got him was how Malvo and his people had gone into hiding. He couldn't really blame them because they were losing far more soldiers than he was in the war. The way he saw it homeboy realized that he wasn't built and folded.

"Niggaz is soft, cuz." Loc Dog chuckled and shook his head. Screwing the cap on his 40 oz, he headed across the courtyard to check on his traps.

****

Malvo sat slumped in the confinement of his truck on the dimly lit block across the street from the Jordan Downs projects. Seeing that he was losing in his ongoing war with Loc Dog, he decided to fallback to find a strategy to defeat his nemesis. Having ended the call he'd just made, he looked at the time on his cell phone's screen and giggled. Loc Dog was in for a big surprise tonight, a real big surprise. Twenty minutes after the O.G had closed the door of the unit he had entered, police cruisers swarmed the projects. Moments later a police helicopter came soaring across the sky, shining its bright light down on the tenement he'd just entered. Malvo watched as the police broke down the door of the unit that Loc Dog was in. A few minutes later he, Goose, One-Punch and a few of his Baby Locs were escorted out in handcuffs. He laughed hardily, tears dancing at the corners of his eyes as he slapped his knee. He had finally gotten that mothafucka, he had finally beaten him. Seeing the police leave the unit with an AK47, a couple of pistols, and a few freezer bags of crack, he smiled and shook his head. His rival was washed up. This was his third strike so he'd never see the streets again. When he saw his face the boy looked sick, like he was about to throw up.

Malvo was one of the cleverest dudes that had ever been pushed out of a woman's womb. He called the precinct and told them that Loc Dog and his people had a little white boy and girl held hostage inside of the apartment that he'd forced into prostitution and child pornography. With a call like that being placed he knew for sure that The Boys were going to come flying down there…and they did. Feeling triumphant, Malvo fired up his truck and drove off.

****

"Nigga didn't waste any time selling his people out." Eureka shook her head, thinking back to Lavonte, Arkane's cousin. "All so he could have his wife to himself, where the fuck is the loyalty?"

"In this world loyalty is as mythical as leprechauns and wizards." Fear answered.

"Ain't that the truth?"

"These niggaz gone feel my pain," Fear said scowling, rolling down the block. "We're going after the whole lot of 'em. We're gonna dismantle The West Coast Connection one man at a time."

"What the hell?" Eureka frowned as they pulled into the driveway. Anton staggered out of the house holding the back of his head, appearing disoriented.

Fear hit the hazards, the AC, and knocked on the dashboard. The stash spot shot out displaying his fully loaded .9mm automatic. He didn't have to cock that thang because it was already ready to go. Throwing the Charger into park, he threw the door open and hopped out of the car. He made a mad dash up the steps to Anton.

"What happened? Someone's in the house?" Fear rattled off question after question.

Wincing, Anton shook his head and said, "No—mommy—," he grimaced in pain. "She knocked me out cold."

"Why? For what?" Fear asked confused. Before Anton could answer, a light bulb came on inside of his head and his eyes widen. He darted into the house.

"Ant, are you okay?" Eureka asked, slamming the car's door as she approached.

Anton took his hand from the back of his head and it came away with blood.

"Jesus, Ant," she took his hand and looked down at his red palm. "What—"

Eureka was cut short when Fear came staggering out of the house. Seeing the look on his face froze her where she was. Anton turned around wondering what had grasped her attention.

Fear rested his hand on a pillar as he stared down at the ground at nothing, with a faraway look in his eyes. He looked like he'd been dumped by the first love of his life. He was breathing sporadically and was trying to catch his breath through quick sips of air, looking like a pregnant woman in labor.

"Are you alright?" Eureka inquired.

"She—she took—she took my safe." Fear uttered, still harboring the faraway look. "That was all of the money that I had in the world!" his eyes became glassy and his top-lip twitched as he gritted his teeth. "It's all—it's all *fucking gone!*"

"Fear?" She slowly approached him, taking cautious steps in his direction.

Hearing her voice snapped his attention in her direction. He was coherent now. He pointed his banger at her and her hands shot up in the air. Her heart quickened. She was scared.

Fear's eyes glinted with madness. He was gritting his teeth so hard that his top-lip twitched."Y'all set me up!" he grumbled, motioning the gun between her and Anton.

"Fuck are you talking about?" Anton asked.

"We didn't set chu up!" Eureka frowned. "Fear, I swear to God we didn't know that this was going to happen! You gotta believe us!"

"Fuck y'all! Both of y'all!" Fear shouted, eyebrows arching and nose wrinkling. "I ain't gotta believe shit! You die now!"

Chapter Twenty Two

Ding! The elevator chimed before its double doors slid apart and a group of men filed out. Ronny wore a mask of determination as he moved down the corridor with Vladimir by his side and his men bringing up the rear. Every man accounted for held a shotgun, handgun, or assault rifle of his own. They walked around with their weapons out in the open as if that shit wasn't illegal. Stopping at a green door with #9 on it, Vladimir hoisted up his M-16 and wrapped its strap around his fist. He then turned to Ronny, looking him over before eventually speaking. "Is this the right place?" he asked.

"Yeah, this is the right place." Ronny frowned and gritted his teeth, causing the veins in his neck to bulge. They looked like they were about to explode. Malvo had violated and now his ass had to pay. "Step aside," He kicked the door at the lock. *Boom! Boom!*

****

Malvo came through the door of his apartment and went straight to the kitchen where he poured himself a drink. With Loc Dog out of the way, his people could hustle without having to worry about looking over their shoulders. On his way home, he'd already sent a text out to all of his workers, letting them know that they were open for business again. Now that that situation had been handled, it was time to address the others.

He had something in mind for Siska and his crew, but he was going to take a different approach with Eureka. He didn't want her dead anymore. He wanted her brought to him so that he could torture her little ass. Ernie's man had gotten caught up and was still fighting those murder beefs in the county jail. But he did plug him in with someone that could possibly help him. He had planned on hitting him up and setting a time and place to meet to discuss business right after he called to check on his wife and kid.

Picking up his glass of brown liquor from the kitchen island, he journeyed into the living room and plopped down on the couch. He took a sip of his drink. He was about to punch a number into his cell phone when it rang and vibrated. When he saw Faith's parents' number on the screen, he couldn't help but smile being that he was just about to call her. Sitting his glass down on the coffee table, he lay back on the couch and kicked off his Timberland boots. He pressed answer and placed the cell to his ear.

"Hey baby?"

"What's up, boo?" An older gentleman's voice responded.

The lines on Malvo's forehead deepened and he said, "Who the fuck is this?"

"Take a wild guess."

Malvo's eyes snapped open and he sat up on the couch.

"Siska."

"What did I tell you, Malvo? What did I tell you, huh?"

"Daddyyyy!" Heaven's voice rang out in the background.

"Malvoooo!" Faith's voice rang out after her daughter's.

Hearing his wife and daughter in distress caused his heart to skip a beat.

"Look, man, I got the money. I can…"

"No. No! No! No! Fuck the money, you pay now, with their lives."

"No! Wait, I..."

Boc! Boc!

Shots echoed from the other end of the telephone and the call disconnected. Malvo dropped to his hands and knees on the floor, choked up by what he'd just heard. He stared ahead at nothing, making a weird groaning sound. His eyes welled up with tears that ran down his face. He felt like someone had torn his beating heart out of his chest. He couldn't fathom the pain he was experiencing because he'd never felt it before. But the people he had victimized throughout his selfish existence of a life had. Now it was *his* turn.

Boom! Boom!

His front door rattled and his neck snapped in its direction. Something told him that it was Karma that had come to pay him a visit and he grabbed his banger off the coffee table. He rose to his feet and pointed the gun at the door. If it was death coming to claim him on the other side of that door he wasn't going out without a fight.

"You wanna bang, cock sucka?" He barked, spittle flying from his lips and tears sliding down his face. "Well, let's bang!"

****

Giselle moaned as she slowly began to stir awake, her head bobbling about as if it were loosely attached to her neck. Her eyes peeled apart and she looked over her surroundings with blurred vision. She didn't know exactly where she was, but wherever she was it was dark and hot.

The first thing she thought was that she had died and woke in hell. But that idea quickly dissipated when she didn't see any fires or see any demons ambling about. As her vision came into focus, she was better to assess her surroundings. There were large rusted pipes woven in and out of the ceiling with fat beady eyed rats scurrying across the lengths of them. Off in the distance she could hear water dripping into a puddle, coming from one of the marred pipes no doubt.

She glanced to her left and there was a bluish light that shone through the gated window high above the floor. Her eyes swept back across the room, settling on a large chair made of black leather and metal. It was comprised of several straps, metal bracelets, and shackles to keep its sitter held in place. Its attachments were a variety of bladed weapons ranging from spikes to electric saws. Sitting beneath the chair, enclosed in what she assumed was shatterproof glass, was some sort of power generator with wires running from it to underneath the seat of the chair. Giselle figured that it was rigged to the seat of the chair to electrocute whatever poor soul that was restrained in it. Now, she didn't know exactly who had made the chair, but whoever did had to be wickedly brilliant to craft such a deceitful piece of furniture.

Feeling something crawling on the side of her face, Giselle went to swat it and her hand stopped just at her cheek making a clang sound. The skin on her forehead bunched as she wondered what had snagged her wrist. When she looked, she saw that her wrist was shackled to one of several pipes that ran from the floor to the ceiling. Getting upon her feet, she yanked and pulled on the length of the chain, making the metal clasp together. Once she'd grown exhausted with her futile attempt to break free from her restraint, she turned back around. Her head snapped in each and every direction, looking for anything she could use to free her wrist from the shackle. All she could hear was the beating of her heart in her ears and her labored breathing.

Giselle bowed her head and began to sob, thinking that she'd never be able to escape her imprisonment. It wasn't until she heard what sounded like a match stick sweeping across the black strip of a match book that her head snapped up. Her eyes searched the darkness trying to locate the noise she'd just heard. Feeling something at her feet, she looked down and saw a spent match. When she looked back up she saw an ember in the darkness and a repugnant odor invaded her nostrils. The odor she'd smelled couldn't be mistaken for anything else. It was familiar, it was weed.

Giselle held a hand over her brow and narrowed her eyes as she tried to make out who it was that the shadows were hiding.

"Who is it?" She panicked, wanting to know her kidnapper. "Who's there?"

Suddenly, the shadows began to stir as someone was moving within them. A moment later a hooded person stepped before Giselle, blowing a cloud of smoke and dumping ashes on the floor. She tried to peer closely to see who it was standing before her, but her efforts were useless. The shade that the hood provided, coupled with the darkened room hid the person's face.

"Who…who are you?" Giselle asked timidly, her heart thumping inside of her chest. It was so hot that sweat rolled down her face and obscured the vision in her right eye. Taking the sleeve of her jacket, she wiped her eye and face.

The person stopped in front of Giselle and she was able to make out the face through the bluish light that shined through the gated window. The person licked their lips and smiled evilly.

"I am the devil and this…" the person spread their arms apart and looked about the room. "…this is Hell." Constance laughed hard and manically.

"Oh, shit, helllllp! Hellllp me," Giselle screamed as loud as she could, yanking the chain her wrist was shackled to, trying to break free. "Helllllp, oh God, *pleaseeee*! Somebody helllllp meeeeee!"

While Giselle screamed and yanked on the chain, Constance continued to laugh manically. *Hahahahahahahahaha!*

To Be Continued…
The Devil Wears Timbs III
Hell on Earth

299

301

303

* 9 7 8 1 7 3 2 7 9 2 2 9 6 *